PRAISE FOR MALONE RIDGE

In this lovely coming-of-age novel, Dill evokes Malone Ridge as a place to leave. Then, slowly, as life will, it becomes central to the heart. This is Malone Ridge, the place and the book together, a story as indelible and welcoming as home.

—David L. Robbins, *New York Times* bestselling author of *War of the Rats* and *Isaac's Beacon*

James K. Dill crafts some vivid and memorable characters in this new adult drama that will pluck at your heartstrings and emotions, leaving you wanting more. Eve's story kept me fully invested until the very last page. This is a riveting slice-of-life story that I highly recommend.

—Pikasho Deka for *Readers' Favorite*

James K. Dill's *Malone Ridge* pits perseverance against circumstance with a compelling premise that lends characters incredible complexity, allowing readers to accompany a destitute girl on a journey toward womanhood.

—IndieReader

I found the story to be relatable on so many levels. Enjoyable to see running and humility provide Eve the strength and will to follow her heart and pursue her dream and most desired need (family). I love a good heroine!

—Judy St. Hillaire, Road Race Champion and United States Olympian, 1992 Barcelona Games

Running is a wonderful catalyst to find out about yourself and being fortunate to do so at a young age can set you up with the strength and resilience to overcome obstacles and "take a chance on life!" Jim does an amazing job of weaving the joys of running through a story involving the individual life challenges of his lead character that positively influences his many other characters in their paths.

—Anne Audaine, three-time Olympian, Commonwealth Games Champion, and New Zealand native

Malone Ridge is a remarkable story of resilience and a revelatory look into a young girl's tremendous family struggle and personal triumph. An uplifting story ... James Dill tells it brilliantly.

—Kim Jones is a US Marathon Champion with podium finishes at New York, Chicago, Boston, and other major marathons

Malone Ridge is a captivating story that explores the personal challenges and family struggles faced by a former high school champion distance runner who turns back to running as salvation for her entire being. There are many unforeseen twists and turns, and I couldn't put this book down as the main character and I both raced toward the finish. I highly recommend this book for runners and anyone who faces challenges and obstacles in life.

—Gary Cohen, founder of
www.garycohenrunning.com (GCR) and
author of *'All in a Day's Run'*

Also, by James K. Dill

Racing Shadows

MALONE RIDGE

A NOVEL

JAMES K. DILL

Published by Little Star

Richmond, VA

Malone Ridge is a work of fiction. Names, characters, places, and incidents are either a product of the author's imagination or are used fictitiously, and any resemblance to actual persons, living or deceased, businesses, companies, events or locals is entirely coincidental.

Contact the author at www.jameskdillauthor.com

ISBN 978-1-7358872-8-9

Book and cover design by Wendy Daniel

Printed in the United States of America

For Wendy,

Meaghan, John, Leona & Theo,

and Quentin, Bekah, Georgia & Weston

The pine trees stand alone near my old Virginia home
And that silver haired mother of mine
I can see her smiling face in that old familiar place
In my home among the hills.

E.W. James

MALONE RIDGE

Nitro, West Virginia

One

Family is hypothetical. It's a flip of the coin how we arrive in this messed up little world. Anyone who says it's about blood doesn't have a clue. Dad romances his two mistresses, scotch and work, while Mom prefers the seductive curves of the wine bottle. I see stronger families on the street all the time; strangers bound by survival and loss. Family bound by blood is a myth.

—Margaret Smallwood, *The Asp: Tales of a Private Investigator*

❖

Eve folded the corner of the page, sighing. She slid the graphic novel into her mostly empty backpack, the book her only excitement, her life lived vicariously through the PI's exploits. Life after graduation wasn't supposed to be like this. Eve changed slowly from scrubs into jeans, her movements labored. The door to the changing room burst open. Marcy appeared like a thunderclap on a blue-sky day, forcing a smile despite Eve's foul mood.

"Why so glum, Twiggy?" Marcy opened the locker next to Eve and winked, her cologne overcoming the Pine-Sol scent of the room. Marcy was the only one who could get away with the nickname, her voice drippy with West Virginia twang, her nickname coming out twig-eha.

"I've gotta' get out of here." She banged her head gently against her locker. "This isn't what we had planned."

"Get changed, Eve." Her hand touched Eve's shoulder gently. "We can't do anything about work tonight. Let's go to the carnival, listen to music, drink some beer, and dance. I'm buying. The boys are waiting outside."

Marcy pulled off her scrub top and dropped her bottoms next to Eve's, her curvy figure straining against the department store lingerie and her café-au-lait skin tone so in contrast to Eve. The two were complete opposites. Eve's body had changed little since high school; her running bra and boy-cut shorts hung more than clung to her willowy figure and near translucent skin. Eve ran a gelled hand to spike her bleached white hair while Marcy swept her long dark hair into a ponytail.

"Let's blow off the boys and go alone," Eve's voice was sharp and clipped.

"Get dressed, Twiggy. I promised the guys." Marcy tossed her a tee shirt. "You know I'd like nothing more than for the two of us to go out tonight, but we've made plans. Come on, let's go."

Eve dressed with effort, pulling on the tee. "Going out with the guys doesn't do it for me, Marcy, nothing does around here. I don't feel anything about anyone and I'm so done with this podunk town. I'm ready to start my life somewhere else, anywhere but Nitro-freaking-West Virginia. Work sucks, home sucks, and everyone knows everybody else's damn business."

Marcy ignored her, spraying more cologne which filled the small space. She shut the locker and handed Eve her backpack. Arm in arm, the two joined the boys at Marcy's truck outside the nursing home. Greg worked in the cafeteria, a member of their senior class. Sam was new to town, one of the few African Americans in the community. Marcy, whose momma was white and daddy from Jamaica, didn't count according to Eve. The Caribbean was on their bucket list one day, Eve to travel and Marcy to find her grandparents. Marcy drove while Eve fiddled with the radio, the guys talking about fishing in the back seat. Marcy pulled into a cornfield to park, following the man waving a flashlight. A bluegrass band could be heard nearby with the screams from the midway. The smell of hot grease, sweets, and the barnyard filled the night air.

Just inside the entrance was the first attraction, a shabby dunking booth and clown. Both had seen better days, his red wig off-kilter and makeup blotchy. Dirty overalls completed his costume and he may have been a little drunk. His bloodshot eyes peered over a trembling Solo cup.

"How'd you three misfits end up with something like that?" He sneered in Marcy's direction, sliding suggestively on his perch while his hands gripped the cage. "I'd like to have that swing in my backyard." He brayed like a donkey then took a swig and grimaced. "Come on, boys, try and dunk me."

Maybe it was the wolf whistle or that he'd thought she was one of the guys. Eve shot him a glance. "Ass-clown," she muttered.

"Whoa, sorry about that, princess. I thought you were one of the boys. Don't worry sweet-thang, you'll have bumps like that one day." He guffawed again loudly. "Come on, you should try and knock me off. Bet you can throw better than those two ding-dongs yer walking with." He brayed again.

Marcy reached for Eve, but she shook her off. Grim-faced, Eve grabbed a lopsided ball from the shelf. The barker continued flipping through his magazine, happy to have someone take a shot at his obnoxious partner. Eve tossed the lopsided ball from one hand to the other to get the feel and weight, never taking her eyes off the bullseye. Varsity softball wasn't so long ago. She measured the distance in her head before taking several steps backward into the small crowd watching. Eve rocked back onto one heel then stepped forward quickly. Her shoulder led, followed by her arm, wrist, and fingers, the throw slightly sidearm. She released the wobbly ball straight for the clown's head, causing him to duck before it dipped ever so slightly and found the bullseye. It was the same throw she'd performed hundreds of times, picking up a grounder down the third-base line and winging the ball to Marcy's waiting catcher's mitt at home plate. Clang, the ball struck the red center, sending the clown butt-first into the water. The Solo cup floated, while the clown cussed and coughed.

"Looks like you flushed a big turd, Eve. Let's go." Marcy pulled Eve away.

"Nice throw," Greg chimed. "That clown was nasty and had no clue you could throw like that. Bastard deserved it. You nailed him big time."

"Fuck." The clown thrashed about, not caring who heard him. He called for Eve to come back and pay for the pitch and try again. Her thin smile returned.

Eve walked arm-in-arm with Marcy through the crowd, the boys taking the lead and looking for dinner. The first stop was the barbeque shack. The boys chose sandwiches, messy with sauce to line their stomachs for the beer they'd consume at their next stop. Eve chose a fried Twinkie and Marcy, a corn dog.

"I'm ready for a beer," Eve announced. The four passed the swirling rides and games of chance to get to the beer truck down by the river's edge, the carny music fading to the bands playing on the nearby stage. Greg and Sam stepped right up while Eve and Marcy fell behind and stalled, pulling out their fake IDs. The procurement of the well-used cards had been a rite of passage a year earlier. The beer man barely glanced at Eve's, following Marcy as she walked to the tap. Beers in hand, the four sat on an empty picnic table near the back where they could hear the band that was setting up. Greg lit a cigarette.

"Do you ladies have any plans for the summer?" He took a big gulp of beer. "I'm going to Baltimore later for a ball game with my Daddy. We got family up there. What are y'all's plans?"

Eve and Marcy erupted in spontaneous laughter. Marcy spit foam and snorted while Eve covered her mouth, her shoulders shaking.

"What did I say that's so funny?"

“Never mind, it was something me and Marcy were talking about earlier. No, we don’t have any plans. We’re both saving money for community college this fall.” Eve paused at the sight of the big man in khaki uniform and Smokey Bear hat. His gold badge flashed in the glare of the tent lights, his gun at eye level in front of the four.

“You all old enough to be drinking?” They nodded. The boys began to pull their IDs out. “I don’t need those, boys. Put ‘em away.” Eve glanced at Marcy, swallowing a harsh sip. Busted for underage drinking at the fair by the local deputy wasn’t the plan for the night. He knew Eve and Eve knew him. “Any word from your daddy, Eve?” He waited, but she didn’t answer, staring at the straw floor. “It’s been nice and quiet around here without him. I aim to keep it that way.”

“We haven’t heard anything from him or when he’ll get out,” she murmured without looking up. It wasn’t the deputy’s business, her momma would say, and besides, family is family. “We’ve been enjoying the quiet too, Momma and me.”

“I bet you have. Well, let me know if you hear from him. I busted that man once, and I’ll bust him again no doubt and send his sorry ass back to jail. I won’t have meth labs or arsonists blowing up homes in my county. Nitro is known for making ammunition, but I won’t cotton to no meth labs blowing up homes and families.” Eve turned pink. The deputy gave her his card. “You call me now, ya hear?” She nodded. Smokey strode off, the four collectively exhaling.

Eve chugged her beer and stood, letting the card fall to the straw floor.

“It’s okay,” Sam spoke for the first time. “That’s why my mother and I moved back here to my grandma’s. My father’s in prison, too. He was dealing oxy.” Greg and Marcy nodded silently. Eve walked away without acknowledging Sam’s confession.

Marcy jumped up to follow her friend. “I better go with her. She’s really keyed up. Get another beer, and we’ll meet you over by the band.”

Eve was livid. “It’s this, Marcy. This,” she flung her fingers outward, “is not enough. Nitro friggin’ West Virginia and Deputy Dog back there. Everyone knows everyone else’s business, and nothing good ever happens. I’ve got to get away.” Eve was breathing rapidly, a tear in each eye. “I want to leave. Let’s get away from here and live.”

“Hang in there, Eve, and remember the plan. We get our associate degrees, then work as nurses, then we’ll move somewhere once we have some money. You and me, we’ll make our way out of here. I can’t leave my momma yet, and neither can you.” Something big splashed in the river.

"I hate to tell you, but it's not going to happen like we planned, Marcy. I have a feeling, a bad feeling I can't shake. Look at me—my father's about to get out of jail soon and we live in a shitty trailer with no indoor plumbing. I don't stand a chance at anything close to normal." She turned to the river, wiping the stream of tears with her wrist.

"We can't do anything about that tonight, Eve. Let's get another beer and leave all this shit on the dance floor." She took her friend's arm, steering her back along the river to the beer seller and stage.

Eve took a few deep breaths to calm herself. It was what she'd done before shooting a free throw, stepping up to the plate to bat, or listening for the starting pistol to be fired in cross-country. Eve could focus and center herself. Deep inside, she liked knocking the asshole clown into the tank. She also liked buying beer and fooling the deputy about her age and her daddy's return. If she had to admit it, she liked the murky smell of the river, the catfish splashing, the big harvest moon overhead, and the rinky-dink carnival that had been the highlight of her summer all these years. She also liked Marcy, a saving grace in the evolving drama of her life of late. But something loomed. Change was coming and it unsettled her.

❖

Eve and Marcy lay on the single bed in Marcy's room as they'd done since kindergarten. Gone were the pajamas and soda pop of those innocent days, replaced by tee-shirts and a six-pack of cheap beer. Clothes were discarded across a room that featured posters of country rockers. The two friends had grown up in this room.

"So, when does life get interesting?" Eve finished her beer and belched loudly, giggling into the wide mouth of the green bottle.

Marcy took a long pull from hers and matched Eve's burp with one of her own, louder and more drawn out. Eve hit her friend with a battered, stuffed giraffe, laughing. Marcy's mother yelled for the two to keep the noise down. "Let it go tonight, Eve."

Eve fanned away the smell of the burp. "I think about the scholarship sometimes. I could be at university right now. Life would be very different." Eve popped open another beer. They were both a little drunk.

"I could come and visit you in your dorm room, just the two of us on our own." Marcy's face was close to Eve's, her gaze intense. Marcy leaned in, her eyes partly shut. "Kish me," she whispered.

"I'm not kissing you." Eve laughed, shoving her lightly aside.

"You've kissed me before," Marcy pouted.

"We were younger then and didn't know what we were doing. I'm sorry, Marcy, you're my best friend, but I don't feel about you that way. I want more, too, but kissing you wouldn't mean anything and don't take this wrong, but it would be a little gross. I need you as my friend now. I hope that's enough?"

Marcy rolled back toward Eve, the space between the two minimal. Eve didn't mind. She snuggled with her friend.

"We'll get out of here one day, and we'll both know how that kind of love feels, I hope." Eve pulled Marcy's hair from her face into a ponytail. Marcy's eyes fluttered shut. Her soft breaths feathered Eve's face.

❖

Morning light filtered through the collection of green bottle trophies from the previous night on the nearby table. Eve slid out of bed and pulled on her running shorts, tee shirt, and shoes. She smiled at Marcy's rumpled form.

Marcy stirred and sat up; her hair tousled from the pillow. "My mouth tastes terrible. That beer last night was crap."

"It was crap. You were breathing on me all night." She tossed a small donkey wearing a sombrero at her friend. "I need to go check on Momma. I'll see you at work."

"You want a ride?"

"No, I'm going to run off the beer."

Marcy swung her legs off the bed. "About last night."

"No worries, Marcy. I love you, too, but not that way, Lesbot. We'll figure things out. I'll see you later." She was out the door and settled into a slow jog to warm up, moving smoothly through town. Her mind wandered to Marcy and her attempts at affection. If they had made out, then what? The night wouldn't have ended with kissing. Marcy wanted sex, her vibes palpable. It bothered Eve that she didn't have such desires. Eve hadn't kissed anybody that mattered, boy or girl. She wondered if she was different with no feelings. Eve stopped at the one light in town. She faced the bank, the Piggly-Wiggly, the ABC store, the one Chinese food joint, and the sheriff's office. She spotted the deputy's car. Bastard. She ran on.

Eve liked to run, a better cross-country runner than infielder or point guard. Their school was small, so Eve ran cross-country in the fall, played basketball in the winter, and softball in the spring. She was a natural at all three sports but a three-time state champion in cross-country. Her performances led to the scholarship offers. Eve noticed the billboard for the university up the river in Huntington. It would have been fun to go there for college. WVU would have been too far away. Both made offers and the scholarship would have helped, but it wouldn't have been enough. Her family had no money for her to go to school.

The differences between Eve and the other recruits had been apparent on her visit to the university. The other girls had French braids and wore cute outfits. Eve arrived in old jeans and her high school sweatshirt, her spare underwear and toothbrush in her backpack. The other recruits wore new training gear. Eve felt pitiful in old trainers and shorts, sitting outside while they shopped at the campus bookstore, loading up on hats, tee shirts, and other gear. Eve purchased two small key chains—one for her and one for Marcy. The coach asked to meet her parents, but Eve could only show him her bus ticket. The training run was the only part of the trip when she felt she belonged. Eve kept up with the upperclassmen no matter how hard they pushed, loping along and breathing easy while the other recruits stopped halfway to walk back to campus. She was different, both in her ability and lack of means, but it was one small thing in the end, a difference that was undeniable. The question from the other recruits loomed like a vulture overhead, its presence unsettling.

"No, I don't have a cell phone." Eve would explain patiently.

"How do you live without one? I couldn't live without my phone," each would ask and answer, not really interested in Eve's response, snapping selfies and constantly checking their status. It was annoying. Eve stayed in her room and reread her dog-eared copy of The

Asp for most of the visit. But it was more than money. It was also class and family. Her family came up short in those categories, too, the only recruit as far as she knew with a father in prison and mother in rehab. Eve's world and theirs were a universe apart.

Eve let her college dream disappear like the billboard behind her. It was how life turned out and she'd accepted her lot. She didn't mind providing for her and Momma. She jogged away from the billboard, her dreams smaller with each step.

Walking across the gravel lot, Eve stopped at the Minimart part way up the ridge on her way home. She wiped the sweat from her brow and entered, choosing a packaged cinnamon bun. She nuked a sausage biscuit from the freezer and picked-up a small orange juice. She paid, stuffing her goods in the small backpack. Bigun, the proprietor of the adjoining tattoo parlor, pulled up in a tiny sedan covered in stickers that looked like it sloped to one side. He unfolded more than stepped out of the vehicle, tall and lanky, his tribal tattoos ran down his arms from under the Nitro football tee-shirt. His beard was trim and he had his hair up in a man-bun, island style. Eve waved. Bigun was her friend and the source for the graphic novels she loved. Bigun waved back with a slight nod. The road climbed just outside the parking lot, much more than a hill, her home a few switchbacks above on Malone Ridge.

With each turn the homes became smaller and more run-down. The front porches sloped or caved in, many of them covered with creeper. Most of the small cabins had a broken-down car or two and all had yard dogs, terrifying if you weren't from the neighborhood. Eve knew them all, their wagging tails a sure sign of safe passage.

The trees changed from the scraggly crabapples to taller pines and oaks, the daylilies in bright bloom along the roadside. Eve leaned into the last switchback, the sun on her forehead, breathing hard up the last hill to the top of the ridge. The faded blue metal of the trailer she and Momma called home was just ahead.

Two

Momma was stretching her legs in the sun on the small stoop of the trailer. Her painted toes matched the bright emerald green serpent tattoo on her left ankle and foot. The snake's mouth was open with long yellow fangs, a red forked tongue and black beaded eyes. It was the most exquisite art Eve had ever seen. Momma lit a cigarette. "There's my baby girl," her voice low and sleepy.

"Morning, Momma." Eve hugged her, breathing in menthol and something sweet and salty like caramel. "Sorry, I'm a little damp." She stretched against the post, then opened the backpack for the orange juice. She gulped from the bottle. "Do you want some?"

Her mother shook her head, a dual stream of smoke plumed from her nostrils. She held out her coffee cup. Momma was beautiful without makeup, sitting in her nightgown with her hair long over her shoulders.

"All that running's keeping you skinny. You need a little padding." Eve didn't mind the comment. It was her momma's duty to say such things.

"I like to run. It gives me time to think. There won't be much time for running once I start school this fall." She finished the juice and opened the cinnamon bun, licking the icing off the top. "I got a sausage biscuit for you with your coffee." Eve had to keep an eye on her mom's calorie intake. She'd quit cooking once they'd moved into the trailer.

"Thank you, baby. There's something I need to talk to you about." She paused, taking a deep draw. "Let's go drink our coffee in the garden where it's peaceful. Can you get me a refill when you get your cup?" Momma called the family burial plot the garden. The small cemetery sat on the backside of the property known as Malone Ridge. They crossed through daisies, black-eyed Susan's, and Queen Anne's lace that seemed to thrive in the charred ground where grass once grew. Elaborate ironwork formed the gate, once black but now showing rust, and set in walls made of stacked stone. The grass inside was short and well-manicured. Eve and Momma sat near the headstones of Eve's grandparents, facing the valley. Sunlight filtered through the big walnut tree behind the enclosure. Eve's cat, a stray that lived on the property, jumped on the wall and padded up, sniffing the biscuit bag. The two sipped their coffee and nibbled on breakfast without talking. A woodpecker pounded in the big tree while the cat purred in the sun, impatiently marching in front of them with its tail bristling.

"Your Daddy will be home soon," Momma started. Eve closed her eyes to conjure a picture of the man, but she couldn't see him.

Eve asked, "Do you think he's changed?" She viewed the charred remains that had been the family home for generations. The brick front and porch that ran down to the road was a pile of rubble. The only thing still standing were the twin stone fireplaces, the mantles long gone and the rock charred. In between was a mess of burnt timbers, pipes, and odd pieces of junk. The cops said he was running a meth-lab, but there was little evidence after the blaze. Her father had been arrested for simple possession that night, receiving an eight-year sentence. She couldn't say she missed the man. He'd burned down her home and was responsible for her grandparents passing soon after with nowhere to live. They'd gone to the poor-home and passed quickly, first Grandma and then Granddaddy. Momma fell apart after that, her solace the little white pills that were so easy to obtain. It was all his fault and they'd lost everything except their name because Momma never took his. They were the last two

Malone's on the ridge and though they'd lost their home, they wouldn't lose their name.

"I don't know if I want him back, Momma. It's perfect here with you and me. I'm working and getting ready to go to school and there's only enough room in the trailer for the two of us. You've done so well in recovery. I don't want him messing that up."

"I have to be true to your Daddy, baby. That's the way I was brought up. The two of us are married, and he's my man. I'm sorry, but we'll have to make do." She lit another cigarette.

"I'm working, and we have your disability. We could get an apartment somewhere. Daddy could stay here, and we could see how it all works out. He can have the damn trailer."

"He wouldn't stand for it and watch your language. I still love the man, or what was the man." Momma seemed lost for a few moments, debating something. She cleared her throat. "No matter what, I want you to know you can always come here to the garden. This place is yours now. It was mine from my Momma and Daddy and his parents before that. It's a safe place, and you can figure things out here. Your Daddy won't bother you and knows he's not welcome in the family plot." She pulled at the rock behind her mother's headstone. The curious cat crept up, sticking its paw into a small crevice to fish behind the stone. "Remember this if I'm gone. You come here and find what you need. I get strength from my parents and grandparents, and you can, too." She shooed the cat away. Momma pulled out a small ornate silver frame in a plastic storage bag. The picture showed her and her mother in high-necked white blouses, their hair up. Her mother wore a large cross. Momma reached for a second object, the cross from the picture, also wrapped in plastic. The gold cross had a gemstone mounted at the end of each point, a ruby in the center with pearls woven throughout the chain.

"Oh my God, your mother's cross. I thought those were lost in the fire."

Her mother smiled. "Some things need to be kept safe. These belonged to my grandmother, then my mother, and now me. It was my job to keep them safe for you." She handed the two objects to Eve. "Keep them safe, honey." Eve fingered the pearls of the rosary.

"Don't talk that way, Momma. You're not going anywhere." She paused to change the subject. "If you could go anywhere, where would you go? Not with Daddy, but by yourself or with me?"

"I always wanted to go to Charleston, the one in South Carolina. Grandma talked about it. It's warm there all year with the ocean and palm trees. But Charleston is kind of far, so I'd most likely go to Alexandria." Eve cocked her head, surprised. "It's not so far and sits on the Potomac River over yonder on the other side of the mountains. My mother took me there as a child. We stayed with her sister. I'd never seen a city so beautiful. The way people live there—the boats, not coal barges like on the Kanawha but powerboats, houseboats, and sailing boats. People dress up to walk around the open-air market. The nation's capital is just up the river with monuments, parks, museums, and just about anything you can imagine. I remember a merry-go-round and ice cream and being so happy, but that was a simpler time. It's funny that such a place could exist so close yet be so far from us and our way of life. It was the best summer of my childhood."

Eve wondered when she'd have her best summer. Despite the calm of the moment, and the discovery of the treasure, it wouldn't be this summer. A hawk screeched somewhere over the valley, bringing her back to the remains of her childhood home. Her best summer was there in simpler times. Grandma and Granddaddy had a big room on the first floor. Momma and Daddy had a room down the hall on the wing above. They had a bathroom upstairs and down, plus the big kitchen and living room. The floor beams were smooth so she could run barefoot through the hallways. Best of all, a porch ran the length of the upstairs that she could step onto and look at the valley below. Most mornings she went out that way and down the back stairs to see Kitty and play in the wildflowers before Grandma's breakfast.

But that was a long time ago. Daddy was working at the auto body shop, and Momma worked at the home for seniors. Then Daddy got hurt at work, crushing his foot. He came home to take care of things as best he could, but the house became shabby. He'd always been a partier, staying out late with his boys, but he'd always come home, and everything returned to normal once Momma started talking to him again. He took pills for the pain in his foot and that became a habit.

Daddy started working in the basement, keeping the door bolted. He and his boys would work all hours and go out by the back steps. That was when strange smells started coming from the basement. One night there was a loud noise like a wind blowing through the house, followed by screaming, fire, and caustic smoke. Everyone made it out that night, but the house was gone with nothing left but rock, brick, and rubble. The officers came after the fire department and took Daddy away. An ambulance took everyone else to the hospital to be treated for smoke and fumes. Someone brought a hunting trailer for them to live in after a couple of weeks in the motel down by the river.

Eve was angry, her happy home blown to bits by her father. He'd taken away everything she loved. She glanced from the rubble to the trailer covered with mud and mold. They had no bathroom, using the old outhouse by the woods' edge. Water was carried from a hand pump. She understood why her mother was depressed most of the time.

"So, what was the best summer of your adult life?" Eve knew the answer, smiling broadly.

"The summer you were born, of course." Momma didn't hesitate, taking the picture and heirloom cross back from Eve. She sealed the two items in their plastic bags and stuffed them back in the crevice, pushing the rock into place. "Keep these here while he's home. They're yours now."

"Maybe we can go to Alexandria sometime, Momma."

"I'd like that, honey." She drew the smoke in and sighed. "But enough of the past for now. How about you? Did you and Marcy have fun last night?

"Yeah, we had fun. Marcy's going through something. I don't know what she wants or if she knows what she wants. I think her mother might be driving her nuts." Eve laughed, thinking about Marcy's pass.

"It would be good for you to have more friends, maybe a boy or two to see."

"I'm happy, Momma. Having you and Marcy in my life is all I need. You always took care of me and now I get to help take care of you."

"Do you have to work today?"

"Yeah, I have to get ready. When's Daddy getting here?"

"I don't rightly know, but soon. He called me at the clinic." She lit another smoke and finally turned to survey the remains of her family home. "Gonna need the car today, hon. I need to go to rehab. Can you get a ride from Marcy?"

"Yeah, no problem, you go on to rehab." Eve had a feeling in her gut, unsettled but manageable.

Three

The Asp was skating in Gotham in search of a missing kid. Skating in the big city along the river in expensive sunglasses was a pleasant dream. She put the book away and sighed, preparing for work and the events at home crowding out her private eye fantasy.

She would need a plan for her father's return. Hopefully, he'd be different but circumstances could get ugly real quick. She would need to be tough and look out for Momma. Maybe the two could disappear to Alexandria. The city was far enough away so Daddy couldn't find them, but not so far that the beat-up Corolla couldn't get them there. They could start over, find jobs and get a proper apartment. Malone Ridge had been there for a hundred years, and it would be there when they returned. She decided she would come back and rebuild one day.

❖

Work was tedious at the women's home. Marcy made things better, forever the cheerleader. Eve perused the course catalog for nursing school at the JC, highlighting the classes she wanted to take in the fall semester. Thinking about college and investigating courses made helped her forget about her home life.

Eve changed into her nursing scrubs and Crocs, going down the hall to check on Mrs. Smith. She knocked, and hearing the welcome, stepped inside. The little woman waited patiently, reading a thin volume of poems.

"Good morning, Mrs. Smith. How are you today?"

"God has blessed me with another day and I'm grateful. And you, my dear?"

"Some good and some bad. Momma's doing better. Would you like to go outside? It's a nice day for the rose garden if we stay in the shade."

"That sounds lovely, but you seem flustered. Tell me as we go." Mrs. Smith loved to talk with Eve about life and Eve enjoyed her company. She helped her into the wheelchair.

"My father's coming home from prison soon. We heard he made parole. Momma's done so well in rehab with him gone. I don't want her to slip away again." They wheeled into the little courtyard with a fountain and rose bushes. Eve parked Mrs. Smith in the shade. Some of the other residents were also out, reading or knitting. Eve leaned against the wall. "We've been happy enough. Now he has to come home and spoil it all."

"Do you know he will ruin things?"

"I'd like to trust him. He's my Daddy and he wasn't always so bad. The last time he was home things were horrible. He ruined our home and I lost my grandparents. I'm worried about Momma. She's not strong."

"I've read in the paper about the drug problems you young folks face. Keep an eye on her and don't trust him to do the right thing. It sounds like he's only concerned about himself, and prison most likely didn't help much. She's going to need you. It's not always easy for women, living in a man's world. I was married for sixty-two years, and most of it was very nice. But my husband could get angry. Those were the younger years when life was tough. We matured, and his temper did too, thankfully. I miss him now."

Eve smiled. "Would you marry him again?"

"At my age?" She chuckled. "I have no regrets, and if I could go back and do it all again, I wouldn't change anything. We lived in the city, but he had a farm in the country. It was more of a farm-in-progress, but we had horses, goats, chickens, and cows, and a small vegetable garden. I was an energetic young woman and enjoyed hiking in the Blue Ridge and the Appalachian Mountains.

I'd camp, often by myself which was unheard of in those days. I was independent, you might say. My father was a Presbyterian minister and quite strict when I was growing up. My job was to watch the children from his second wife. He married her right after my mother died and the first baby came shortly after the wedding. That woman was hopeless at everything except getting pregnant. She had seven children. So, I became their nanny and it kept a roof over my head. Life wasn't easy in those days, and we all had to do whatever we could to help. Eventually, I left and worked nearby. I'd hike on the weekends with friends to get out of the city fumes and breathe the good air. One weekend, I hiked down the mountain to get supplies and found my future husband and his farm. I never left."

"You stayed that first night?"

"No, no, not the first night. I must have left something out." The two laughed quietly at the thought. "I meant that once we met, we never saw anyone else. Love at first sight, I guess."

"It sounds wonderful. Was it wonderful?"

"For the most part, yes, it was. We had three girls and a full life, but there were struggles and my children have had their struggles. They all live a ways away and I rarely see them or my grandkids. But I can't complain, it's been a wonderful life. You seem to be a strong, purposeful young woman. You'll get through this time, too. Just don't expect it to be easy."

"I have this feeling that things are not going to be all rosy. I'm not worried about myself but for my Momma. I'm not the same child who watched her house burn. Something happened to me that night; it hardened me, like the Asp."

"The Asp? He was a character in Little Orphan Annie in the Sunday comics, a big Indian fellow with a turban. Is that who you mean?"

"No, my Asp is a private investigator in a graphic novel. It's a book that's written with pictures like comics but more serious, more real. I like her spirit, like yours. She roller skates on the boardwalk, and you hiked the Appalachians. I've never done either. I run, so I could probably hike or skate." Eve checked the clock. "Shall we go in for lunch?"

"My dear," Mrs. Smith placed her hand on Eve's, "whatever you do, be resolute and know you can overcome even the worst of circumstances. Sometimes even when it seems we can't bear life a moment more, we come out on the other side. Then the real work begins, putting the hurt, and anger, and pain behind. That's what we women do. I think you'll do fine." She patted Eve's hand. "Yes, I'm hungry. I feel like I've hiked ten miles. I do love talking about the old days."

Eve wheeled Mrs. Smith into the lunchroom. She waved across the room to Marcy, who looked both ways to see if anyone was watching, then pulled her top aside just enough to show off a bit of her lingerie. She ran her finger down the fabric then across her lips to blow a kiss at Eve before hiding in the big, curtained window behind her. Eve stifled a laugh. Marcy was such a flirt.

❖

A beat-up pick-up parked in front of the trailer meant trouble. Eve's stepped from Marcy's car tentatively. "Fuck," she muttered.

"What is it, Eve?"

"Looks like he's back. Wait here and let me check on Momma. I'll grab my stuff and be back out if you'll let me stay tonight. I'll only be a few minutes." Eve opened the door with her eyes closed.

"Lookie, lookie at my baby girl. Come hug your daddy, baby." She walked over and leaned toward him, unsure if she wanted to have him touch her or not. He seemed foreign, smelling of sour whiskey and smoke. The hug lasted too long, Eve holding her breath until she could pull away from his greasy hair and whiskered face. "You look like your momma when I met her, thin as a twig. Don't worry, darling. You'll fill out and turn heads like her one day, too." He was looking her up-and-down, which was unsettling.

"When did you get out, Daddy?" Eve shook off the comment and his inspection. It wasn't love she felt.

"A couple of days ago. I thought my family would be there for me and bring me home. Damn shame no one was there to greet the man of the house after he's done his time. Damn shame." He paused with pursed lips and thin eyes, sipping something from a Solo cup. "But hey, I'm home now."

Tough shit, no one was there to pick you up. Eve smoldered.

"Party with us tonight, daughter, you're old enough." Daddy lifted the cup. Eve remembered how it started, mixing Jack Daniels and Mountain Dew. Later, they'd light the pipe, carrying on until morning.

"I got the Jack-N-Dew out. Missed drinkin' in prison. Jack-n-Dewwwwwwwwwwww!" Daddy threw back his head with a rebel yell. Eve hadn't heard that cry since he'd left.

Momma stared sadly at her feet, her toes deep in the dirty shag carpet. She then stood slowly to shoo Eve out the door. "You go on now. Can you stay at Marcy's tonight?" Eve nodded, and then hugged her mother. It was difficult to leave, but that was the deal. Once the party started, there was nowhere to disappear in the trailer.

Eve whispered before she pulled away. "We're gonna get out of here, Momma." She walked briskly back to Marcy's truck.

"What are you going to do, Eve?"

"Stay with you tonight, maybe for the rest of the summer. I'm not sure what I'll do. I might need to find something of my own. Maybe I can get a second job. Like I said the other night, I have a bad feeling. I have to be here for Momma because she won't leave him. Maybe they'll work things out, but I doubt it." The two reached Marcy's home. Eve brushed their teeth and crawled into bed for an unsettled sleep.

❖

Eve walked to the trailer the next morning alert and apprehensive. His truck was gone, so that was good. She didn't want to face that man first thing in the morning. Eve stepped over a pizza box on the floor. There were red Solo cups scattered here and there, half filled with unknown liquids and snuffed out cigarettes. She set about tidying up the place, filling two large garbage bags. Eve tossed them into the yard to put in the trash bins later. Then, she made coffee and cleaned dishes.

Eve peeked in the door of the tiny bedroom where her mother slept. She was lovely in her sleep, pale and peaceful. A small pipe lay on the bed stand. Eve picked up a small crystal next to the bowl. Her mother's cigarettes and lighter lay next to it.

"No, Momma, no. You've done so well." Eve threw the little rock as far as she could into the scrapheap outside, one more blemish on the beautiful face of the mountain. The breeze hit her face, and she took in the valley below, a pretty picture other than the scab that was their home. She couldn't leave, not yet.

With a sigh, Eve tied her shoes and headed down the back trail of the mountainside to sort life out.

Four

Daddy turned out to be an infrequent visitor, stopping by to party but living elsewhere. He never left money; his contribution to the family's welfare was a fifth of Jack Daniels and a liter of Mountain Dew. Occasionally he brought dinner, a greasy bag of fried chicken and taters from the convenience store. Eve slept on the couch in the space they called their living room when he wasn't there, her clothes in the same box the Salvation Army gave her after the fire. The box had seen better days, like most things in the trailer.

Eve heard the party as she pulled up after work. The old truck looked derelict, muddier and more rusted than usual. Music poured from the open window, some country outlaw. She considered turning around to visit the tattoo shop and waste time, but first, she needed to check on Momma.

Pausing on the porch, Eve put her hand on the knob. She thought of the knob in the old home. Turning the big brass handle unlocked Grandma and Grandpa's house, her room, and happiness. Now she didn't know what the small aluminum device would reveal.

The door swung open from the inside, surprising her. A skinny young man in ripped jeans, dirty high tops, and a rebel flag tank top stood before her. His mouth hung open under stringy, reddish-brown hair and a face pocked with pimples. The yellow green remains of a bruise colored one eye. The boy blocked her way, his smile widening to show mossy teeth.

"Who are you?" Eve tried to squeeze by.

"J-JJ," he stuttered. "You must be Eve. Pop talks about you all the time."

"Pop? Who's Pop?"

"Come in here, Eve. You need to meet your brother, JJ." Eve's father stood in the center of the room, arms crossed.

Eve looked to her mother, who wasn't acknowledging much of anything, her gaze out the window at the old house site. Either by pills or pot, she'd left the room.

"I don't have a brother." She turned to her father. "Who is he?"

"He's my son. Not your mother's boy but my son and your half brother." He stood next to the boy, the resemblance clear. "Now, when we have a little party, you'll have someone to keep you company."

"Not gonna happen, Daddy. Trailer is crowded enough, and you bring this kid home?"

"Don't get your panties twisted darling. I want you two to be close. Your Momma isn't too happy finding out about him. The other woman didn't mean anything, but family is family, blood is blood. Get used to seeing the boy around here, right, JJ?"

"He ain't my blood, Daddy. I don't have to get used to anything."

Daddy put a firm grip on her shoulder, spinning her around to face JJ, his grizzled jaw in her ear, and stale cigarettes on his breath. "You'll do what I tell you in my house. I know how your momma has big ideas about her Malone name and this property. But I'm the man here, and I say what goes on. We're gonna' have a little party tonight, so clean the damn place up." He shoved her toward the sink and piled dishes.

Eve did as she was told. She washed, cleaned, and straightened the small space. JJ slumped on the couch, silently watching her which was annoying. Daddy sat at the table. Momma went to the bedroom to lie down. When she finished, Eve went out to the garden, watching Daddy and JJ pull out to buy the booze and who knows what else. A plume of dust followed them down the road. Her ideal life on the ridge with Momma had become a nightmare.

❖

Sullen JJ rarely spoke, and then only a few words. He lurked, following Eve from a distance, which creeped her out. She moved out to the garden, building an encampment in the fortified space behind the rock wall in a two-person tent she bought at the Walmart. Eve kept a change of clothes, a water bottle, and a sleeping bag in the tent. Someone had gone through her clothes box in the trailer. She hoped it was only Daddy looking for her earnings and not JJ looking for who knows what. She kept her money in a safety box in the cleft in the garden wall. Marcy wanted her to open an account at the bank, but Eve was hesitant, wanting to be ready in case she needed to move.

JJ watched while she sat on an old beach chair in the garden, reading. She had a stack of magazines, a couple of books, and some graphic novels borrowed from the tattoo parlor, her ersatz library. Bigun, her friend and librarian, called her a blank canvas, eager to put his ink on her. Eve held off, not wanting a tattoo for the same reason she didn't want an intimate relationship with Marcy; it had to mean something.

JJ peered over the stone wall, startling Eve.

"Stop creeping me out, JJ. What's your deal?"

"W-why are you always out here reading?"

"Because it's too small a space in there with you and Daddy, and it's starting to stink. I like it out here."

"He's your father, too."

"I don't know about that. Daddy burned any relationship we had with the house. I'm done with that man."

"But Daddy said blood makes us family. So that means you and me is family." She flinched at his grammar. "I ain't got much. Momma quit taking care of me. Daddy came to fetch me from the institute when he got out of prison. I'm grateful."

"Good for you. I'm not happy he's home. My summer has gone to shit, but Momma won't give up on him. She's like the beautiful butterfly that's attracted to dog crap."

"Don't say that. The old man ain't that bad."

"We can argue all day, but I bet that shiner on your eye didn't get there by itself. What's up with you?"

"I-I-I," he stuttered. "I have to take medication. I see things and hear things that aren't there sometimes. I had to go to the hospital for a while. Can I look at your comic book?

"It's not a comic. It's a graphic novel. The woman is a detective who solves crimes and helps people who've lost family or been cheated on. She's called The Asp, like the poisonous little snake."

"C-C-Cool." He got it out. "Maybe you can lend it to me when you're done. I don't read much 'cause the words get all messed up in my mind.

"Are you on meds?"

"Yeah, but Daddy took them. I haven't taken what I'm supposed to in a few days. I'm a little jumpy right now. Things are starting to look a little funny, too."

"Stand up to the bastard. Take your meds back. I know from work how important it is for people with health issues to be on their meds." The boy hung his head. Eve let out a sigh. "Fine, I'll get them."

Eve put down her book and brushed by the boy. She went in to check on Momma, still in bed. Momma was rarely up before Eve went to work since Daddy had returned. When she was up, she didn't speak much.

"Come on, Momma. Let's get you up." Momma was compliant, sitting with a sigh. Eve went to the bucket in the kitchen for a washcloth and filled a plastic tub with water. "Bath time, Momma." She shut the door and pulled off her mother's tee shirt while she sat on the edge of the bed. Lifting her arm, she ran the cloth along the length of her arm and underneath. She didn't let herself think how it had come to this, tending to her mother like the little old ladies. She gave baths all the time, but somehow bathing Momma as she had once been bathed was another reality. Eve washed both legs, her feet, her back, and neck to freshen her up from living in the close quarters and no air conditioning. Eve then delicately washed her mother's face, dabbing her eyes and ears. She had her lean back and rinsed her hair, hand drying her locks gently with a towel. She placed a clean bra and panties next to her mother on the bed.

"I'm going to tidy up the room, Momma. Run that washcloth around down below and change into your clean underclothes, so we can get you dressed." She turned away as her mother washed and changed. Eve went through her father's things quickly, finding the plastic freezer bag. Several of the brown plastic bottles had JJ's name on them. She put them in her backpack and stashed the bag where she'd found it. She then pulled off the bed sheets, stuffing them in the pillowcase with Momma's dirty clothes. She'd add her items to wash later before she left for work. Eve made the bed and then came back for her mother.

"Let's make you look pretty, just like the picture you showed me, Momma." Eve pulled her mother's hair back, braiding the long strands. She put out a clean tee shirt and jeans for her. Eve then applied a little foundation, eye shadow, and clear lip gloss. "There, gorgeous and ready to meet the day." She hugged Momma, earning a fey smile. "It'll get better, Momma."

The two walked out together.

"I'm going out before work, but I'll be home later," she announced. "I'll get JJ to get y'all some food." She kissed her momma goodbye. Lilly followed Eve out, lighting a cigarette and stretching out on the porch in the sun. JJ sat on the stone wall of the garden. Eve walked over and tossed him the pill bottles.

"Take your meds. And keep them close. Don't forget to get them refilled when they start to get low. Those two can't do much for you anymore. I'm going out for a run to clear my head before work, and then I'll be home later. Keep an eye on things. Oh yeah, go down to the Minimart and get a bucket of fried chicken, taters, and rolls. There's no food in there and Mountain Dew and Doritos ain't gonna' cut it. Everyone needs to eat." She handed him a twenty and jogged off into the forest.

Running on the trail made the world better, everything falling into its rightful place. The beauty of the land displayed at her feet. Mountain laurels bloomed knee-high, minnows darted in the stream that ran down the hillside beside her, and dragonflies skimmed the water, secret companions on her daily journey. It felt good to leave her worries behind with a rush of adrenaline and a soft breeze.

Five

Eve shoved her book in her back pocket when the dryer stopped tumbling. She stifled a yawn and began unloading. She wasn't supposed to use the laundry room at the nursing home, but no one ever said anything and she'd come in early anyway. Eve folded the sheets, then her clothes, loading everything into the paper bag, and stuffing it into her locker with her book. She locked the door to the hallway, then moved the mop, buckets and cleaning products aside from the janitor's closet to take a shower. After a quick wash and shampoo, she rinsed, dried, and dressed quickly for another day.

Eve helped patients wash and dress for the day, then took turns pushing them from activity to lunch to another event and finally dinner while thinking about Momma. She wasn't going to rehab anymore and slept most of the day, depressed. Daddy had not been around much, though JJ had become a fixture, a stray left behind like Kitty.

❖

"What is it, Momma? You're so quiet, and you haven't been eating." Eve inquired on a balmy summer morning. She'd made toast and juice for her mother who seemed to be living on coffee alone. She was skeletal. "Have some toast at least."

Momma didn't answer, looking out over the ridge. "He has someone else. That's why he's not here that much."

"Bastard. Let's leave, Momma. It's time and there's no reason to stay."

"I can't honey. I'll wait for my man. I've always known there was someone else. The boy is proof." She never called him JJ, just, "the boy." It was distressing to see her so withdrawn. The happier version that enjoyed support group had withered since Daddy had returned.

"If having JJ around reminds you of her, we can get rid of him. I'm not afraid of JJ, and I'm not afraid of Daddy. But nothing is going to get better if you don't try, Momma. Why don't you go back to your support group?"

She huffed, blowing out smoke. "Those poor souls can't help me none. Those women have their own problems. They've been left, they owe a fortune, and they've either lost or are going to lose their home. Most of them have nothing left, including their teeth. There's no support there. I'll make do and wait for him to come home." She'd finished her cigarette and went back inside.

Eve went to work perplexed. Watching her mother succumb wasn't something she was prepared to do. Mrs. Smith was dressed and waiting when she arrived.

"You look nice today, Mrs. Smith. Where shall we go?"

"We can stay here and wait for lunch if it's okay with you. I'm a bit tired. How are things for you, my dear?"

"It's not so good at home and I'm worried about my Momma. She's depressed. Daddy's not home that much and he brought home some kid who's supposed to be my half brother. The whole situation sucks. Oh, sorry."

"It's okay. I could tell something was troubling you. How can I help?"

"Tell me if I'm too nosy, but it sounds like you didn't care much for your father. How did you deal with him, living in his home?"

"You're not too nosy. I'm happy to share my life with you. My father was an icon in the community and he could be very strict. It was my job to keep the children unseen and unheard unless he asked for them. I dressed them for Sunday church and dinner. It was not a bad childhood, but it wasn't happy, either. I had a roof over my head, and I worked hard until the day I was old enough to leave. That home and work was better than no home during the Great Depression. I missed my real mother terribly and still do. One day, I said goodbye to my stepbrothers and sisters, who I was quite fond of, and left to work in town.

You know the rest about the young woman who liked to hike and eventually met her husband at the farm." She smiled.

"You give me hope I can get through this, Mrs. Smith. Let's go get some fresh air before lunch." Eve smiled and took a relaxed breath for the first time that day.

❖

Returning home, Eve found the door ajar. The party must have broken up early that night. She found the chicken bones piled in the sink. She nibbled on a tater wedge that was still in the bag, relieved her father was gone. JJ was gone too. Momma was sprawled in bed. A pipe lay on the table next to a mostly empty fifth of Jack Black. Eve picked up the pipe, a crumpled crystal still in the bowl like a dried pea. For a moment, she was tempted, the lighter still on the table. It would all go away with a puff of the pipe, at least that's what they said. She put the pipe down and tossed the rock in the garbage where it belonged. Impulsively, she took a swig from the Jack Black bottle, coughing from the burn on her tongue. She spit what didn't go down into the sink and rested, wiping her brow, then methodically cleaned up the kitchen and unloaded the laundry before heading to her tent for the night.

Everything was in order when she arrived at her new home. The opossum grinned from the branches above her.

An owl, higher up somewhere, hooted his soothing song, preparing for the hunt. Eve climbed inside and prepared to zip up the tent, waiting for her cat. He came inside with tail up, happy for shelter. She said goodnight to her little family, safe within the confines of the garden.

Footsteps approached through the wildflowers. Eve unzipped the tent and stepped out quickly in her tee shirt and running shorts, the grass cool on her bare feet. JJ stood outside the gate, illuminated by her lantern.

"What are you doing here?"

"I thought we could talk some more. It was nice of you to get my meds back. I wanted to say, th-th-th-thanks. I feel better now." He smiled and held up a six-pack of Old Milwaukee.

"No, thanks, JJ. I worked today and I'm tired. I have to work tomorrow, too. You should see about a job yourself."

"Hard for me with my past and meds. Daddy says I can get a disability check to help out when I'm old enough."

"Don't listen to him. Talk to your doctor and go out and look for a job. There are lots of places you could work, even with a medical condition. I have to go to sleep, so can you leave? I won't be able to with you out here."

"I'll go back, but thanks. It's nice talking with you. I don't have many friends. I imagine you're just like that lady in your book, helping everyone." He trudged off, leaving an unopened Old Milwaukee on the rock wall.

Eve took the beer and popped it open, chugging the contents and watching JJ to make sure he entered the trailer. She crunched the can and dropped it outside, letting a small belch erupt into the night air. She crept back into her tent, content with the cat asleep on her feet.

❖

The morning sunshine was warm through the tent. The cat ran out as Eve unzipped, jumping to the rock wall to clean itself in the sun. She needed to pee and squatted behind the big tree to relieve herself, taking her time and enjoying the morning sun and the mountain in all its glory. Standing to pull her shorts up, Eve was surprised to see JJ directly across from her sitting on the wall. He and the cat had been watching her. He grinned with no shame, then lit a cigarette and played with something between two fingers.

"What the fuck's wrong with you, JJ? You never watch someone doing their business." She blushed, wondering how much he'd seen.

"Just came by to see if you enjoyed your beer. It looks like you did." He nodded at the empty can. "Sorry I caught ya' squattin'." He casually lit a small firecracker, his grin possum-like. JJ tossed the lit cracker to the cat, which pounced as it popped. Kitty screeched, bounding over the wall her tail bristled. Eve reacted at the same time as the cat. She scooped up one of the black walnuts on the ground, spun and released. The nut thumped JJ's forehead right between his eyes. His high tops were the last thing she saw as he disappeared behind the wall.

"You're an idiot. That's my cat." A low groaning yowl came from the woods below.

JJ stood, rubbing a big red spot and black walnut smut on his forehead. "Where'd you learn to throw like that?"

"School. You should try it sometime. What's wrong with you? That animal is defenseless."

"It's just a cat, a stupid animal. We eat animals. What does it matter? I eat squirrel, opossum. Maybe I'll try cat!"

"God, you're insane. Go away and get out of my life." JJ shuffled off, cursing and rubbing his head.

Eve called for the cat, but it wouldn't leave the woods, only coming back under cover of darkness later that night.

❖

Ridge Works Tattoo made a nice stop her way home that day.

"Hey," Eve waved as she entered the tidy store. For some reason, she always expected the shop to be a bit dog eared, but Bigun kept it neat with plants set about in the windows. Today he had on a Hawaiian shirt to complement his Nitro football shorts and sandals. He smiled as she entered.

"Hey, back atcha. Just get off work?"

"Yeah, thought I'd hang out if you don't mind. Any new magazines?" He pointed to the rack.

"It's going to be slow tonight. Why don't you let me give you your first ink, on the house?"

"I don't know. I wouldn't know what to get or where." She picked up one of the oversized design books, but all the examples seemed clichéd to her. She passed over sweet and naughty Tinkerbell, sad Eeyore the donkey, the rebel flag, and various slogans. None of them meant anything. Besides, where would she put it? Eve flipped to the section with the tribal designs. It confused her further, the symbols for war, earth, spirituality. She closed the book. "I think I'll just read for a while."

Bigun turned up the volume on the sound system, then resumed reading The Wall Street Journal. Eve picked up a horror comic but only clutched the well worn pages, staring into the mirror in front of her. Her angst bubbled inside her once again. What was she doing with her life, hiding out at the tattoo shop while Momma waited for Daddy, the cheatin' bastard. His double life pissed her off and she decided it was time to leave. Eve tossed the book back on the pile. She stopped at the door.

"Gotta go, Bigun."

"Come back any time, Eve. We can talk, you know."

He really was sweet. "I know." Eve smiled at him shyly and waved, stepping out the door into the night.

Six

The drive into Huntington would have been a nice diversion on her day off except that Eve was on a mission. She passed the university that should have been her home, a snug room in one of the dorms with teammates, a real bathroom, private shower, and the training table. Even better, she could have been free from the drama on the ridge. Eve wouldn't let herself become bitter, never quite allowing herself to indulge the full fantasy. Going off to college was just a dream. She'd won races and everyone said state champion was a big deal, everyone but Daddy. He told her in front of her coach and team how their folk didn't go to college, how she wouldn't fit in, and that she was wasting her time running and studying.

The tall bank buildings passed as she turned off the interstate and reached the shabbier side of town. Eve pulled across the street from the low brick office that may have once been a school. Ratty old men smoked out front, looking for shade on the hot summer day. Eve stepped out of the car and stood under a tree to wait. Eventually, more men came out from the parole office, all pausing to smoke in relief. Daddy came near the end, lighting up like the rest. He saw her and walked across the street slowly, taking a long drag.

"Whatcha doing down here, baby girl? Guess you were missing your Daddy or did your Momma send you to check on me?" His wide grin changed to a thin line.

"Had the day off and thought I'd come to see where you go all the time." She paused and took a deep breath. He was a bit greyer and a little stooped. Prison might have done that. His belly had rounded, too, no longer flat. "Momma knows, Daddy."

"Momma knows what? She hasn't been herself lately. Don't go listening to her about nothin'". He lit a new cigarette.

"Momma knows you got someone else down here, someone besides JJ's mother." She'd been fueled with anger on the ride down, but somehow it evaporated standing in front of him. She still had feelings for the man. Eve fought her emotions, wanting to hang onto her resentment for his philandering but he was just a man, her father getting older.

Daddy drew long from his smoke then stomped it out and took Eve's hand, surprising her. "Come on. I want to show you something. You're old enough now I reckon."

Eve walked with him. The two passed slowly along the empty street, trying to keep under the shade of the trees. The day was scorching hot. He stopped at a gas station. Two bays were open with cars parked in various states of disrepair. "I work there. It keeps me busy. I'm a grease monkey which ain't a bad job. I'm good, and I make a little bit." Someone yelled, followed by a wolf whistle. "That was for you. I guess they saw us." Eve blushed.

They came to a residential section of town with smaller mostly run-down cottages and bungalows. It seemed natural walking next to her father and not so different from a few years before when Eve was little, down by the river fishing. They were father and child once again with few cares. The thought melted with the hot breeze that sweated her forehead. They'd reached the end of the street and stood in front of a nicely manicured trailer park. Two blond girls in pigtails and matching swimsuits splashed and squealed in a plastic pool next to his truck. They might have been six or seven. They spotted Eve and Daddy, waving.

"Joe! Joe's home." The two hopped out of the pool and ran to him. A teenage girl got up from a folding chair and went inside the trailer. Eve glanced at her father.

He nodded. "That was the babysitter that watches them while I'm at my parole meeting. Hey, girls. Are you having fun? Sadie and Sarah, this is my daughter, Eve."

Eve's spell with her father evaporated. The two children gathered around her with big eyes.

"She's pretty," Sadie said.

"Like the Frozen princess, Elsa, but with shorter hair," Sarah added. "Can you sing the song?" Both launched into the theme song, dancing around father and daughter. "Are you going to fix us lunch, Joe? Can she stay and be our big sister?" Sadie held one of Joe' hands and Sarah the other just as Eve had moments before.

"I don't know, maybe. You want a peanut butter sandwich, Eve?" Mesmerized by the little family, she didn't answer. "You girls run on up. I'll be along shortly."

"Are they yours, Daddy?" Her voice was quiet. She didn't accuse him, more curious than anything else.

"Naw. Their momma needed someone to rent out a room. I needed a place so I could be close to parole. I helped out and took 'em to eat some. She was lonely and I was lonely, so I moved into her room. They call me Daddy because I sleep in the mommy-daddy bed, but they got a real one somewhere. You mad?"

"Mad at you? Yes, I am mad at you and the way you treat Momma, but this, I don't know what I feel. Those two are precious. You look after them when you're home." The pitch of Eve's voice rose. "What about Momma, my Momma? It makes me sad to think of her alone up there depressed all the time and you down here with another woman."

"Like you said, darling. She knows - has always known. A stray dog gonna wander off sometimes but always comes back when he needs rest or food. I love that woman, but I can't stay in that shit-house trailer with her full time." He lit up again. Sadie and Sarah stood on the front porch waving. Eve waved back. "You were just like them once. It was nice. I was working and we lived in the big house with your grandparents. I'm sorry everything went to shit. I want you to give me a chance. I promise I'm trying to get rehabbed, and I'll be back for your Momma. We'll all be happy again. Maybe we could rebuild the old home." He wiped the corner of his eyes then held out his arms to hug her. Eve complied, folding into her Daddy. Like her Momma, she had become a butterfly.

"Gotta' go, Daddy." Eve pulled away. He looked old and defeated. "Momma will need me. When will you be home again?" There was no answer. He stared at Sadie and Sarah, exhaling smoke.

❖

Eve's thoughts raced as she drove back to the ridge. She felt something for the man, but she wasn't sure if it was love or obligation. Did he even deserve that? Momma, now that was love –a deep desire to care for the woman that cared for her. Then there were Sadie and Sarah.

They were innocent and didn't deserve his disruption in their lives. She wouldn't let him destroy what little bit of happiness or opportunity they had in that double wide if she could help it. "Fuckin' stray-dog, my ass. He needs to leave them be."

Eve stopped at Ridge Works.

"Hey," she waved to Bigun.

"Hey," he waved back. "I wondered if you were coming tonight. It's been slow, and I was going to close early if you didn't show."

"I was coming back from Huntington and thought I'd hang out for a while if you want some company." Eve bent down with her back to him, going through the stack of magazines on the shelf that she knew all too well. She felt him watching her, her shorts a bit low and her tee shirt riding up. Bigun was the closest thing to a friend Eve had on the ridge. She smiled. He could look if he wanted. He was kind and she felt safe with him, one of the first men in her life who hadn't cheated, stolen, or lied to her.

"Why don't you let me give you your first ink tonight, Eve? I saw the perfect place just now." He laughed.

"I bet you did." Eve joined him with a laugh.

"Pick something out, maybe a Celtic cross or ivy, and we can get started. Don't have to finish tonight." He sipped his ice tea from a WVU cup.

"Sometime Bigun, but not tonight. I want something that means something, something beautiful that will last. Guess a tattoo is like a relationship, but I'm in no hurry for one of those either." Eve plopped into the barber chair next to him to read a Stephen King novel that was missing a cover. A few pages in, Eve laughed out loud, "Look at us. We're just like an old married couple, aren't we? You read the paper and me a book and neither of us talking."

"Huh, what's that?" Bigun stretched his arms in the air, his tee shirt revealing muscular arms and a bit of his tight stomach."I don't know anything about being married. Do you want to talk? I can go next door and get a six-pack of brew and we can talk for a while." Eve nodded. Bigun shuffled out to the convenience store. He returned quickly with a twelve pack of beer and a bag of chips. "Dinner," he announced. "You still runnin'?"

"A little. I run to stay fit or get around town when I don't have the car. I thought about competing for the university but that dream's over." Eve popped open the beer. "Do you ever miss football?"

Bigun poured two beers into his cup and opened the bag of chips, returning to his chair, a king on his throne. He passed the bag to Eve."Ladies first. I don't really miss football. I volunteer now as a coach and it helps me stay fit. Back in high school I was playing for a scholarship but blew out both knees my senior year. I had an operation and knew my playing days were over. While I was recovering, I found a book on tattoo art and started studying and drawing. I got my first ink in Charleston near the hospital." Eve seemed to remember Daddy talking about him playing ball for Nitro when she was in middle school. She wanted to see his tattoo.

"What was it? Can I see?"

Bigun rolled up a sleeve of his shirt to reveal a small Hawaiian dancer with long black hair and firm round breasts. "She reminds me of my dream. I want to go to Hawaii one day where my people originally came from. I didn't go to school but saved everything I could and found this place. I study investments and read the Journal and drive that beater of a car. One day I want a really nice shop, and travel to the islands. At first I lived in the back on that old mattress. By the way, you're welcome to stay anytime, with everything that's happened up on the ridge. I like having you here, in case you hadn't noticed. Heck, we can finish this brew and you can stay tonight if you want." His puppy-dog face and dark brown eyes looked hopeful.

"Aw, thanks, Bigun, but I need to get home and get ready for work tomorrow. Besides, I need to check on Momma. See you later." Eve drained her beer and waved goodbye, trudging into the darkness. Her day had been weird. Her surprise feelings for her Daddy and then his surprise with the two girls. Bigun had checked out her ass and may have just asked her to spend the night. She'd enjoyed him watching her and the thought of kissing him set her humming deep inside. Eve rolled down her window to cool the rising heat.

Seven

Eve and Marcy stalked the cosmetic aisle of the Walmart, pretending they were in New York and not West Virginia, the lipstick, eyeliner, and nail polish another form of diversion. The big-box retailer was as close as they could get to the glamorous models in the ads, a tease for a bigger world outside Nitro. Eve was applying mascara and eye shadow in dark shades of violet and black like the Asp. Marcy tried various shades of bright red or pink lipstick, puckering in the mirror. She was only partially listening to Eve about her recent visit to Huntington. Marcy was uninterested in Eve's travails, which was odd. Eve left out her last stop last night to see Bigun. Marcy didn't like anything about the man or his shop.

The two moved to the clothes selection which both agreed sucked. "What are you not telling me, Marcy? What's up?"

Marcy held up a bra and panty set in blaze-orange camouflage. "I'm wearing this underneath." She grabbed

Eve by the hand and pulled her out of the store to the parking lot, both laughing hysterically.

"I need to tell you something, but no judgment." Marcy stopped to catch her breath. Finally, she blurted, "I met someone, Eve." Her face was the color of her new nail polish.

"You met someone. Who is he and do I know him?"

"I said I met someone. I didn't say he." Marcy looked away, dodging Eve's inspection.

"Marcy," Eve grabbed both hands. "Spill and tell me everything. This is fantastic. Do I know her?"

Marcy shook her head no. "I went to pick up a pizza. I was waiting at the bar, sipping a Coke. The new bartender is super cute. I'd never seen her before. She asked me if I wanted something stronger. I told her I didn't have my ID, but she poured us each a vodka. We shot those and then did another. When the pizza came, she wrote her number on the box." Marcy pulled a torn piece of cardboard out of her back pocket. The scrap had the number, followed by the words, 'TEXT ME, heart, heart!'

"Oh my God, Marcy, you slut. You got picked up at the pizza parlor."

"No, it wasn't like that. Well, it was like that. I didn't know what to do. I almost didn't respond because of Mom and the whole thing if someone saw us. I finally got my courage up and texted her. She told me when she was off and I snuck out and met her. We smoked a joint in her car then made out." Marcy paused and took a deep breath. "Then we went back to her place. I spent the night with her." Marcy gushed, somewhat out of breath. "Eve, it was amazing." She fanned herself.

Marcy had been searching for a while and finally found love or it found her, a big old smooch target. Daddy had those feelings for the woman he was shacking up with in Huntington, and Momma still had those feelings for Daddy. Eve wondered where her feelings were. Conflicted, she turned back to her friend.

"So, when do you see her again? Do we need to go back in and buy makeup for your next date?" She made air quotes as she said date.

"That's the thing, Eve. I've texted her a few times, but she doesn't answer."

"Let me see your phone." Marcy handed over the sequined phone. She scrolled through the text. "Good lord, Marcy. Is that you in those pics?" Eve chuckled. "First, no more pics or texts until she calls you. Second, that's not a few messages." She handed the phone back. "If you run into her at the pizza joint, then talk to her. But don't stalk her. You may have been a one-night-stand."

"But she's my first love."

"Not love, Marcy. For God's sake, you had sex."

"We did have sex and it was wonderful. I don't want to stop having sex, and I want her."

"She'll call - give her time. Who could say no to all this?" Eve made a heart shaped silhouette with her fingers. "I've got an idea. Want to go get a slice of pizza?" Eve grinned wickedly. "Come on, at least I can see her. We can say nasty things about her if she doesn't talk to you, or I can try to make her jealous." The two ran across the lot to Marcy's truck, hand-in-hand.

❖

Later that night, Eve stopped at the Handy-Mart for a few supplies. JJ's beat-up Trans Am was parked out front. She came to the counter with wipes, deodorant, a bag of chips, and Gatorade. JJ stood near the vacant-eyed checkout girl. She blew a large bubble from her gum, snapping it to acknowledge Eve's purchases while wrapping a finger in her blond hair.

"How're you doing, sis?" JJ inquired.

"I told you not to call me that, dumbass." Checkout girl watched, slowly ringing each item on the register.

"This here's Patsy. She says she might go out with me when I start working. Got to find a job."

"Good for you, JJ. You need a job. I'll see you later." She didn't wait for a reply or to acknowledge Patsy. Who was she to get in the way of love, even if it was JJ? He needed all the help he could get.

Eve waved to Bigun at the tattoo shop then got in her car and headed to her campsite to prepare for bed. She laughed, thinking about the scene at the pizza parlor. The barmaid ignored Marcy and Eve, sitting in a back booth with their heads together. Eve wanted to leave a napkin with foul names and drawings of her private parts. She wasn't exactly super cute but she'd heard her Daddy says that vodka and last call could make anyone desirable. Marcy grabbed the napkin with Eve's scribblings and stuffed it into her pocket, mouthing the words, "call me," to the uninterested bartender, her thumb and pinky extended to her ear and mouth.

Marcy had found something like love and Eve was happy for her. Even mossy-toothed JJ had found someone, which she found hard to believe. Whatever. Eve was content for now with camp and taking care of Momma. She snuggled with Kitty, a large moon rising above the tent.

Eight

The next time Eve saw Daddy, he asked her if she'd told Momma about her visit to Huntington. She told him she hadn't. The partying returned to the ridge - Daddy, JJ, Momma, and sometimes strays from the old days. Daddy tried to get Eve to join, but she stayed in the garden or at Marcy's. Morning always looked the same with spilled drinks, empty Jack Daniels bottles, pipes, and pills. She'd clean up, only to have the place trashed the next night. Such was her summer.

Eve pulled into the gravel drive to check on her momma and prepare for work. The door to the trailer ajar. She walked inside, greeted only by the faint scent of mildew and held her breath, performing a quick survey. Daddy sat at the table, head in hands, asleep or hung over. JJ was sprawled on the couch, his mouth open, snoring. Debris from the party covered the floor and countertops. Eve opened a window to let in air. She slid into the bedroom, her mother still under the sheets. Thick white pills adorned the nightstand. She placed her hand on her mother's shoulder. There was no warmth. Eve had no desire to go further, forcing herself to move, her breath rapid, not wanting to confirm what she already knew.

Eve pulled back a strand of Momma's hair. The skin along her jaw was the faintest shade of blue. She placed her lips close to her mother's. There was no breath, her skin neither cold nor warm. A small amount of yellow fluid had soaked the pillow by her mouth.

"No Momma, no. You can't leave me. We're getting out of here together. You can't leave me." Eve crawled in bed next to her mother and hugged the limp form tightly. Tears ran down her cheeks onto her mother's hair and onto the sheets.

It was sometime later when she got up. She was unaware of how long she'd been there or what to do next. Momma was gone. Eve covered her mother with the sheet. Thank God her eyes were shut, their clear, bright blue now only a memory. Eve walked out; the two men unmoved.

"What happened, Daddy?" Her words were measured and quiet.

He lifted his head, his eyes half shut. "I don't know. Your momma was like that when I got up this morning. I think she took oxy. I'm sorry, honey. She wasn't well. Bound to happen. Shit, I don't know. I fucked it all up again, I guess." He put his head back in his hands.

Eve put aside her loss. "Why haven't you called anyone?" She looked from her father to JJ, still reclined on the couch. "JJ, go down to the Mini Mart and tell Patsy to call an ambulance." She kicked his feet and he sat up, rubbing his eyes. "Run!" she screamed.

Daddy stood up and pulled on pants over his boxers, grabbing a shirt. "I gotta go," was all he said, leaving JJ in a trail of dust from his truck. Eve prayed he'd never come back and went to the garden to wait. As she sat on the wall, she said a prayer of sorts to her grandparents, hoping Momma was with them. She said goodbye over and over, crying until she exhausted herself, calming until the tears would begin again. The cat joined her, quietly circling her feet, mewing its concern.

"Looks like it's just us. You're my family now, Kitty." Tears blurred the view of the valley below, an ambulance siren in the distance. She continued to sob openly. A truck pulled up by the trailer. A man in jeans with a symbol on his jacket approached.

"Did you call about a woman dying, ma'am?" Eve pointed to the trailer. "Can you show me?" She led the EMT to the trailer. The man's head swiveled from side to side, taking in the poverty and debris from the party. They made their way into the small bedroom. Eve waited outside on the couch in shock. She heard the man on the radio and then another EMT joined him. The two carried her out on the stretcher, covered by the sheet. The EMT came back. "Would you like to come with us, ma'am? There'll be questions and we'll need your help." She followed the man out, sitting in the back of the ambulance. On the way to the hospital, she held onto Momma's toe from under the sheet on the gurney knowing it would be the last time she touched her.

Everything was a blur at the hospital, from the doctor's questions to all the forms to sign. The deputy showed up, wanting to know about the party. Eve told him what she knew. He said he'd check it out, perturbed she hadn't called him about her father's return.

❖

The deputy stopped by the ridge to put up crime scene tape at the trailer. "You stay out of there while we investigate. I wish you had called me, Eve. Maybe your Momma would still be alive." Eve didn't need him to tell her that. She had thought of little else. Thank God Daddy was gone now. JJ had disappeared, too. Eve gave the trailer a wide berth. She preferred her camp in the garden, anyway.

The deputy's comment stung. Maybe it was her fault. "You can bulldoze that place for all I care." She told him. "I'm done with the trailer." Numb to the world around her, Eve couldn't forgive herself for not getting to say goodbye. In a silver lining of sorts, her mother would be buried next to her parents in the little plot. The Baptist church down the road took up a collection to cover the cost of the burial even though the Malones weren't members. The church gave her a small stone engraved with Lilly's name and the years of her birth and death. The grave lay where Momma loved to sit. Eve stared at the stone that marked the cleft above Lilly's headstone. Her treasures were where they should be, with her mother and grandmother.

Eve fidgeted under so many eyes at Lilly's funeral. Marcy brought Eve a new dress and shoes and helped her get ready at the church. The reception was held in the social hall. The people who attended were friendly and sang Lilly's praises. Eve had never seen most of them before and probably wouldn't again. Almost all of them asked her what she would do now. She had no answer. There was lots of food, none of which she could keep at camp. The preacher was sincere, telling Eve to come by and that he and the congregation could help her. A few of the well-wishers asked about her Daddy but she'd look away and not answer them either, silent in her grief and anger at the man who caused it all. Marcy and her mother came to the service at the church and were the only two at the gravesite for the actual burial. Eve watched Bigun drive by. He slowed with the window down, his hands together in a sign of prayer, his head dipped. Marcy held onto her friend's arm while a man filled in the hole.

"Eve, you can't live here any longer. Come home with me and Mom. We'll get ready for school this fall." Eve's tent was down for the funeral, but Marcy knew it would be back up soon. Eve's habits of late seemed a bit macabre.

"Thanks, Marcy, but I can't leave her yet. I need to stay with Momma for a while." Eve smiled a sad little smile while resting her head on Marcy's shoulder, unable to share that she wasn't going to be going to school. Everything had changed and there didn't seem to be any reason to stay here where it would only be sad and cold.

❖

Summer passed to fall, and Eve only left the ridge to work or make a run for groceries. She stayed in the tent, adding a tarp to cover the camp and the bare spot where her mother had been laid to prevent the summer storms from turning the camp muddy. She picked Queen Anne's lace and Black-eyed Susans from the wildflower patch for bouquets in a little vase at her mother's stone. The cat stayed close, a small comfort. School and dreams of an apartment in town drifted away like stormy summer clouds.

Marcy did her best to stay in touch, but Eve withdrew from her friend. Sleepovers became a memory. Mrs. Smith held Eve's hand and patted her when she stood silently behind her chair. They all meant well, but what was the point? The one person she loved was gone. Nothing could bring Momma back.

❖

Daddy returned with the first breath of autumn, JJ in tow. The police tape was down from the trailer.

"Girl, I was worried about ya. That's why I came back. Daddy will take care of you now. I know you loved your Momma, and I did, too. It's a damn shame she overdosed like that, damn shame. I think she was sad. Nothing we could have done."

"She was sad because of you, Daddy. You made her depressed, running out on her, and worse, you gave her the pills. You took her parents, her house, and her possessions. Then you took her pride, bringing that piece of shit home." She nodded toward JJ slinking in the corner.

"Don't talk that way. He's your kin. You be nice. Now we gonna go back to normal and be a family. You be quiet around town about me being here. I know the deputy's been askin' about me. You can take your Momma's place and look after the place and you can contribute to the family budget, too."

"Sure, Daddy. Whatever you say." She wouldn't fight him, knowing she'd be leaving soon, freedom's whisper strong in her ear now.

"JJ, go get some Mountain Dew. I have a bottle of Jack we can open and get the party started. It will be just like old times, and we can remember Lilly, my wife and your mother." He let go a loud, "JacknDewwwwww." On the way out to the car, JJ practiced his own version that sounded like nails on a chalkboard.

Daddy brought a new woman home after a while, her makeup clownish. She was lumpy in the wrong places. Worst of all she smelled of cheap cologne that barely rose above the trailer's mildew. Eve stayed to herself at camp. They could have their Jack-n-Dew, stink-hole, love-nest.

Eve slept next to her mother in the graveyard and stayed late at the tattoo parlor, turning things over in her mind. Her first acknowledgment of the change taking place within her came when she decided on her tattoo. It gave her something to look forward to and something to think about other than Momma. Bigun sketched the tattoo to her approval then made a stencil which he delicately transferred to her wrist. He began outlining the intricate design with black ink. The big man moved around her gently, his grip strong but his movements delicate and soft. Bigun always wore shorts, even in the crisp autumn air on the ridge. She breathed in his cologne, musky like the forest but bracy like the sea shore, his long hair swept up, his beard occasionally tickling her arm when he was closely looking at his work. He laughed easily at the slightest things she said and he had a kind smile, his eyes twinkling when he laughed. To distract herself, Eve inspected his his tattoos, the black ink in contrast to his cocoa skin. Her fantasy with him blossomed as he worked on her design, a young woman's harmless whimsy and an escape to the arms of someone she trusted with a small part of her body.

Eve imagined his soft hands touching other parts of her, his face close to hers as he worked. She could slide an arm around his neck and open her lips. That would start things no doubt. He'd put down his needle. Eve stifled a chuckle. She could move in with him and they could become a couple. His place was probably as neat as the shop. There would be kids, probably several since she was pretty sure they'd be "doing it" all the time. She'd never given the thought of having a grown up life, not to mention kids a second thought but here she was with a man she liked and who liked her and it was all she could think about. It gave her a thrill deep inside. At first her imaginary children were blond like her and looked like Sadie and Sarah, but then morphed into smaller versions of Bigun with wild hair in tee shirts, and gym shorts. She laughed.

"What's so funny? What?" He'd stopped for a moment, squinting at her.

"Oh, nothing... something I was dreaming about. Did you know that besides Marcy, you're one of my best friends?"

He smiled. "I don't think she likes me much."

"Marcy shouldn't judge. Who knows, maybe one day she'll get a tat."

Bigun rested a hand on her shoulder, setting the tattoo gun and shaking out his cramped fingers for a moment. Eve fell back to her fantasy with his touch, which didn't last nearly long enough, the tattoo gun whirring again. It didn't hurt as much as she thought it might, the ink jetting into her wrist, now bright emerald green. The sound and vibrations relaxed her, and she could dream about a bigger, better life. Bigun wiped a smear with his rag. Their affair would begin on Bigun's chair with her on his lap, the two locked in an embrace, Eve facing him and moving ever so slightly. What would sex with Bigun be like? Marcy said it hurt, but what did she know? They'd watched her father's porn videos and it all seemed strange and the people stupid. The actual act in real life and love must be okay because people did it all the time. Bigun had an old mattress on the floor in the back storage room. He'd probably invite her back with wine and candles. She pictured him on top of her, crushing her with his size. The thought terrified her and excited her at the same time. She took a deep breath, a shiver passing down her arms and legs.

"I remember your mother's tattoo. She was a beautiful lady, and I enjoyed working on her serpent, some of my best work. I'm sorry you lost her. I came to the burial." Her fantasy dissolved with the mention of her mother. Eve returned to the present.

"Thanks, Bigun, I saw you."

Eve chose the same tattoo as Momma but in a different place, a place where she could see it and remember her candy and menthol scent. The emerald green serpent wound around her wrist several times, beautiful and elegant. The tail pointed to her elbow while the head opened on her wrist, the same fangs, black-beaded eyes, and curvy pink tongue as Momma's. She wanted the head in her palm, but Bigun said it would hurt more and was harder to heal. Besides, she could cover the tat on her wrist with a long-sleeved shirt if she didn't want it seen. It was beautiful, like Momma's.

On her first day back to work after the tattoo, Eve wore a long-sleeved shirt. Marcy figured something was up and pulled her sleeve up to examine her wrist. Usually, Marcy would take delight in something new such as a tattoo, a sign of rebellion and counterculture.

"Eve, you're living like a hermit on a mountaintop. You sleep in a tent in a graveyard for God's sake, and now you have a tattoo. You're not doing anything with that hairy, old tattoo guy, are you?"

"I've only handled his mechanical tool if that's what you mean." Marcy gave her an expression of disgust. "No,

Marcy, I'm not fooling around with Bigun, though I could if I wanted to." Eve grinned at Marcy's discomfort. "I can't stand to be near Daddy or that trailer, so I spend time and help out at the tattoo parlor." Marcy wanted to look at apartments in town, but Eve declined her invitation. She felt relief when she unenrolled at the JC and was happy cleaning and organizing at Ridge Works in exchange for her new art. She was waiting for change, trusting her instincts that she'd recognize when the time was right for her.

Coming home one day, her father stopped her before she could get by. "I want you to move in, darling. I want you to be a part of this family. You can cook and clean for us like your Momma did. Oh yeah, and I want you to contribute to the family welfare."

What a genius, Eve thought. What kind of idiot does he think I am, asking me to move in with a murdering parent and give away my money?

Daddy's voice startled her. "You hear me? Anyway, you can party with us. I want you to be a sister and help JJ. He's a lonely kid and a little touched in the head. You're out there in that graveyard by yourself. It's not right for you to be out there with the dead."

Eve didn't feel like arguing. It was time. She'd never escape if she didn't leave now. Relief swept over her. She'd been patient. The tattoo had come in its own time, and so had leaving. She'd start a new life and almost smiled, keeping a straight face in front of her father. Eve studied the serpent, small and deadly. She'd travel to Alexandria and take her mother's memory to a place where she'd once been happy. Maybe she could find happiness there, too.

"Sure, Daddy, I'll move back, but I need a few things." Eve pulled her box back to the bedroom and shut the door. She got out jeans, a winter coat, extra underwear and other necessities. She stuffed everything in a bag and threw it and a blanket out the back window, then went outside and pulled on her sneakers. She walked around the trailer to get the bag and blanket. Eve stopped at the garden to say goodbye, filling her pack and retrieving her book. The cat circled her ankles.

"Bye, Momma. I have to go. He can't hurt you now." She patted Kitty. "Stay away from the trailer. You know where the trash is to get food. I'm sorry I can't take you. Keep her company for me." A small garter snake slithered by her foot, unusual for that time of year. The cat pounced, but the snake disappeared into the stone wall. It was a sign. Momma wanted her to go. Eve picked up her backpack and walked down the backside of the property, leaving Malone Ridge.

Nine

The bus pulled into the Roanoke station. Daddy had taken her Corolla, his truck broken down like him. It didn't matter; she could barely afford the bus much less gas for a car. She reread the postcard before she dropped it in the mailbox.

Dear Marcy,

I'm doing it! I'm leaving Nitro and I feel like I'm in one of Mrs. Smith's stories. Tell her goodbye for me, I'll miss her.

I'm sorry I didn't come to say goodbye, but it would have been too hard. I'll call you when I get settled. I already miss you!!! We will make it, I promise you. I'm headed to Roanoke and then Alexandria.

Wish me luck!

Love, Eve.

She mailed the card then found a pay phone. Eve dialed the Sheriff's office first, leaving an anonymous tip for the deputy, her Daddy was back on Malone Ridge dealing oxy. The bastard could sit in prison where he couldn't hurt Sadie or Sarah, or JJ ever again. The stray dog was going back to the pound. She laughed sadly. It felt good to help Sadie and Sarah but her thoughts of her father were mixed. She didn't know what she thought about JJ, her brother from another mother with so many issues, he wouldn't make it long in the real world. Hopefully, Patsy would look after him. Eve was free.

❖

JJ walked into the trailer with his slew-footed gait. Daddy sat at the small table playing solitaire. "Guess what, Daddy? I got a job today."

"You got what?"

"I got a job. I'm working at the gun shop in town. I work in the storeroom and drive the forklift." The old man motioned for him to sit. JJ took a seat across the table,wary of a cuff to the ear. Maybe Daddy would be proud.

"Well, I'll be. That's great JJ, but don't do anything stupid and get yourself fired. Workin's gonna make it hard to claim disability. Does the boss know about the way your brain works?"

"Yeah, they know. A boy from the hospital helped me get this job. I won't get fired. I need to earn some money."

"Well, show some backbone and work hard and you can do good. Where'd that sister of yours go? She's a tough nut and you could learn from her, but I'm hungry and I need her to fix me something. We can tell her your good news and drink a little whiskey to liven up the mood around here."

Sirens could be heard coming up the ridge.

"Shit, son. Guess someone turned me in. You haven't been talking, have you? I heard you been hanging out with that little tramp down at the Minimart."

"Daddy, I ain't talked to no one, I swear, and I didn't say anything to Patsy."

"Patsy, huh. Well, I guess you're grown-up now. Go get ya some, boy." He stood up and ruffled JJ's hair, both grinning.

Multiple cars screeched to a stop outside in the gravel followed by doors slamming. A digitized voice called out. "Joe Ball, come out with your hands up."

"Alright then, let's get this over with. Looks like I'll be warm this winter and get my three squares." Joe walked out without a second glance to JJ, his hands behind his head.

❖

The bus station was like every other—huge, dark, and made of concrete. It smelled of dampness, popcorn, and urine. Eve quickly made her way to the nearby shelter, following the homeless who migrated along the railroad tracks toward the dodgy side of the city. One look at the institutional beds and sad, pinched faces told her she needed to move on. Now that she was on her own, all the overnight rules seemed oppressive. She stayed for dinner, and then ducked out before bed check to catch a ride at the nearby Sheetz station. The trucker was nice and said he'd take her as far as Warrington. She'd have to find a ride east from there. The land was pretty in Virginia. They rode through a beautiful valley of farms hemmed in by the Appalachians on one side and the smaller Blue Ridge Mountains on the other. The mountains were truly shades of blue and green in the fading sunlight, with spots of red, yellow, and brown in the valley down below. After a while, a huge moon moved over the mountains. The size and speed of the big rig impressed her. Everything in her new world seemed bigger and faster. Momma would have loved this, headed for Alexandria in a tractor-trailer, the land changing by the mile.

The thought of Momma brought tears to her eyes. She imagined Kitty prowling around near her old campsite and Momma's grave. She lightly ran her finger over the green serpent on her wrist and knew Momma would be happy for her. She clutched her bag a little tighter as she turned her gaze to the road ahead.

The trucker dropped her off at a truck stop that made the Walmart parking lot in Nitro look small. The last thing he told her was to be careful and not get in just any truck. Finding a ride east at the terminal would not be hard, but finding the right ride could be difficult. She walked down row after row of idling cabs, the men grinned or waved, signaling Eve to come up. Eve would holler, "East," then wait for the thumbs up or down. Their friendliness set her on edge-Asp mode, ready to kick-butt if she had too.

The beefy trucker seemed okay, his truck gleaming under the huge parking lights. He invited Eve into his cab with a friendly wave and thumbs up to her direction of travel.

"Come on up, sugar. Now, where you off to? Running from something, I'd guess."

"I'm starting over. My Momma died. I'm headed east to Alexandria."

"I can take you as far as Springfield, and then I head north toward Pennsylvania and the turnpike. It's a two-hour ride if traffic is good. You can get to Alexandria from there, twenty to thirty minutes is all." She stowed her pack at her feet and fastened her seat belt and relaxed a little. She'd be in Alexandria in three hours or so.

The trucker smiled through tobacco-stained teeth, then flipped a small switch that locked the doors, the diesel engine idling. Without warning, his thick hand gripped her knee. She pulled away, dodging a slobbery kiss, his breath foul. "Ah, come on now. No one rides for free. Thought we'd get acquainted."

"Get away from me and let me out." Eve's eyes darted to the locked door. She tried the handle which didn't move. Don't freak out, she repeated to herself.

"Before we leave, honey, you have to pay your way and I ain't talking gas money." His hand moved to his zipper. "Get in the back and drop them jeans." Eve tried the door handle again. "It stays locked until you put out, sweet thing." He turned up the country music. "Just in case you get loud, and by the way, I like it loud." His hand slid up her leg. "Now come on, this can be easy or hard." His grin grew broader.

What would The Asp do? "Okay." Eve unsnapped her seat belt. The man drooled, unzipping his fly and dropping his suspenders so he could shimmy his pants down. He spit out the tobacco pouch into a cup of brown goo. Eve shrunk back in her seat, lifting her knees to a crouch while leaning back against the door seductively. Slowly, she moved a hand toward the snap of her pants. His eyes followed her fingers.

"Hurry up, sweet cheeks, I'm ready for some fun. You want me to help you there and we can do it right here? I'll set you right up here on the wheel." He reached for her with a gargling laugh.

Eve swiveled and thrust her legs straight at his face, the bottoms of her shoes flying past his swinging arm and connecting with his chin. The trucker's head smashed into the driver window, her feet pushing him back in his seat. He roared, grabbing his head and swatting at her with the other hand. Eve gave him a second quick shot with one foot that connected with his nose, making a sickening crunch. Blood spurted onto the steering wheel. She reached over his belly to hit the lock switch. Being so close to the man made her sick. Grabbing the handle with one hand, she swung the door open. He was still screaming as she fell from the truck to the parking lot below. Eve pulled her pack on, spat out the bile in her mouth and ran to the truck stop.

"I need help." She told the first person she saw, out of breath. Someone pointed to the counter. "A trucker wanted to hurt me," she told the counter man. "He wanted to." She was unable to say the word.

"No hitchhiking or propositioning the truckers." He pointed to a sign.

The trucker came stumbling in, blood smeared on his face and tee shirt. He was roaring epithets about what he was going to do to Eve. His nose looked strange—larger, flatter, and blue.

"Gimme that little bitch. I'm gonna kill her." The counter man moved between Eve and the trucker.

"Now you leave." He spoke directly to the man. "Hospital is up the road in Winchester. Looks like you're going to need some help there before the night is over.

Move on and I won't call the police. The young lady here says you were assaulting her. Rape is a serious charge and I choose to believe her. Now go on, get out of here." Several other workers from the kitchen filled in as backup. The trucker slunk out, pausing at the window to glare malevolently at Eve.

"You gotta leave, too, honey. Go the other way, but not out by the rigs. You're not safe here. Word will spread on the CB and there's no telling whose side they'll take. It's pretty mean out there at night. You can hitch from the highway, just not here."

"Can I buy a few things?" He nodded. She collected herself, walking slowly down the aisles, picking up jerky, gummy bears, and water. She paid at the counter.

Ten

"Did you really do all that to that trucker?" A young man stood behind her while she paid.

"Yeah, guess I did. I was scared," Eve answered quietly. She looked at a small spot of blood on her jeans. "I need to wash up a bit."

"That was badass. He was way bigger than you and you really smashed him up. Where are you headed?"

"Alexandria." Her stomach roiled.

"We're headed that way. My classmates and I live nearby. We're going home for the weekend. There's no football at VT this weekend. Do you want to ride with us?"

"I'd like that. I can pay for gas." She blushed.

"It's okay, we have money. You can tell us your story. I'm Rob." Eve nodded, then followed him to the Honda sedan where two friends were waiting. As Rob opened the passenger door, Eve ran to the back and heaved loudly, discharging her dinner from the shelter where it splattered on the tarmac. She braced herself and heaved a second time. She hung her head while long threads of drool reached for the ground. After a few minutes that seemed like an eternity, Eve stood wearily and wiped her mouth, slightly dizzy. Rob handed her a tissue. She began to shiver.

"Here," Rob wrapped her in an old blanket and handed her water. "You're probably in shock." She wrapped up, sitting shotgun. Eve closed her eyes, leaning her head on the window.

The four set off for Alexandria quietly. Eve slept a little while the boys talked football. Eventually feeling better, she sipped her water and ate a few gummy bears. Eve told the boys her story as the miles passed. After dropping off the other two, Rob and Eve headed to his house in Fort Hunt. He walked her to the door.

"My parents will be cool. You can stay in the guest room. They'll be asleep since it's late. I'll let them know you're here in the morning."

The guest room felt like another world. Eve used the bathroom and climbed into bed. As she drifted off, she thought she could hear whispers, a voice of concern. A door squeaked open, and then closed quietly and she didn't care.

❖

The next morning was a revelation. Eve luxuriated in the soft bed and clean sheets, not wanting to stir. Soft light came in through pretty curtains. The guest bathroom was even nicer, the clean towels and warm water a treat. She showered for a long time enjoying the scent of the soap and shampoo before changing into clean underwear. She came downstairs to the smell of bacon in the grand home. Eve hung back at the door before Rob motioned for her to come in. He introduced her to his parents.

“Do you go to the university, too, dear?” Rob’s mother had a worried look. She brought over a plate with pancakes and melon.

“No, ma’am. I’m from West Virginia, and I’m traveling to Alexandria. I hope to find work and a place to live there. Your son was nice enough to give me a lift and a warm bed for the night.” Shit, that came out wrong. Rob’s parents exchanged a glance.

“Dad, Mom, geez. You always preach kindness, and she needed a place to stay. That’s all.” Eve exhaled, looking at her food. She was starving.

“Oh, do you have family here?”

“No, ma’am.” Eve was nervous in the intimate environment, speaking low and slow. “I’m hoping to start over. We had some family problems. I lost my Momma recently. I want to go to school, but I have to work and save first.”

“I’m so sorry, dear. You must be having a rough time.” Her expression lightened, turning to Rob’s father for support. He continued to read the newspaper.

Rob came to the rescuer. "Mom, enough with the interrogation. Eve, have some pancakes and bacon." Rob's father glanced over the edge of the paper at her tattoo. He sipped his coffee and smiled. The food was wonderful. Eve had a second cup of coffee and nibbled the bacon.

After breakfast, Rob and Eve went down to the basement to play Warcraft. She'd never had much time for video games but could keep up with him and his online friends. Eve's chose an Elfin Princess with a deadly spear for her avatar.

"Sorry about my parents. They mean well, but they can be protective. If they only knew the shit I do at college." Eve liked his smile. "Dad likes your tattoo by the way. He was checking it out, the old dog." Rob laughed, punching his controller. Eve realized the pain on both sides of her face was from smiling. She laughed for the first time in weeks.

"It's okay, you're lucky. They love you. It's nice."

"Are you okay, losing your mom? I mean, I know it's not okay, but can I ask how you cope? I couldn't do what you're doing."

"I have good days and bad." Eve speared an Orc then swung the spear like a sword. She mowed down the small horde, her brow furrowed in concentration. "We were close. A part of me is gone and I mourn that loss. I miss seeing her face, feeling her close. She would have loved being here, meeting your parents. She loved people, she loved me. I have to carry on for her. I know she wanted me to move on." They played in silence before taking a break to walk around the neighborhood. Rob showed her the river path. "Look, Mom and Dad said you're welcome to stay the weekend, but you have to leave when I do. I guess they're surprised I brought in a homeless girl." He paused. "I'm sorry. I shouldn't have said homeless."

"I hadn't thought of that, but I guess I am homeless. I had a home in West Virginia. I don't have one here. Maybe I am homeless. It's so weird."

"Anyways, I thought they'd let you stay for a while. But they want you gone after I leave. You're welcome to come back to Blacksburg with me. You could stay in the dorm for a while until you find a place and work? No one would mess with you. I think you're cool."

"That's so sweet of you. Don't worry. You've done enough for me and I'm grateful. I understand how your parents feel. I'm not family and they don't know me. You all have been wonderful to open your home. Alexandria is where I want to start my life." She smiled.

"But what will you do? Where will you go with winter coming?"

"I have a little money. I can get a room and look for work. Which way is Old Town?" Rob pointed. "I'm going to pack my things and head out this morning. I'm excited to see the city that made my momma so happy. I hope I'll see you again." She hugged him. It felt good to touch someone who was nice and didn't want anything from her. She gave him a quick kiss on the cheek. Rob blushed. Eve grabbed her pack when they reached the house, excited to be back on the road and what lay ahead. She turned once to wave at Rob who watched, then set off.

ALEXANDRIA, VIRGINIA

Eleven

The path along the river was lovely, like a fall scene from a painting at the rest home. The river was wide with reedy marshes, the path leaf-strewn, and there were lots of boats and birds on the water. Bikes whizzed by along with moms who power walked their strollers on the paved path. Eve came up on the south side of the city and stately brick townhomes. The front facades and doors were all painted in colonial red, white, and a pale shade of blue. People hung flags and even in the cool weather there were flowers blooming from boxes under the windows. She passed a large church made of gray stones and several taverns busy with lunch. There were few pickups like home. She saw instead sleek sedans, a jeep here and there or high-end SUVs, all clean and no mud, no rebel flags, and no deer hunting stickers on the back windows. It appeared that everyone went to college from the stickers on windows she did spot. Her world had changed dramatically.

Eve worked her way to the center of the old river port, the stately municipal buildings around the large square. She followed the cobbled street down to the water's edge. There were boats bobbing on the blue water, with happy people drinking and laughing. Did anyone work, she wondered? Momma was right, the city was beautiful. She'd arrived at a place of pleasure and beauty.

Help wanted signs were scarce and she had no phone or address for a call back at the few she inquired about. Her backpack broadcast that she was homeless which scared prospective employers. Night was falling and she needed a place to stay. She located the shelter which gave her a private room for her first night. She had dinner and slept, safe from prying eyes. Eve restocked her necessities at the thrift store the next day and learned about Box City, a short walk up the river path. The shelter was noisy and she didn't like the looks she had received as the new girl. She decided to take her chances at Box City.

The homeless camp sat in a culvert along the pathway that ran along the river. She followed the smell of smoke and something else, something more primitive and mustier that rose from the tidal waters that lapped the shoreline. A boy she'd seen at the shelter store introduced himself and showed her an empty refrigerator box she could use next to his.

"I'm The Kid." She didn't question his name, more intrigued with her new home that had once housed a major appliance and was now covered with a tarp and leaves for insulation. The leaves were everywhere in the old forest, mid-calf deep. The discarded leaves, the Kid pointed out, also helped so you could hear someone coming. The camp code was simple. Look out for yourself, keep the peace, and don't piss off the boss. He lived below with his boys in an old army tent set up on a pallet at the water's edge.

"What brings you here?" The boy asked through the cardboard walls. Their two boxes sat above the main camp, away from the smoke and noise of the communal gathering area and marketplace by the boss's tent.

"I lost my Momma and home. My Daddy can't be trusted so I had to leave."

"Sorry, that had to be tough."

"Yeah, he burned our home down, and then let my Momma overdose on Oxy. I called the Sheriff on him and hope he's in jail. He ruined everything." She sighed. "How about you? How did you get here?"

"Pretty much the same story. I was living with my dad and his meth addiction got out of control. He disappeared and I had nowhere to go. I was getting picked-on at the shelter, so I came here."

"What do you do when you're not here?"

"Panhandle. I have a corner down near the courthouse. I make twenty or thirty a day. I'm saving to catch a bus to Florida. I want to be somewhere warm this winter and I have family near Miami."

"Is panhandling hard?"

The boy stood and dumped the contents of his Big Gulp cup. He held it out. "Change, sir?" He moved the cup sideways. "Change, ma'am?" He moved the cup in the other direction. "That's it. Honestly, easiest gig ever. The trick is finding the right space, look 'em in the eye, and smile. Don't ever take someone's spot that lives here, that's another rule. Most of the guys take a street corner near the highway exits where there's more traffic. I haven't seen a girl panhandle before. Find a space, stay there all day. I make a lot because people feel sorry for me. I look younger than I am. Hardest part is not spending it or getting ripped off."

She mulled the idea, watching him stuff newspaper in his clothes.

"For insulation." He handed her a Sunday edition. Eve started stuffing. She would panhandle the next day, the only job available with no address or phone. She'd save her money in her fanny pack and eventually get a place. It was going to get cold soon, but The Kid told her they all survived the winter and if it got too cold, there was always the shelter. Panhandle by day, get warm food at the 7-11, and pile under blankets and paper at night.

The fire flickered from the can below, the smoke wafting up to her new home. Eve wore her coat, jeans, and wool hat, wrapped in her blanket on the cardboard floor of her box. She settled in for the night, oddly comfortable. The camp didn't seem so bad. The sounds of humanity floated up the ravine: whispering, moans, coughs, and screams. She and The Kid made a pact to watch out for the other. It was so different from Rob's house just a couple days before, but it was better than back home and seemed better than the shelter. Deep down, she missed Malone Ridge, kitty, and her tent.

❖

Eve's first day on the job dawned crisp, clear, and cold. She walked down from the camp, passing through town. She stopped by the marina in front of a building that appeared to be an artist gallery. She didn't have the nerve to ask anyone at first, holding her Big Gulp cup out in front of her while looking down. She watched people pass by, headed to work, or to get coffee. Shops began to open for the day. A young man a few years older than Eve walked his pretty white Labrador from a boat in the marina. He returned shortly, the dog wagging his tail and panting, the two entering the studio. This spot would work, she reasoned, the center of the tourist area and high traffic from the coffee shop. Eve also hadn't seen anyone from the camp. She had a good feeling, though her toes were cold. Winter boots would be her first purchase from the thrift store.

Eve needed to get her nerve up and ask for money. So many people had passed by without a second glance. She stepped out from the shadow of the building and held out her cup nervously toward a man who passed her and then a woman who looked the other way. The people hustled by trying not to make eye contact. The first few hours passed quickly, her biggest haul, a few bills from the man with the dog after he purchased his coffee. She took a break with just a handful of dollar bills and some pocket change. Too many pennies and not enough paper. She needed to pee from the Diet Coke she'd bought that morning to get her cup. The security guard shoved her out the door of the artist colony. "No bums. Stay out, Miss." Her change cup gave her away.

"I'm not a bum. Jerk." Eve muttered. She really had to go. Ducking around the building, she saw a stand of overgrown azaleas. "Just like the garden at home." Eve ducked between the bushes next to the building and pulled down her pants, squatting where she couldn't be easily seen. The man with the Lab was coming down the path towards her.

Eve hurried to get herself together, pulling her pants up and her panties bunching underneath. The dog greeted her with tail wagging and licks of his tongue.

"Sorry you had to see that." Eve petted the dog.

"I didn't see anything," the man answered. "Oscar saw you and was pulling hard on the leash. I thought he saw a squirrel or something." He was being nice. The azaleas weren't that thick. "Well, I must get back to work. I have a model coming in today. Stay warm." He smiled.

Eve found herself smiling despite the circumstances of their meeting. She watched the artist walk away and smiled.

Twelve

Trying to stay warm, Eve thought about the artist who lived on a boat with his dog. He would be nice and warm right now. She lived in a cold box and begged for money. Despite their differences, her circumstances at the moment couldn't be helped. She had to start somewhere. Eve began to ask for money more boldly, making eye contact and smiling. "Dollar for lunch, sir? Spare change to get a cup of coffee, ma'am?" Dollar bills began to replace the coins as strangers caught her blue-gray eyes. After lunch she counted out twenty-six dollars. A month or two of this and she'd have an apartment or cheap hotel room. Damn, it was cold. She walked up to 7-11 to get a hot chocolate and an oatmeal cookie. Her toes thawed for the first time that day in the warm store. Later, she could see the artist in an upper window facing the street corner where she worked. He appeared to be watching her. A woman hustled past, almost bumping into Eve. She sobbed openly and muttered, "Fucking creepy artist." Eve watched her leave. He was still watching her or the other girl who glanced back up to the window and flipped him the bird. Eve decided to call it a day on that note.

Eve finished the last spoonful of beanie-weenies later that night. She tossed the can into a nearby barrel, then popped the top of a tall-boy, sharing it with The Kid on the stoop of their boxes to celebrate her first day of work. The beer tasted delicious. She drained the last sip, noticing a greasy man walking up the hill. He stood in front of them.

"Boss wants to see you. Rent's due. Come on." The Kid nodded for her to go. Eve walked down the hill with the man, staying a few steps behind. He stopped at the Army surplus tent, stepping onto the pallet. "Wait here." He pulled back the flap and entered. "Come on in," a gravelly voice called out a few moments later.

It was dark inside. Eve was aware of several watching her while smoking. There was a small light at one end. Eve was on high alert in the cramped, dark space. "You work today?" A gruff voice nearest the light asked. Mildew, smoke and funk filled her nose.

"Yeah, my first day."

"You make anything?"

"I did." She held her breath.

"First day working and first day of the month go to the camp. Rest is yours. They's the rules." The voice went quiet. Eve reached in her pocket and pulled out a roll of bills. She handed it over to a shaking hand. "That it?"

"Forty-four dollars. That's what I made today down by the marina. I pay my way."

"Not bad for your first day. No funny stuff if you stay. Don't bring the cops. Pick up yer own trash and burn it, especially if you on the rag." Someone snorted. "You need anything, drugs, booze, whatever, you let us know. We keep it quiet and peaceful here."

"Can I go?"

"One other thing. We'll let you know if we need anything from you." The tone was slightly threatening. A snicker came from one of the others. "Get on, then." He grunted.

Eve walked out and up the steep slope to her box and breathed deeply in the crisp air.. She felt a mix of chill from the night and fear from her transaction in the tent below.

"Well, I guess that wasn't so bad." She lied. Fear and resentment mixed inside her with having to give up her first day's profits.

"They ain't drinking with your money yet," The Kid said, tucking in under his blanket.

"What's that mean?"

"They all want it young. They ain't angels or the Salvation Army. They take what they can get. A couple of them come up here one time for me, but I run off. Figure they'll want you before me now. But don't worry, I'll watch out and we can run faster than them. The leaves and this hill give the old fuckers away. We'll be okay and this is better than the street. You keep watch tonight." Within a few minutes he was softly snoring, his confidence made her feel only a little better.

Thirteen

Eve became comfortable with begging and camp life, losing track of the days. Festive lights were going up in town. The only bad part was the cold. She was never warm. She nibbled on a cheese sandwich in front of her box. Her meal tasted like the cardboard that surrounded her. The first winter snow dusted the leaves. Eve bit into a mustard pack and sucked the condiment out for flavor. She handed half of the sandwich to The Kid, then popped open a Coke, walking to the barrel fire for warmth.

"You know, it dawns on me I never asked you your real name. I'm sorry."

"Don't worry, it's cool. I'm just The Kid. Been called that for years and probably always will. Shit!" He pointed down the hill to the tent.

"What?" Eve followed his finger. Two men came out of the tent to smoke. They were looking up the hill in their direction and laughing.

"We need to watch out tonight. Looks like they're gonna party. It's not good they're looking this way.

Probably got in a supply of pills. No doubt some was Viagra, the limp-dick motherfuckers can't get it up anymore."

"Should we go?"

"No, they'll wait until dark. There might be someone posted on the path. We'll wait til dark, too, then sneak away. Get dressed. We can't stay here tonight. Take only your pack and blanket."

Eve pulled on her hat and mittens, already wearing her coat. She double tied her shoes like cross country and slid on her pack. She drank the Coke to settle her stomach, watching the sun set slowly.

Dusk settled when two men emerged from the tent, headed up the hill through the leaves. "Let's go," The Kid said, running quickly up the hill. Eve followed, passing him after a few strides. She could hear cursing and shouting. The men had spotted them but couldn't keep up.

She ran as fast as she could, knees high, arms driving. Her blanket trailed like a cape. She reached the top of the path, tripping on the raised asphalt path. The Kid skidded to a stop, out of breath. "Which way you going?"

"To town, how about you?"

"South to the highway." He pointed, out of breath. "I might as well head to Miami with winter coming."

"Good luck, we better split here. Thanks for everything." Eve waved, but he'd darted into the darkness. She began running down the hill toward Old Town, wary of anything that moved. It was dark, almost black with the forest on either side, and she had to watch her footsteps. A shadow reaching for her like a black bear startled her. She twisted as the arms grabbed, ripping her blanket away. The man fell to the ground cursing and pulling Eve with him. She was on all fours for just a second before snatching the blanket and launching herself like a sprinter from the blocks.

"Come back here, you little bitch. We're not done with you."

Eve ran, putting distance between her and the camp. She only slowed once she reached downtown, resting outside the stone church. She tried the doors, hoping for a warm place to escape but the church was locked. The overhead lighting from the streetlamp was a small comfort. She walked into town, warm from the run and breathing fast. Her body heat wouldn't last long in the night air.

The fire in the cozy restaurant was roaring. People were eating and drinking. Eve looked through the window, envious of the environment just beyond her reach. She walked on, the scene disappearing behind the window panes, fogged from her breath. It was late when she sat down on a bench near the boat. She needed to be alert in case anyone came to look for her but figured at least people out and about could help her if she called for help. Eve went to the trash can nearby and found newspaper to stuff in her clothes, her feet already cold. She lay on the bench with the blanket tucked around her, allowing only one tear to run down her cheek. It crystallized on the bench as soon as it landed.

Fouteen

Eve awoke to heavy breath and a rough tongue on her cheek. She sat up quickly, rubbing her red eyes with stiff, swollen fingers. It was the white Labrador and his master.

"Did you sleep here all night?" The artist asked. She nodded, stretching. Oscar relieved himself, never taking his eyes off her. "You must be frozen. Would you like a coffee or hot chocolate and something to eat? I'm going to the shop across the street after I walk the dog. Why don't you come with me to warm up?" Eve walked stiffly, shaking out newspaper from her pant legs and taking out the paper from her coat sleeves as they walked like it was normal. She dropped the paper in a bin and followed him back to the boat, folding up her blanket and storing it in her pack while she waited on the dock.

The coffee shop was busy with activity. The espresso machine sputtered and bluegrass music played in the background. Baked goods, pastry, and cinnamon perfumed the air of the small shop. It felt dreamlike.

"Get whatever you want. I'm buying and I'm sorry, I've never asked your name?" He held out his hand to shake. "I'm Baker."

"I'm Eve."

"That's a pretty name. What would you like?" Eve chose a bagel with cream cheese, hot chocolate, and a cinnamon roll the size of a small plate. She tried to minimize the happy noises as she ate and drank. Baker smiled. He picked at his croissant and sipped black coffee.

"It smells so good in here," Eve breathed deeply, and then stretched out her fingers. "It's so nice to be warm. I've watched people come and go for the last few weeks and wondered what it was like inside." She dipped her finger in the frosting of the roll, tasting the confection. "Oh my God." She shivered.

"I'm glad you came with me today. Do you mind if I ask where you stay? I'm assuming the bench last night wasn't your first choice."

"I used to stay at Box City." Her answer was a whisper

"The homeless camp up the river? It's a pretty dangerous place from what I've heard, especially for a woman."

"I can take care of myself, but I can't go back. A bunch of them came after me last night. That's why I ended up on the bench. Those men were bad, but it's the cold that kills you. It's cold all night, and then you step out into the cold day. I'm never warm anymore. Probably go to the shelter tonight."

"I can't imagine. It gets cold on my little boat, but I have a space heater and Oscar." The two sat silently and watched people pass by through the little window, drowsy in the sunlight.

Baker seemed deep in thought. "I have a question for you and there's no obligation." He stopped for a moment and sipped his coffee. "First, I want you to know that I've been sketching you from my window. I hope you don't mind?" Eve looked surprised, furrowing her brow. She'd seen him watching her. "You have a presence, a look that captivates me as an artist. Would you like to come in from the cold today and let me sketch you in the studio? I'll pay you a sitting fee, so you won't lose money."

Eve lowered her voice and eyes. "Would I get to keep my clothes on?" The young woman with the tears running from his studio came to mind. She knew a little about hustlers from The Asp.

Baker laughed. "I'm sorry." He leaned back, covering his mouth with his napkin. "I didn't expect that response. Yes, clothes on. It's your face and hands I'm trying to capture. I'm practicing. I'm not sure for what, but you've brought back my creative spark."

She'd take a chance. "Okay, you can sketch me. It will be nice to be warm. Will Oscar be there?"

"We'll go get him. He'll be glad for the company. We get lonely."

They walked across the street. Baker introduced her to the security guard so she could come and go. Eve brought Oscar his biscuit from the cafe and the two became immediate friends. Oscar followed her around the studio while she studied Baker's paintings.

"Are you ready to get started?"

"Can I use the bathroom?" She was embarrassed by her state, realizing he was about to sketch her. It was her first human contact in quite some time, her last shower at Rob's house when she first arrived in Alexandria. Baker pointed to the door.

"Just down the hall."

Eve walked to the bathroom. She closed the door and immediately felt the warmth from the radiator in the small space, the seat in the stall warm and luxurious. It had been a while since she'd had privacy and toilet paper. Eve flushed and came to the mirror. She took off her travel stained coat. Her jeans showed wear, but no stains, thank God. She pulled off her heavy sweater to look at the white tee-shirt underneath. Eve washed her hands, her arms, her face, scrubbing away the smudges from living rough, then wiped under each arm with a wet paper towel and soap, aware of the odor. She left a little soap for a better scent. Her hair was a mess. She was lucky it was short, running wet fingers through the tangles and pulling it back. She had no makeup. It would have to do. Eve walked back to the studio, unsure of what would come next.

"Wow, you look great. I like your hair that way. Now sit over here by the good light of the window. We can break whenever you need, and if it gets cold, I can turn up the thermostat." She placed a book she had in her coat on his desk, and then hung up her coat on the rack next to his. Baker picked up the book. "Ah, graphic novel. Is it any good? I haven't heard of this one, but I like the cover art." Baker took a second look at the resemblance between the heroine on the cover of the book and Eve. "Is she like you or are you like her?"

Eve blushed, unused to compliments. She shrugged. "Both, I guess. Can I ask a question?"

"Sure." Baker posed her on the stool, touching her for the first time, perched facing the window, her arms wrapped around her knees.

"Why me?" She spied the sketch of a nude woman, the model who had bumped into Eve. She sat in the same pose but naked, the sketch discarded in the corner. The model had been upset as she rushed past. Eve was conscious of his closeness.

"I saw you, a pixie panhandler, and it's all I've been able to think about. I want to sketch you. To tell you the truth, I want to paint you, which I haven't felt motivated to do for some time. You're perfect for my new vision."

"What about her?" Eve nodded to the nude.

"Francine wasn't what I needed. She didn't inspire me so we parted. Don't worry, I told you these will be sketches of you, clothes on, I promise. And now we work." He walked around her, sketching in his pad. He'd stop, staring at her bare hand or foot. He got close to her face, moving a few stray strands of hair behind her ear with his pencil. "You don't mind, do you?"

She shook her head no but felt the tips of her ears and cheeks redden. Bigun was the last one to touch her so intimately. She couldn't think that way, not here and not now. She fixated on the nude, wondering who she was and why she had been so upset.

"That's good art, too." He pointed to the small emerald snake, sketching the tattoo on his pad. Baker picked up a green colored pencil to shade in the snake's coloring.

"My Momma had one on her foot. I wanted one like hers to remember her. She's gone now."

"I'm sorry. I lost my mother, and my father isn't well."

They took a break later that morning then took Oscar out before a late lunch. Baker ordered sandwiches and Diet Cokes from a local café that delivered. Eve wolfed hers down.

"How did you end up on the street?"

"My father messed everything up and I had to leave. My mother died because of him. I'm from Nitro, West Virginia. It's just across the mountains."

"I'm sorry about your family. Did you like living in West Virginia?"

"Malone Ridge, my home, was a wonderful place to grow up but not so much anymore. Coming here was my first time away from home. How about you? Your situation seems ideal. An artist with a studio and you live on a boat."

"Oh, you know the same old boring story. Jilted by the woman I loved, my father's ill, living above my means in an expensive city in an old boat that requires upkeep. I've been struggling with my art for so long. Now I meet you and suddenly, I'm drawing and want to paint again. You've inspired me. Can I ask what you will do tonight, after we break?"

"I'll go to the shelter, even if it's not the best place. Can I come back tomorrow? You don't have to pay me. I can help out and clean around here. Looks like it could use a little cleaning." Eve and Baker chuckled.

"Yes, I want you back tomorrow but not to clean for me. I have another idea. Come to work for me full time. You can stay here at night until you have enough to get a place of your own."

"You'd let me stay? Don't you worry I might rip you off?"

"There's nothing of value here so no, I'm not concerned about you ripping me off. Besides, it'll be short term. There's a blanket, and you can sleep on the daybed. I'm out on the boat if you need anything. You can use the bathroom down the hall to wash. Just lock yourself in the studio at night. You'll be safe here. I can't bear to think of you at that camp in the cold."

"That's the nicest thing anyone has ever done for me." Tears filled her eyes. Eve hugged him, deciding a kiss was out of the question, though she felt like planting one on his cheek. "Thank you. It'll be nice to be warm."

"Good night, Eve." He paused at the door with Oscar.

"Good night, Baker. Eve closed the door.

❖

"You seem to be happier today. Why so chipper?" Eve greeted Baker. She had a coffee for him and Diet Coke for her on his desk.

"I visited my father last night. We had a good time together. How was your night?"

"Being safe, warm, and full is so nice. I had a bowl of chowder at the place across the street you told me about. It was amazing and they didn't even charge me for the crackers." She showed him several unopened packs on his desk. "Snacks! The daybed was comfortable and the blanket soft. Thank you for all of this."

Baker moved on from drawing her hands, now sketching her torso, head, and face in various poses, drawing her full form. He wasn't sure what was next but was confident he was on the right track. His paints, brushes, and pallet, also arrayed on the desk next to the crackers.

"So what do you do when you leave here?"

"Oh, I work at a little restaurant down Union Street."

"The one all lit up with the small lights out front and the big fire inside?"

"Yeah, that's the one. Want to come with me tonight? I'll buy you dinner."

"That sounds like fun. Will they let me in?" She looked at her jeans and tee shirt.

"You'll be fine. We can get you some gear from one of the shops up the street before we go if you want."

"Thanks, I'll pay for it." She paused, "I read some of your painting books last night. Can I ask you something? What's with the naked women and their fat bottoms and tummies? They're all in strange places and doing weird poses with fruit and animals, and angels."

"That's the way they painted nudes back in the day. Their full figures were a sign of wealth and fertility, and they'd choose a setting to depict what was happening at that time."

"Do you paint nudes?" Eve thought back to Francine.

"I do mostly abstract art these days. It's not very good, at least that's what the critics have said. I'd like to do more work in the female form, something modern. I've enjoyed drawing you and I think we're almost done. I'm not sure what comes next. I'm waiting for more inspiration."

Eve wasn't sure what that meant and fretted all day as they worked. Several times he had to ask her to smile.

Late in the day, Baker asked, "Do you mind if we take a break so I can take a nap? I'm exhausted. Why don't you and Oscar go for a walk, then we can buy you some clothes and we'll go to the pub." Baker covered himself with the blanket, breathing lightly as the door clicked shut, Oscar's nails clipping happily down the cement hallway.

Fifteen

The bar and restaurant were alive with late afternoon activity. The colorful woman in the white chef's jacket was hard to ignore. She was a friend of Baker's and she'd seen her come and go from the boat occasionally. The woman called her staff together, lecturing the attentive faces, then sent them off in various directions. There was a soccer game on the TV with the sound turned down so the upbeat instrumental music could be heard. The bartender read from a well-paged book, glancing at Eve every so often. She walked to the fire to warm her hands, self-conscious in her hoodie and jeans with all the dressed-up people dining and the servers in their black pants and white shirts.

Baker stopped by to take Eve's dinner order and make sure she was comfortable. She studied the menu, quickly choosing the Pub Burger, fries, and a Diet Coke.

"So, you must be the muse." The woman in charge stood over her, hands on her aproned hips and didn't attempt to conceal that she was checking Eve from head to toe. The bright red tourist hoodie Baker had bought her suddenly felt even more inappropriate than her travel clothes.

"This is Eve, Cora. She works for me at the studio. Eve, this is Cora, and I work for her most nights," he said offhand. Cora rolled her eyes at his introduction.

"I have two rules in my place, sweetie. You're either buying or you're working. Doesn't look like you're buying."

Eve wanted to disappear, trying to become as small as possible.

"Wand to help me out? I pay a lot better than Baker."

"Are you asking me if I want to work for you?"

"I'm short a barback tonight. I lost a server recently because Baker can't keep it in his pants and so Francine quit." Baker did an embarrassed, 'who me' shrug. "If you want to fill in it will help me a lot. I'll pay you for the night, plus dinner. Everyone gets a drink after work, too. You're legal, aren't you?" Eve nodded hoping her ID would stand up to inspection. "Baker, get her an apron and find an extra white blouse. That sweatshirt is hideous. Larry, our bartender, will get you started. Do everything he says and make him happy." She leaned in to whisper, "That's how you make your tips." The woman smelled wonderful - kitchen smells of carrots and onions and maybe beef, not at all unpleasant, and something floral, like roses in the garden. Eve relaxed and smiled when Cora added, "We're one big family here,"giving her a hug.

Baker introduced Larry and the evening became a blur. Eve washed glasses, fetched ice for the bins, and cleared plates and dirty glasses. She carried wine and beer in cases up from the cellar. She also watched the patrons come in and out. Baker passed by every so often to make eye contact and give her a reassuring wink or nod.

Eve wiped down the bar as the staff drifted in after shift. It was after one o'clock in the morning. She set out glasses as Larry directed while he poured drinks. Cora thanked everyone for a good night. Larry counted out tips and gave Eve her share. It had been a good night.

"Larry, pour Eve a glass of the Vouvray." He picked up a green bottle from the chiller.

"I don't usually drink wine, ma'am. Wouldn't Miller Lite be better?"

"If you want to keep working here, honey, you need to learn what we sell. Also, I'm not ma'am. That's my mother. I'm Cora, queen and chef of this little establishment. Now, try the wine and tell me what you taste."

Eve was self-conscious with the whole staff looking on. She took a tiny sip, surprised by the taste. "That's good. It's not sweet like the wine I've tried. It's crisp."

Cora smiled. "My work is done here. Do I have good taste or what? That is a Chenin Blanc from France. It's not too expensive but delicious and a big seller with our seafood. We'll try reds tomorrow for the meat dishes if you want to come back. If you're still with us at the end of the week, we'll make it permanent and see about moving you to server or hostess." Baker stood behind her with a big grin.

"Thank you. I'm not used to such generosity."

"I know Baker. He wouldn't bring me anyone I can't trust. Everyone needs a job. You can't live on what he pays, and he can't afford to pay you what you're worth. I can. So, will you come work for me?"

Eve nodded. She took another sip, the wine even more delicious with the second taste, her prospects changing dramatically. As she swirled the wine around her tongue, she gazed out at a street she had recently passed on her way to the night on the bench.

"Take care of my girl, Baker. And don't let him try anything funny." Cora leaned heavily on Baker, grasping his shoulders then walked back to the kitchen.

Eve clinked glasses with Baker. His was smaller and round with an inch of amber liquid and one ice cube.

"What are you having?"

"Scotch, Johnny Walker"

"Is that like Jack Daniels? Daddy always drank Jack Daniels. It tasted nasty, like rubbing alcohol so we cut it with Mountain Dew." A far-off memory of a rebel yell interrupted her reverie.

"Scotch is a different type of whiskey. It's from Scotland and an acquired taste. I don't cut it with anything other than an ice cube." He held it to her nose. Eve shook her head in disgust. He asked her, "So how do you like my family?"

"I love them all. I can't wait to work tomorrow."

Baker and Eve walked back to the boat; the studio locked tight for the night.

"It's a little cramped, but you can stay here. I have two bunks and Cora stays all the time. Don't worry about Francine. She gave me what I wanted but I couldn't give her what she wanted. I'll tell you some time - it's complicated." Baker invited Eve onboard, Oscar happy Eve was in their company. They walked him a short way before going below. Eve was so tired from work she didn't stop to think about sleeping in Baker's boat and in the same cabin with him or his conquests. He'd been a prince so far. She snuggled under the blanket in the spare bunk, exhausted and thinking of Momma. She'd have loved sleeping on the water and working in Old Town with Baker and Cora. Eve slept deeply that night, content and warm, two feelings she hadn't felt together for quite some time.

Eve and Baker skipped sketching the next day, sleeping in. After walking Oscar, the two drove to McDonald's for breakfast and then to Walmart. Eve picked out two pairs of black jeans and several white shirts, a sweater, and a new winter coat, hat, and gloves. She also got new black athletic shoes to complete her outfit, paying with her tip money and Baker's sitting fees. Later that week she found an affordable apartment in a sketchy but nearby part of town. Baker took her to the thrift store for furnishings. Last, at Cora's insistence she purchased a cell phone.

Eve made her first call. Marcy's phone rang, a hesitant voice answering, "Hello, this is Marcy."

"Marcy, it's Eve. I have a cell phone." She squealed, slightly louder than Marcy.

"Oh my God, Eve. I got your note when you left, but I've been so worried. I'm so glad you called. Where are you? Tell me everything." Eve filled her in on the trip, Box City, Baker, and the pub. "And you have to meet Cora. I've never met anyone like her. When can you come?"

"I have a break at Christmas and could come for a couple of days."

"Great, you can stay with me. I can't wait to see you."

"It's been so quiet here without you, Eve. School's going well, but I miss you so much. I can't wait to visit."

Marcy filled her in on the goings-on about Nitro and JJ sightings. Malone Ridge was quiet as far as she knew.

❖

Christmas arrived in Old Town. Eve felt like a character in a snow globe in one of the Christmas shops. There was a light powder of snow over the old cobblestone streets that were filled with the smell of pine and burning oak wood. All the shops and old homes went all out with decorations. It seemed long ago and so far away that her home had been decorated the same way. There had been a tree by the hearth, music, and presents. The memory seemed hazy as Eve decorated her new apartment with a small, pre-lit tree. A big, freshly cut fir tree had been placed in the entryway to the pub, the lights visible outside to passersby. Presents from staff decorated the floor around the tree. Cora had even hung stockings with staff names around the hearth. Eve felt that Christmas had already arrived with her new clothes, friends, and apartment. It was the first real Christmas that Eve had had in a very long time.

❖

Marcy arrived late from traffic, meeting Eve at Union Street. Eve sat her in the corner of the bar and brought her crab puffs, boiled shrimp, and a glass of wine, making sure Larry gave her a tall pour. Eve, now a server, couldn't help but hug her friend whenever she came to the bar with her drink orders. Marcy hadn't changed a lick, beautiful and huggable.

With the shift finally over, Eve introduced Marcy to Baker and the other servers. Most of the staff drank the special Christmas Ale from large mugs. Surprisingly, Cora was not there. The leader of most celebrations, she could be seen hovering behind the kitchen window.

"Baker, what's wrong with Cora? I want to introduce her to Marcy."

"I think she's already seen her. Look at her being coy behind the window. She can't take her eyes off your friend." Eve looked from one to the other. Marcy was lovely as always in a fitted white sweater and Christmas scarf, her dark hair loose around her shoulders.

Baker went to the kitchen to fetch Cora. She walked slowly, checking her hair and wiping her hands on the towel at her waist. He introduced the two. Cora held her hand out daintily, a slight blush on her cheeks. Eve choked on the foam of her beer and giggled with Baker.

"Come with me." Baker took Eve's hand and led her to the Christmas tree. He reached toward the back and handed her a green and gold foil bag draped with ribbon. "Merry Christmas, Eve."

Eve pulled the shoebox out, opening it with a gasp. "Danskos." She held one of the black clogs up. "Just like the other girls." She slid them on. "Perfect, I love them, but they're too expensive. You're too good to me, Baker." She hugged him tightly for a moment, then kissed his cheek.

"You've helped me so much, Eve. I'm glad you like them."

Eve fetched a bag from her backpack. "It's not much, but Merry Christmas." Baker pulled out a braided leather dog leash with a sturdy copper clasp. There was a matching collar with Oscar's name branded in the leather. Last, she pulled out a smaller braided leather bracelet with a copper clasp like Oscar's collar. "I found a cool leather shop. I hope you like it." Baker snapped on the bracelet, admiring it, then hugged her, holding on a little longer it seemed. Baker nodded to the back of the bar as he let go. Marcy stood close to Cora. The two were deep in conversation and it appeared their fingertips were touching.

"I think Cora's found a new friend," Baker said. The two walked back to the bar and their ales. Marcy came over with Cora. "Eve, I hope you don't mind, but is it okay if we catch up tomorrow? Cora invited me to a late dinner. I don't know when I'll get in and I feel terrible since I just got here." She glanced from her friend to Cora.

"Go have fun and stay out as late as you want. You've been dreaming of this forever. But I expect to hear all the details tomorrow." She hugged her friend while Cora beamed.

"Looks like it's going to be a Merry Christmas." Baker raised his glass to the three women.

❖

Eve met her friend the next day, early in the afternoon. "I love her, Eve. I really love her." The two friends sat in a small Italian bistro. Eve ordered an Italian white wine.

"Marcy, she's a great gal, but you just met her. You're in lust, and besides, the last time you gushed like this was after the pick-up at the pizza joint."

"Eve, last night was wonderful," she paused. "I can't describe what it was like."

"I'm happy for you and Cora. She's been lonely, too. I think it's fabulous. Just go slow, okay?" Eve squeezed her friend's hand.

"That's just it, I didn't know what to do and I was ready to get naked and just go for it." Both giggled, same old Marcy. "But Cora slowed everything down and we talked almost all night. I mean, I know nothing. I felt like such a child, and you know how I've struggled with who I am. With her, everything was normal. I feel whole and loved with her."

"So, was it only talking, Marcy?"

"Maybe a little kissing. Wonderful."

Eve fanned herself. “Can we talk about something else? It’s getting pretty steamy in here.”

“Let’s talk about your love life. How about you and Baker? You two look happy together.”

“He’s done so much for me. I care about him, but our relationship is not like you and Cora. We’re good friends. Between his art and our work at the restaurant, there doesn’t seem to be much time for a relationship. I wouldn’t want to live without him in my life, but I don’t know, maybe something’s wrong with me. I haven’t felt anything for anybody since Momma died.” Eve didn’t mention the warnings from the female staff that he had a reputation for one-night stands. “Maybe I’m not the relationship type? I’m happy on my own and just being his friend.”

Marcy patted Eve’s hand. “Don’t give up. Love will come when you least expect it. It sure as hell surprised me. You’ve done so well, Eve. I was so worried when you left. I almost went to see the deputy to see if we could find you. But coming here was the right thing for you. Besides, you introduced me to Cora.”

Marcy and Eve spent the day together, hanging out, shopping, and catching up. They dropped in on Baker at the studio. Marcy studied his drawings. He’d hung several of Eve’s face in an exhibition space in one corner. Eve walked Marcy to her car, taking her friend’s arm.

"I have to go home tomorrow, and Cora's taking the night off tonight. Do you mind?"

"Cora is taking off? She never takes off."

"Cora's going to get everything started at the restaurant and then she's taking me to a little French restaurant she likes, La something."

"Le Refuge. It's up the street a few blocks. I've walked Oscar by it before. Baker and Cora go there sometimes. It's French. He says the escargot is delicious, but I don't know about snails." Both made faces and laughed.

"I won't see you before I leave, and I'm sorry we didn't get more time together, but I promise I'll be back."

"It's okay, Marcy. I'm happy and you're happy and I actually have a freaking cell phone finally to call you with."

"Thanks for understanding, Eve. Call me tomorrow, okay? And by the way, judging from what I saw in Baker's studio, he's crazy for you. His drawings of you are incredible and I'm telling you, that boy is in love. Don't push him aside for too long." The two hugged. She took her time on her way to her apartment to get ready for work. The black leather of her Danskos glistened. He was sweet and handsome and there was an attraction. What had Momma told her?

"That's what being grown up is all about, Eve. You decide to love someone. Sometimes it's obvious, and sometimes it's not. It's not always roses and chocolate. Sometimes it's respect and care and the little things someone does that make you love them. But it's your decision and it will feel good to give your love away."

Sixteen

The studio was a mess with drawings, the air warm, when Eve stopped in the next day before work. Baker had finished drawing her - hands, chins, ears, a leg or foot, a smile - parts of her dotted the wall. He wasn't sure what would come next, his brushes and paint idle on the small table next to the wall. Eve walked around with Oscar at her heel, casting a critical eye. What had Marcy seen that she hadn't? She examined the strand of hair, her ear, an arched eyebrow. He made her look beautiful but was there anything more? Baker was asleep on the sofa, resting before work, his face peaceful. He was so carefree around her, able to sleep with her walking around. She watched him. What would it be like to crawl onto the daybed next to him? Warmth spread through her body, her heart beating rapidly. Eve decided to leave before things got out of hand. She walked to the restaurant, pushing away her thoughts of Baker. She was happy.

Cora surprised her at the restaurant, calling her back to her office next to the kitchen. Eve walked slowly, unsure if she'd done something wrong. She sat in the small office. "I'm going to shut the door so we can have some privacy. Would you like a latte or anything?"

Eve shook her head no, unsure what was about to happen.

"I want to thank you for sharing Marcy with me. I know she came to see you and I ended up monopolizing her the whole weekend. You've both been through a lot, and you probably had much more to talk about. I should say I'm sorry, but I can't. She's lovely and I so appreciate you allowing us time together." Cora smiled.

Eve relaxed, seeing her boss with her guard down. "Marcy is lovely." The word lovely was a grownup word. "She was all I had when Momma died. I hated leaving her, but she had school and her own momma needed her care. I've missed her so much, but I love seeing her happy. You don't need to apologize. I've never seen her so full of life and plans. I hope she'll come back soon, even if it's only to see you." Eve laughed in relief.

Cora stood and hugged Eve, then fanned her eyes. "I'm sorry. I'm all emotional and that hasn't happened for so long. I really like her, and I hope she comes back, too. I'm a little stuck with the restaurant or I'd head to Charleston this weekend."

"Nitro," Eve huffed in jest, "but you'll learn the difference. Marcy has been looking for someone for so long. Baker told me a little of your story. I hope you don't mind. It's fitting Marcy should come here and meet you. She's happy and I guess I am, too."

"I haven't had anyone in my life, other than Baker. He can be a rascal, but he's been a good friend. I sleep in the guest bunk sometimes when I get lonely and when I wake up the world is a happy place and so am I."

"I know, right?" Eve smiled. "Maybe it's not Baker. Maybe it's Oscar, the chick magnet." The two laughed.

Eve could see Baker folding napkins outside but watching the two women intently. She laughed once again.

Seventeen

JJ's boss held out a gleaming revolver. "This is the new Colt .45. Same as the old lawman's gun, but with new action." He showed JJ the pistol. Next to his Trans Am and Patsy's backside, it was the prettiest thing he'd ever seen. "I get to keep it for a few days and test her out. The rep said I can let other employees try it and you could too, if you want. You live up on the mountain where you can't hurt anyone, right?"

"When can I? I-I-I-I'd like to hold it. I'd like to shoot it."

"Now don't get all lathered up, JJ. There's a list and you can wait your turn. You can try it out after Christmas, okay? You keep focused now and do your work and I'll let you try it out for a few days." After Christmas seemed like forever.

JJ stopped at the Minimart after work. "You want to come up to the trailer after work tonight, Patsy?" He bought a drink and pork rinds.

"I don't know. There's nothing there except what you want to do. I'm tired of doing that. I want to go to a movie or the mall or something fun."

"You like to shoot guns."

"Yeah, you got one?"

"I'm gettin' one. Gonna have it after Christmas. A real peacekeeper - a Colt .45 like in the Westerns."

"Alright then. Maybe I'll come up. But clean that shithole up. I ain't coming to any dogpatch. I'm a lady. Get some food and some lite beer and we can have a little party." She smiled a not unpretty smile. JJ showed off his mossy teeth.

❖

Patsy was generous with JJ. She let him do things with her he'd only heard about from some of the boys at the hospital. He felt like a man when he was with her and didn't miss his Daddy when she was around. Daddy was in jail so that made JJ the man of the house. He had his woman, his home in the trailer, and a job. Soon he'd have a gun. Life was good, though a little cold on the ridge. The services had been turned off. He lit a barrel outside at night to warm-up, burning garbage and wearing two or three layers of clothes in his sleeping bag.

He heard about his father's death from his supervisor at work.

"You want to take off a few days, son?"

"No, it's warm here. I like working."

"What do you mean it's warm? What about your Pappy?"

"My Daddy's gone. Nothing I can do I reckon. Working is best, they say. What about the gun? That'll take my mind off him."

"Boy, I know you're a bit touched, but that is the strangest thing I ever heard. Family means you're there if they marry, they give birth, or they die. You got to go take care of your Pappy."

"Go where? He's dead and we ain't church folks. I wouldn't know what to do. I'm trying to take care of myself. I-I-I-I ha-have a girlfriend. I like to work. It's good for me. I like it here."

"Alright boy. I'll get the gun. You be careful, ya here?"

JJ took the gun reverently and put it and the box of shells in his locker. When he left that day, he stuck the gun in the back of his pants and pocketed the shells. He felt invincible and on top of the world. The gun was on loan, but it felt like a gift. He'd never had a gift he could remember. JJ drove home with his pride swelling, something he had never felt either. Patsy would see the man he'd become.

JJ stepped into the trailer. Patsy sat on the sofa in her parka. "So why am I here?" Vapor came from her mouth as she spoke. The night was one of those cold, mountain nights, their speech coming out like puffs of smoke. He took out the gun and laid it under the candle on the table. "Well look at you. Got a gun, did ya? That yours?"

"Might as well be. My boss told me to take it home and try it out. Let's go."

They went out into the yard. JJ loaded the pistol and spun the chamber.

"Just like in the westerns." He smiled.

"Come on, JJ. You gonna shoot or what? I'm freezing my ass off. Let's get this done."

JJ aimed at the big walnut tree near the graveyard and squeezed the trigger. BANG. The gun fired. He squeezed again, BANG. He pulled the trigger a third time, BANG. The third bullet must have hit the cemetery wall because of the ricochet and small spark. There was nothing else other than smoke and the echo off the mountain. The tree stood as it always had.

"Dang, didn't hit a thing."

"Damn, JJ, you blind or something? I think I could hit a big old tree from across the yard."

"You think so, Patsy? You try." He handed her the pistol.

"It's warm. I like it." She held it with two hands and squeezed the trigger. BAM, BAM, BAM. Patsy ripped off three shots. Again, the tree breathed a sigh of relief with no visible marks.

"Damn. Maybe we try again in the morning."

"Fine. You bring any wine? Let's go get warm and you can do whatever you want. I'm tired from work and want to get under the covers and sleep. I gotta work tomorrow morning. That's about the only reason I'm staying, so I don't have to drive."

JJ threw the pistol onto the small dining table, followed by the box of shells. He locked the front door and headed for the bedroom, dropping his parka and boots and diving into the bed in his sweats. Patsy waited in her sweats and wool socks.

"Hurry up, JJ. I'm still freezing my ass off. I like that gun, but we got to practice some if you're gonna keep it and have it do us any good." JJ didn't hear a thing, his hands moving up Patsy's body. "My God, JJ. Your hands are freezing. Warm them up, you idiot, or keep them to yourself and get me that glass of wine."

❖

Passing her old home in the camp, Eve jogged easily up the trail along the river. She could smell the smoke in the air along with the marsh grass. She sped up to get by, not missing that part of her life one bit. She thought of The Kid and wondered if he'd made it to Miami. After her run, she showered and dressed, searching the college schedule on her phone. Her plan was to keep working and enroll in the fall. She'd take day classes and work nights at Union Street. Her phone came to life with Marcy's ringtone.

"Eve, it's Marcy."

"Hey, Marcy. What's up?"

"Your father. Something happened and I'm sorry about what I've got to tell you." She paused, then blurted, "He's dead, I mean he passed. It happened in prison. There was an altercation, but from what I heard he had a heart attack. I called as soon as I heard. I'm so sorry."

"Don't be sorry. He can't bother us anymore."

"That's the problem. Deputy called me. They wanted to talk to you, but I told him I didn't know where to find you. I know how you feel about him. They're planning to bury him on Malone Ridge next to your Momma and I thought you'd want to know."

"They'll bury him there over my dead body. Daddy won't have the last say. He ruined our home, but he won't ruin the garden."

"That's what I thought. You need to get up here. He's scheduled for burial on Friday in the morning. When can you come? You can stay at my place."

"I'll be up tomorrow on the bus. I have to work tonight but I'll take off the rest of the week if I can. Thanks, Marcy. See you."

"Uh, Eve. Before you go. If you want to bring anyone with you for company on the ride, it's fine with me. I have plenty of room."

"Okay, Marcy. I'll ask Baker if he can get off. I know you'd like to see him and Oscar." She teased.

"Eve, you know who I mean. I'll call Cora now that I know you're coming. There's room for everyone. Baker can stay on the couch, and you can have the spare."

"And Cora?"

"She can stay wherever she chooses. I have to go. I miss you and can't wait to see you."

"Bye, Marcy. See you tomorrow."

❖

Eve and Baker stood in Cora's office before the first serving.

"Cora, I need to go home and take care of some family business. My father died and I have to see to the burial." Baker placed a hand on her back. "They plan to bury him next to my mother and I can't let that happen." Eve looked to Baker and gave him a little smile.

"What are your plans?" Baker asked.

"I thought I'd catch a bus tonight so I can be in Charleston in the morning. Marcy will pick me up."

"Uh, about the bus, Eve. How about I drive? I've got the Bronco. We can all go if Oscar is welcome, Cora, too.

We talked after Marcy called and we've decided to go if you want us to be there for you."

"But the restaurant. Who's going to oversee everything?"

"Groucho will have the kitchen and Larry will run the staff and service. It could get iffy, and it's never a good idea to have two in charge. But it's time I had a contingency plan. Haven't had a day off in I don't know how long. I want to help you, but I want to see Marcy, too." Her face softened.

"Well, thank you, both of you. This means so much. I'm glad you'll be with me, not to mention not having to ride the bus all night."

Eighteen

The road to Nitro was long and bleak, even more so in the freezing weather. The interstate highway through the mountains could be treacherous between Bluefield and Charleston in midwinter. The cars and trucks were covered in road salt and mud. Eve and her party exited the dark tunnel cut through the mountain into bright sunlight that gleamed off the snow piled high on the roadside.

"Thanks for coming with us, Cora. You didn't have to do this on my account."

"Listen, Eve, I love ya and all but I'm doing this for me. I need to see Marcy and I'm not about to drive these roads in the winter. Thank God Baker's got the Bronco."

"You don't ever leave the restaurant, do you?" Eve turned around to face Cora. Oscar lunged to lick her face since she was obviously talking to him. She dodged and rubbed his head with Baker amused, watching in the mirror.

"Sure, I do. I go home to New Jersey to see my family. I have two sisters and three brothers. We're a good Catholic family. I go home each winter after the holidays and each summer up to Cape May. Most of the time I get a chef friend to run the shop, or I close for a few days. Didn't have time this time. I'm hoping they won't burn the place down. Never know with the Marx Brothers." Her laugh was not convincing.

"Your family sounds nice. Do you miss them?"

"I do. I'm the oldest. They come down to visit sometimes. We're close, even though I'm down here and they're all up there. We talk on the phone every week."

"How'd you get to be a chef? Do you mind?"

'No, I don't mind. Baker knows. He's had to hear my story over a lot of late-night bottles of Cabernet. I dropped out of college my freshman year when I caught mono. While I recovered, I worked in a small café. I learned the stations—salad, soup, pastry, sauces. Eventually I ran the kitchen. I never went back to school and fell into the restaurant life, something I'm passionate about but something I have to watch. It can be consuming, being a chef and obsessed with my art.

Eve felt content with the noise of the truck on the road and a reunion with Marcy and her home up ahead. Cora began to snore softly in unison with Oscar, his head on her lap. The time off would be good for her.

"Where to first, Eve?" Baker broke into her revelry.

"Charleston. I want to drive from there if you don't mind. Nitro's my home and I want to come back on my terms. When I left, I never dreamed I'd return with friends." She paused. "I also can't believe both my parents are gone." They switched drivers at the toll road rest stop outside of Charleston. Baker walked Oscar while Eve filled the tank. Cora stretched and refreshed herself. Eve's heart beat a little faster, passing the golden-domed capital in downtown Charleston while following the Kanawha River toward her hometown. She steered the vehicle up the hill toward Marcy's, pulling into the parking lot.

Marcy's apartment was typical Marcy, comfy and tasteful though spare due to her student status. The full kiss Marcy gave Cora amazed her. Marcy acted like everything was normal, ushering them all inside. Oscar got a big bowl of water which he slurped with abandon.

The three sat at the table, while Marcy dished out dinner. She'd brought home a rotisserie chicken from Walmart, which Cora quickly deboned, setting it in a bowl. Succotash and potatoes were poured into serving bowls.

"I'm sorry I didn't cook myself, but that's what a dinner-in-a-bag is for and besides, I had to get myself and the apartment ready." She plumped her hair and gave Cora a little smile.

Baker leaned over to Eve. “Do you feel like the geeky couple on the double date?” Marcy served while Cora sniffed the wine, taking a small taste. She poured with a satisfied smile.

Eve laughed, leaning back to Baker. “I’d never cook or serve Cora wine. Marcy’s brave.”

“I heard that you two. I know what Cora likes.” She smiled broadly. “How can anyone go wrong with chicken and white wine?”

“It’s delicious, Marcy, and everything, including you, looks beautiful,” Eve told her friend. “Thanks for letting us stay with you. I love your apartment and I’ve missed you and our old sleepovers.”

“Well, you get your wish tonight. Everything is going well. I see my mother a couple times a week. We’re closer now that I’ve moved out. School is good or at least not too hard. I’ll have my associate degree this time next year. I told Mrs. Smith about you coming back. She sends her best.” She smiled at Eve and then Cora. Cora was silent during the meal, relaxed and content to be in Marcy’s company. She refilled the wine glasses.

After clearing the dishes, the four settled in the living room to catch up on everything. The wine flowed as Eve made plans for the next day.

Cora yawned. “I’m sorry. I guess I’m not used to being off. I’m sleepy. Do you all mind if I go to bed?”

"It's getting late, and I have to work tomorrow. I think I'll head in, too." Marcy stood.

She went to the closet to get Baker a blanket and pillow for the couch and showed Eve the guest bedroom. The silence loomed large as to who would sleep where?

"Okay, I'm going to bed." Marcy broke the ice with a big sigh. "Cora's staying with me." She took Cora's hand and let her to her bedroom with Cora following happily.

"Goodnight, Eve. Goodnight, Baker." Cora added. The door to Marcy's bedroom closed quickly followed by nervous laughter.

"Well, that settles that." Baker drained the last sip of wine from his glass. He motioned to Eve to take the bedroom. She shook her head.

"You don't have to sleep on the couch, Baker. You can share the guest bedroom with me. You've shared the boat and your studio when I needed a place. I know we're not," she stopped.

"Thanks, Eve, I know what you mean. There's a lot going on right now. The last thing I want is for you to feel awkward about things between us." Baker went into the bathroom to change. He came out in shorts and a tee shirt, then climbed into the double bed, stretching and yawning. Very cute. "The drive wore me out. Good night. Punch me if I snore." Baker rolled toward the wall. Oscar jumped up to take the other side.

Eve surveyed the scene. She changed into shorts and tee like Baker, then turned out the light and climbed in bed, shoving Oscar back to the middle.

Nineteen

Marcy had coffee ready the next morning. Eve stepped into the small kitchen dressed for the day in jeans, and a heavy wool sweater. She carried her parka.

"You look ready for the day, Eve. I can't get over how much you've changed, Alexandria is good for you. It suits you."

"I want to get this over and done. Maybe it's change, or being on my own, or the fact that he's gone. Guess I'm growin' up."

Marcy made breakfast from the leftover rolls and chicken in a fluffy robe and poofy pink slippers. Cora padded out in flannel PJs and bare feet, eagerly taking a large cup of coffee with cream from Marcy.

"Everyone sleep well?" Eve slurped her coffee, looking over the rim. Cora buttered a roll nonchalantly.

Marcy answered, "I know I did." She slid her arms around the chef, holding her tight and burying her head in the woman's neck.

"Me too." Cora bit into her roll and swatted Marcy away.

"Aw, you two." Eve was amazed by the love blooming in front of her. Oscar emerged from the bedroom, tail wagging furiously as he greeted everyone. Baker followed, pulling on his coat. "The coffee smells great, save me a cup while I take Oscar out."

As the door shut, Eve felt the weight of two stares.

"So, did you sleep well, Eve?" Marcy and Cora shared a devious smile.

"I swear, you two are like middle school girls. Yes, as a matter of fact I slept very well and so did Baker and so did Oscar who slept in the middle and spooned with me all night. Now if you can get your mind out of the gutter, Baker and I are going to the deputy's office to see what I need to do. We'll probably run up to the ridge after. What are your plans for today?"

Cora and Marcy shared a glance. "I'm working at the nursing home." Marcy answered. Cora, fixing her caftan.

"I thought I'd relax here and call into work to see how it went."

"Okay, then let's meet for dinner. Lets go to the pizza place if you're up to it Marcy? It's just down the road." Baker and Oscar returned to the apartment to the three women's inspection.

"What did I miss? What did I do?" He checked his zipper which made them laugh out loud.

❖

Planning for Eve's father's remains turned out to be uncomplicated. After providing proof, the hospital gave her his ashes in a box with his death certificate. It stated "heart stoppage" as the official cause of death. Next stop was the deputy's office to call off the burial. He relayed that there was a scuffle, and her Daddy was caught off guard with no one to protect him, ending at the bottom of the pile where his heart gave out. That was that; he couldn't hurt anyone again. He wouldn't be buried on the ridge, either.

Eve drove up the ridge, easing into the curve then gunning the engine on the straight. Baker sat in the passenger seat, his hands white knuckling the armrest; the switchbacks were cause enough, not to mention the snow and ice on the uncleared road.

"Where'd you learn to drive, Eve?" Baker forced his question out with a small burp.

"Daddy taught me. I'd drive his truck down to the Minimart for soda and chips as a kid." She was matter of fact in her response, a thin smile across her face as they passed Ridgeworks with no let-up in pace.

"How about the ashes? What are you going to do with them?"

"I don't know yet, but he won't be near Momma. Last night, I remembered something I need to bring back. Something I hadn't thought of in a long time."

A little further up the hill, Eve eased the truck into a pull off in front of the small trailer on cinder blocks that might have been light blue at some point. Dirt and mud spattered most of the dilapidated shelter. Bags of trash had been tossed out the door and looked like toadstools in the snow. Eve sighed at the state of the old family homestead.

Eve pulled on her parka, hat, and gloves against the brisk wind coming up the ridge. Oscar ran free across the snow-covered field, stopping only to sniff and then leave his mark on the garbage bags. The remnants of an old, burned down house could be seen. Eve dug with her boot, revealing the charred ground.

"This was my home once upon a time. That trailer is what I have left."

Eve marched over to the graveyard. "Come on, Baker." She unlocked the gate and stepped inside, Oscar crowding in. "So, this is where my Momma and my grandparents rest. I think it is the most beautiful garden in the world. Don't pee, Oscar." The dog obeyed, sitting in the snow next to Momma's grave. Eve snapped a photo of the dog and the stone with delight. She dusted the snow off the stone to reveal the names of her family.

Eve looked down at the valley, shading her eyes from the morning sun filtering through the trees. Baker snapped several pictures of her, breaking Eve's reverie.

"What was that for?"

"Your face just now, like the granite in these walls, and your eyes as blue as the sky, the wind picking those strands of hair. I want to remember this scene and paint it sometime.

Eve laughed. "You're crazy. Now, let's see if it's still here." She knelt by the back wall and pulled at a rock. Baker helped, easing the stone from the wall behind Lilly's grave. Eve pulled out a sealed plastic bag.

"The family jewels." She held out the cross and frame, relieved.

"I'm no expert, but that cross is worth quite a lot if those gems are real."

"They're real. It's been handed down in the family for generations. But this means even more to me." She passed the picture. "This is my mother, Lilly, and that's her mother, my grandmother."

"Beautiful women." He placed a hand on Eve's shoulder, her eyes moist at the edges. "I see you in them. Is there anything else in the wall?"

"I don't think so." She stuck her hand in, surprised to pull out a second plastic storage bag. "Papers of some kind." She handed the bag to Baker to wipe her eyes.

He pulled out the papers and gave them a quick inspection. "It's life insurance, Eve. There's one for your father and one for your mother, both for twenty-five thousand dollars. Here's a note." He handed the card to Eve.

"Eve,

I'm likely gone. I was slipping away and couldn't stop. I'm so sorry, Baby. I love you more than anything. This is your college fund. I own these policies and you are the beneficiary. Hang onto your Daddy's policy. If something happens - it's likely - then you'll have double.

Find happiness, Eve. I know you will. I love you,

Momma"

Tears trickled from Eve's eyes, the note dangling at her side. Baker pulled her to him, holding her close in the quiet of the cemetery. Oscar woofed to get out, bored. A hawk screamed above the ridge.

"I'm ready to go." She pulled free and walked away. Baker put the stone back in the wall and followed her to the truck. He drove, much slower, down the ridge. Eve asked him to stop at the tattoo parlor, wanting to see her old friend. She ran to him, receiving a big bear hug, her friend in trauma. Baker moved to the tattoo sample books to look at the artwork.

"Never thought I'd see you again. I heard you'd blown town." Bigun seemed guarded.

"I did leave and I'm sorry I didn't say goodbye. It was hard for me to leave and saying goodbye would have made it harder. I had to come back for my father. He died."

"Yeah, I heard. I'm sorry for your loss. You didn't care for him much though, did you?

"He was my father, but he wasn't a good man." She stopped and swallowed. The situation was not what she had expected. "It's good to see you, Bigun. This is Baker, my friend. He's an artist like you." The two men nodded from opposite sides of the room, Eve between them. Baker walked across the room to shake Bigun's hand.

"I like your work. Eve's serpent is good, and I've used it in my own drawings."

"Thanks. I don't have the biggest or busiest shop around, but I try to do good work. You got any tats?" Baker shook his head but Bigun had moved on, focused on Eve. "Hey, I got your favorite, Eve, a new edition." He held up the thin novella.

Eve took it and held it next to her face, the character on the cover, a young, athletic woman sprinting down the city street. "My twin, except her hair is black and mine is white. What, Baker? You're staring. What is it?"

"Remind me later when we're back in Alexandria. It's nothing important today. I'm glad I've gotten to see you in your element." He put both hands on her shoulders, but Eve pulled away quickly, her face red. She glanced at Bigun who'd turned away.

"Let's go. Can I take this?" She held up the book and Bigun nodded. "I'll be back, I promise. See ya, Bigun."

"See ya, Eve. Glad your home for a while and doing good. Don't be a stranger." She noticed he didn't turn around.

❖

Cora was on the phone, still in pajamas when they arrived at Marcy's.

"Groucho, I can replace you with any of your brothers. Get the orders out tonight. Larry, make it all work and help the staff. You can be replaced, too, and between the two of you, you go first." She hung up shortly after they arrived.

"How'd dinner go last night?" Baker asked lightly, knowing the result.

"Freakin nightmare. Kitchen wouldn't work with service. Groucho claimed they were putting in orders too fast. Service wouldn't work with the kitchen. Larry claimed they stalled and were getting dishes out cold or not finished. I read them both the riot act. Work together or be gone before I return. We can't have another night like that." She shook her head while pacing. "I need to get back,"

"First thing tomorrow, okay? We can meet Marcy for pizza tonight and then roll out in the morning. You'd miss Marcy if we left now, and I know you don't want to disappoint her." Eve raised her eyebrows. Cora relaxed a little, a hint of a smile.

"It's just those two make me so mad. Why did I trust them?"

Eve opened a bottle of wine and related her day. The three freshened up, waiting for Marcy who whooshed through the door, quickly changing into jeans and a sweater for the evening.

The back booth at the local pizza joint was perfect after a day in the snow. "It's not fancy but the pizza here is good. You remember, Eve." Eve looked to the bartender, a past memory and their life, once upon a time. The woman glanced at the party with a curious look on her face. Marcy ignored Eve's smirk. Baker ordered a pitcher of lite beer and Chianti for Cora. Marcy was excited about making a DIY wax-dripped chianti bottle in basket decoration. Eve related her story of the garden that day.

"I had to leave everything important to me when I left. I couldn't risk taking those things on the road with me, though I've thought about them. I was so excited to see the picture and necklace still there." She passed the heirlooms around.

"I remember this picture, Eve. Your mother was so beautiful, and this cross is really something else. It must be worth quite a lot."

"It's a beautiful antique, but her memory, that's its real gem." She passed the small picture around.

"You share your mother and grandmother's beauty, Eve. This is lovely." Baker passed the frame to Cora.

"Then there are the insurance policies. I didn't expect there would be anything like that, but Momma was so smart. I can't really believe it."

"I'll help you with the policies. I have a buddy who's always bugging me to buy insurance, but there has never been a reason so I brush him off. But he can help you file the claim or find someone who can. Now you can go to school and not have to work if you don't want to."

"Wait a minute, Baker. Are you trying to get rid of my best server? I need her at the restaurant and I'm happy to work around your school schedule."

Eve waited until Cora and Marcy had moved on to other topics. She asked Baker in a whisper, "What was with you today? You asked me to ask you later. What was it?"

"Yeah, Baker, what was it?" Cora and Marcy were listening in.

"I'm ready to paint when we return." That was all he'd say, despite their requests for more information. The four finished their food and drink, leaving as they came in and the bartender receiving a private wink from Eve.

❖

After hugs, kisses, and promises to call, Eve, Cora, and Baker set out with Oscar in tow the next morning. Marcy stood in her doorway and waved goodbye. She blew kisses as they drove off. Eve asked Baker to drive back to Malone Ridge before they got on the highway home. “It will only take a minute.”

Nothing appeared to have changed since the day before, although a beat-up, formerly red Trans Am was parked across the street. The car was faded and rusted out in most places, the Firebird logo on the hood barely visible and the undercarriage low in the snow. Oscar ran around sniffing his previous day’s spots excitedly, lifting his leg here and there to mark new territory.

Eve walked to a snowy patch between the trailer and the garden and began to scrape the snow away with her boots. She asked Baker and Cora to help her clear the spot, ten feet or so. Oscar helped, digging after them, running from one scraped surface to the next.

“What are we doing?” Baker asked.

Eve gathered the box with her father’s ashes from the Bronco. “I don’t want to take him back. He can stay here with the ashes he created, away from Momma. I hope the coyotes don’t like to pee here as much as Oscar does,

Daddy." She pulled the bag out of the box and untied the twist. Walking slowly in circles around the open space, Eve spread the ashes, using her foot to spread and tamp down any piles. Baker and Cora stood back holding Oscar on the leash. She finished with a sigh. "Done. We can go now."

"Any prayers?" Baker asked, placing his hand on her shoulder.

"Nope. This is better than he deserves, getting to rest up here. Hope your spirit is free, Daddy. Let's go."

A metallic door opened nearby followed by a noticeable click. JJ stood on the porch of the trailer with a pistol pointed in their direction. "What are y'all doing on my property?" He waved the gun at the group.

"Put that gun away, JJ. That's no way to greet your half-sister and her friends. And just so we're straight, this is not your property, it's mine. It was my mother's and her parents before that. Our Daddy never owned any of this land." Eve walked toward him with the empty box, standing below him.

"Your Momma died so the property went to Daddy and then to me. He said so. You left, so it's mine and this says I stay." He waved the gun in a small circle above her head. "What you spreading around out there?"

"Daddy's ashes. They gave them to me. I wasn't going to let them bury him near Momma. He can be out here with the mess he created."

"You had no right to do that and have no rights here. Now git before I pull off a few rounds and send your asses running."

"JJ, do you have heat or water in there?" Eve noted the head that popped up in the window. "And you're shacked up, too. Is that any way to treat a lady?" She shook her head in disgust.

"She stays out of this. Patsy ain't none of your concern."

"Fine, but here, Daddy left you a present." Eve tossed the box to him suddenly, a two-handed set shot from basketball. The heavy box flew quickly between the two, obstructing his view. JJ fumbled the box, dropping the gun below him. Eve picked it up by the barrel and tossed it down the hillside into the snowy thicket. "You should know better than to pull a gun on people, much less your kin. Now, JJ, this is not your property, and the deputy will back me up on this fact. I won't tell him you pulled a gun on me and my friends if you do as I say and leave. I'm going to have the trailer towed to the junkyard anyway. You best take your little lady and all of this garbage and leave."

JJ slunk inside, muttering something unrecognizable and rubbing his eyebrow where the box struck him. There was a loud meow. Eve's cat walked up, rubbing her leg with its tail up. It quickly sauntered to Oscar who stood bewildered. The cat touched her nose to his, then sat down underneath the big dog and licked its paws, unconcerned.

"My cat. Kitty, you're still here. Baker, can Kitty come back with us? I can't leave her here." She scooped up the cat, holding it close.

Cora smiled. "Looks like Oscar doesn't mind." Baker shrugged his approval. On the way back, Oscar sat unhappily in the cargo area. Baker drove with Cora shotgun and Eve in the back seat, holding the yowling cat in the cremation box they'd cut holes in. She examined the insurance documents on the backseat.

"You really going to have the trailer removed?" Baker asked Eve, catching her eyes in the rearview mirror.

"I think so. I hadn't thought about it until I saw JJ come out. He can't live there like that with a woman and no water, heat, or plumbing. They're like animals, spewing trash all over the place and I won't have it."

"That was a pretty nifty throw of the urn. I wasn't sure what we were going to do. Where'd you learn to throw like that?"

"Basketball back in the day but I guess I just reacted. I really didn't think about it. JJ can't see too well, and his hand was moving all around. It probably wasn't loaded, but even so, I can't have an idiot like JJ with a gun on my family's property."

"Well, if you two don't mind, can we stop at the first rest stop or McDonald's?" Cora chimed in. "I think I wet myself when Wonder Woman disarmed that boy back there."

❖

Patsy jumped up from the bed near the window and poked her head out the door to the living room. "I saw your sister. She's changed a bit, but who were those other folks with the dog?"

"Those was my sister's friends. She told us to git out the trailer. Looks like we gonna have to move to town. First, I got to find that pistol. She chucked it down the hill and I can't go back to work without it."

Patsy peered out the window again. "You don't look like her at all. That boy she's with is nice looking. She took that cat, the stray that's been hanging around. They's taking it."

"That's good, cause if I ever saw it again, I'd shoot and skin the dang thing."

"If you had a gun, dumbass and if you ever learned to shoot straight." Patsy laughed. "When are we moving?

I'm tired of being cold up here all the time." JJ didn't answer, walking out the door and down the hill to search for the gun.

Twenty

JJ ducked his boss all day, dreading the conversation about the gun when he caught up with him. It was already several days overdue for return.

"JJ, I need that gun back. Rep's coming back this week." JJ's boss stood behind him.

"I don't have it." He hung his head.

"What you mean you don't have it? I told you to take care of that gun, son. What happened to it?"

"My sister done chucked it down the mountain. It's buried in the snow somewhere. You can take it out of my pay. I'm sorry. I should be able to find it come spring."

"Sorry doesn't cut it and neither does your pay. I'm going to have to let you go, JJ. I'm sorry, but you messed up good this time. Empty your locker and leave the premises. You're finished here."

Dejected, JJ drove to the Social Security building to file for disability. A woman helped him type his application on the computer to file the form. At least there'd be some money. Back at the trailer, he scoured the mountainside again. A warm spell had melted some of the snow on the sunny side where the pistol might have landed. He sat on a rock and picked at the moss. Life hadn't been fair. He'd lost his Daddy, his job, the gun, and soon his home. That left him and Patsy homeless with a baby coming in the spring. He tossed a rock down the hill. It hit a bigger rock that stuck out of the snow and leaf clutter. He noticed something glinting in the setting sun. JJ sauntered down to the outcropping. The gun was wedged between two rocks. He pulled it out and wiped it down with his shirt tail. JJ aimed at a large rock a few steps away and squeezed the trigger. Bam. Sparks flew from the rock, followed by a loud ping near his ear that set it burning. Blood dripped from his fingers when he touched the throbbing tissue. He then walked back to the trailer to look in the mirror.

"Well, I'll be damned. Shot my own damn self. Must have ricocheted." He wrapped his ear in toilet paper from the roll that sat on the kitchen table in case you had to go to the latrine. He then tied a bandanna around his head and wounded ear. He thought he looked like one of the banditos he'd seen in a movie at the hospital. JJ liked old westerns with Mexicans, Indians, and cowboys shooting at each other. JJ smiled despite the pain, then took two long swigs from Daddy's Jack Daniels bottle and set it beside the paper roll.

JJ showed Patsy his wound and the gun later.

"I'm glad you found the gun, but that won't get your job back. You could have killed yourself, too. Let me see that wound. Can't let it get infected." She cleaned the wound with Jack Daniels while he flinched, then put a fresh toilet paper bandage and his bandanna back on. "I ain't gonna try to sew that up for you. You're gonna have a notch on the top of your ear. You okay with that?"

He nodded.

"I'm gonna get my old job back at the beauty parlor. It pays better than the Minimart and we gonna need the money with the baby coming. Your check from the state won't pay for everything we're going to need and you won't see anything for a month or so anyways. We need to find a warm place for all of us. But I have something to tell you that might be able to help." She opened a Diet Mountain Dew and eased herself onto the couch.

"You got one of those for me?"

"You get your own, shithead." There wasn't much to eat or drink in the trailer. JJ sat across from Patsy with a sigh. Patsy got the last Dew. "I heard something today when I went to the beauty parlor to ask about my old job. It'll solve all our problems." JJ got the Jack Daniels bottle and took another swig. He grimaced.

"Well then, what is it?"

"One of the girl's old man sells insurance. Seems that half-sister of yours filed a claim from your Daddy. She's gonna get fifty thousand dollars or something like that."

"How's that help me?"

"Us, dumb ass. You mean, how's that help us? Cause, she's your half-sister. She gets half and you get half of your Daddy's money. That's only fair. She never had any use for him anyway and you did. You stuck by him. The way I see it, you're her half brother, you should get half the money."

"How we gonna get our half?" He sat up straight for the first time, mopping his greasy hair off his brow.

"JJ, you got to be a man. You gotta fight for what's yours. Ask her for the money and if she doesn't give it to you," Patsy nodded to the gun, "you take it. Now you got a use for that gun. You take it if she don't give it to you." Patsy scooched on the couch next to his chair then maneuvered herself up and onto his lap. JJ's hands slid around her belly. "Want to feel the kicks, Daddy?"

"I like your plan. We take what's ours."

"You like that?" Patsy had a wicked grin. "You're gonna really like what I have in mind now." She moved his hands higher.

Twenty-one

Eve came into the studio with the same trepidation as the first day she'd followed Baker in from the cold from panhandling . She hung her coat on the rack. Oscar got up with a grunt and walked over to her, tail wagging. "Hey boy." She scratched his neck. "Hey, Baker. So, what's the plan today?"

"Ah." He exhaled nervously. "Today we paint!" Baker busied himself, positioning the stool near the window, upright, her feet on the floor and arms at her side. An easel and canvas were close by. His paint kit lay open on his desk, Baker selected red, brown, gold, white, and black paint, arranging the blobs of color on his palette. He then chose several brushes and studied Eve. "When we were on your property, I saw you in the morning light with nature all around us." He showed her the pictures he'd taken. She did look striking. "I want to paint you as I saw you that day. We'll start with something simpler first to get my touch back, an abstract I think."

Eve slipped out of her shoes and sweater wearing a simple tee shirt and jeans. She sat with her chin up, her gaze out the window. She could smell the oil from the can he'd opened and from his brush near her face.

"Perfect, are you ready?"

She nodded. "Are you? You seem a little flustered." He was breathing rapidly and a little jumpy.

"I haven't picked these up in a while." He studied the brush. "Maybe it's like a bike and you never forget. We'll see. Okay, I want the hand with the tattoo facing me. Your position is perfect." She settled on the seat. "Let me know when you need a break."

"I will. I'm looking forward to doing this. Working in Cora's kitchen has been amazing. I've never seen anyone create like she does. Her food is art. You do the same thing with your drawing and painting. It's hard for me to understand art for art's sake. Everyone in my life has always done some kind of work. It makes me wonder what I can do."

"It's Maslow's hierarchy." Baker made a triangle with his thumb and fingers. "When you're fighting for your life, food, and shelter, those first priorities form the bottom of the pyramid. As you get time, security, and income, there is opportunity for things like art and culture, which sits at the top of the pyramid." Baker chuckled. "It's funny, I haven't thought about old Maslow since college. I didn't worry about much growing up, so I was able to pursue my art. I guess I have my mother and father to thank for that." Baker took a deep breath and exhaled. He mixed the black, brown and red, applying it to the canvas in broad strokes to create a background, a dark curtain or swirling burnt-orange cloud. He then chose a fine brush, dabbing it into orange and white to make a creamsicle color for her body against the darker browns.

"How's your father doing?"

"He's not well. I went over yesterday but he wasn't lucid. They're keeping him comfortable. Doing this really helps." Baker waved his brush toward her. "I can lose myself with you and the canvas."

"I'm sorry he's not well. You really love him. My mother and I were like that. I never had much feeling for my father. Maybe when I was little, when things were still good, and we lived in the big house. But I don't remember those days very well. It's confusing." Eve looked to the window.

Baker traced the curve of her leg, focusing on her foot. "Dad is all I have left. The memories of my parents on the boat are special. Maybe that's why it's such a comfort to come home to the Athena at night. My life growing up was fishing, picnics, working on the engine on the weekend. Everything revolved around that boat. That was my boyhood."

"Do you ever take her out now?"

"Yes, and I need to get her tuned up this spring. I use a shop on the Maryland side of the river. You can come with me if you want to. We can take her over to the shop and get steamed crabs and a pitcher at the roadhouse next door. It's a great way to spend the day." She could see him making long, fine strokes as he passed her. He dipped into the green, her serpent no doubt.

"I'd like that. Sounds like a date." Eve showed a hint of a smile.

Baker put his palette down and picked up his sketchbook. "What was that Eve?" He made eye contact, placing the brush in his teeth.

"You asked me out, I think."

"Oh, right." He disappeared behind the canvas with his own smile. Eve could picture a warm spring day on the river with cold beer, minus the crabs.

❖

Artist and model paused late in the afternoon. An empty Chinese takeout box sat on the desk alongside two empty Diet Coke cans. "Let's call it a day. I'm exhausted and need a nap before work."

"It's hard, painting, isn't it? I watch you debating or thinking, whatever it is going on in your head. It looks like you're fighting with yourself. Is it difficult?"

"It can be. I don't want to waste our time on junk. That's the hard part because we don't know what the finished piece will look like. It could end up utter crap. We're going to start with some basic paintings before I paint you, your face and ultimately a portrait."

Eve came around to examine his work. She was surprised that they had spent all day and there was so little on the canvas. A pale figure, female by her shape with a dark background. She was not wearing clothes per se but a gauzy cover swirled about her.

"You're exhausted from that?"

"It's only the start." He had to laugh at the look on her face. "The painting will grow. It's the visualizing and creating that's exhausting. We'll fill in the background and she will fill out, too. Her facial expression needs to be perfect." Their eyes met for a moment. Her face, hot.

Baker set a schedule. The two worked mornings prior to going to the restaurant for the evening. He'd finished the stool scene and several others of her standing in front of the window and squatting against the wall with Oscar, the woman angular and ghostly, the backgrounds explosive, like fire burning through the wall.

After a few weeks, Baker began a close-up of her face, her bones sharp, and her hair wisps light and bright.

"What's up, Baker? I can see you're troubled. Is it your dad? Or," she paused, "is there something else?"

There had been times when he brushed by her, her skin electrified by his touch. Sometimes she'd catch him staring at her, not painting at all. What did he want to ask her? He didn't answer. She decided to clear the air. "Do you want me to pose like Francene?" She nodded to the sketches. "I will if you ask me. I trust you despite all the stories about you at work."

A bit startled by her question; Baker came out of his reverie. "Um, no, I mean yes, I'd love to paint you nude but no. That's not my vision for these paintings or what's bothering me." He paused, his face drawn. "It's my father. They've moved him to intensive care."

"If you need me to do anything, ask me." She stepped off the stool and put her arms around him, her head to his, his hands on her waist. The two synched for the moment, breathing in rhythm. It was nice.

"Thanks." Baker broke the embrace, a relief to Eve. "I'll let you know and it helps to know you're here. Shall we break for the day? I want to go see him before work." Eve watched him close up, the touch of his hands on her hips and their heads together on her mind.

❖

The doorway of the little alcove provided a frame for Eve in a long tee shirt dress with a plunging neckline. The abstract woman stretched the height of the doorway, her fingers grasping the molding, the lines of her body dissolving into the dark behind her like a ghost. He used black, gray, white, and gold—a dream figure, angelic. Her mother's cross illuminated the woman's breast, a star emanating light in the haziness of the painting.

"She's beautiful. I've never seen anything like her. I can't believe you see me like that."

"It's not you, per se, but the idea is from your book. The Asp is dark, but I want you to be a creature of light. I've always seen you this way, I just didn't know at the time. These paintings have more edge. I'd like to do some larger portraits next."

❖

The call came later that week. Baker's father passed in the early morning. He took off from the restaurant with the painting sessions on hold so he could put his fathers affairs in order. Despite her offers to help, Baker disappeared and their work stopped. Eve wasn't sure what to do.

Eve dialed Marcy, getting her voicemail. "Hey, Marcy, it's Eve. Call me back when you can." That didn't help.

Eve next sought out Cora, busy with preparation for the evening in the back of the restaurant. She pulled a stool up to the counter.

"Do you have a minute?"

"Sure, Eve, but you'll have to work with me. Put on an apron. I'm making stock for a risotto tonight. Can you rough chop those carrots, celery, fennel, onion and smash some garlic? Are you here about Baker?"

Eve nodded as she put on an apron. She selected one of the big chef's knives and began to chop the veggies, loading them into the stockpot. From time-to-time Cora came over to adjust her technique, moving the point of the knife on the board, the blade drawing down. She was a good teacher, standing behind her and moving her hands gently. Eve watched in amazement as Cora showed her how to mash garlic cloves with one thump of the knife blade.

"Wow, that is much faster." Cora peeled away the paper skin and rough chopped the smashed cloves. "I don't know what to do. He won't talk and he's kind of disappeared. We'd been painting every day since we got back from Nitro."

"He's mourning his loss. Give him space. He'll come back around."

"But I want him to know I care."

"He knows." Cora smiled.

Eve felt only slightly better. Cora added water to fill the pot and turned on the burner to begin the cooking process.

❖

The pot had been bubbling away for much of the afternoon. Eve moved on to clean and prepare mushrooms for the risotto. Cora had Eve taste the broth, adding salt and pepper, tasting again with clean spoons. Cora was satisfied.

"You did good, kid."

"Wow. I understand why Baker gets so tired after painting. The creative process is hard or maybe it's because I've been yakking your ear off. How do you do this for lunch and dinner every day?"

"Practice, my dear. Most of this is not creating but routine, having done it hundreds of times before. I'm glad you're enjoying this. Come in any time and I'll teach you how to cook. In fact, would you like to move back here in the kitchen and apprentice with me? I'm going to need someone to run this place other than the Marx brothers when I take time off. You would be helping me a lot. You did well today, and you follow directions. You could become a good chef one day, maybe even go to culinary school. Think about it. Nothing against nursing, but it smells a hell of a lot better in the kitchen than most hospitals. Oh, and don't worry about Baker."

❖

The funeral was a solemn affair on a crisp morning, still winter but with the promise of spring. The caisson pulled the flag-draped casket for burial at Arlington Cemetery. The Honor Guard fired their rifles, the shots punctuating the calm of the manicured grounds and serene water. A bugler concluded the burial by playing taps. Baker, Eve, and Cora shed tears on the bright green lawn overlooking the more subdued colors of the Potomac River. Though a somber day, Eve couldn't get over the vista of the graves filling out the acres of grass, the wide river and Monument Grounds on the far side. Cora opened the restaurant for the wake, attended by contemporaries of Baker's father and restaurant friends of Baker. Cora served finger sandwiches, white wine, and beer.

A woman cut through the crowd toward Baker, regal in black with a smart hat and veil perched on her long, dark hair. Her emerald-green eyes took in the room in one glance. Eve brought over sandwiches which the woman waived off. She stayed close to hear in fascination.

"Thank you for coming, April."

"I loved him too, Baker." April said softly. "Are you going to be, okay?" She touched his hand gently. Eve moved behind the bar, shooing Larry to the other end.

"Yes, I'll be fine. It'll be different without him." He fumbled for words, switching the subject. "I'm painting again. That should help."

"I know. I stopped by your studio on the way over this morning and saw some of your work. The new pieces are good and so different from anything I've ever seen you do. Those portraits of the young woman are exceptional. That hasn't been your style. It's obvious you were inspired.

Who is she, Baker?" April swiveled towards the bar to focus on Eve.

"A friend and model. She's been a big help during Dad's illness."

"Oh, I'm sure she has." April huffed.

Eve picked up her tray and moved past without making eye contact. Eve headed to the kitchen while Baker escorted April to the door of the restaurant, their heads together in conversation. Eve watched until the door closed on the two.

"Cora, who was that?"

"That, my dear, is the ex-wife."

"I don't like her much."

"Get in line, honey. That one is stone cold. None of us could figure what the attraction was between them and then she tossed our boy Baker to the side of the road like an old dish rag." Cora glared.

Eve brought out the new tray then walked over to Baker, ignoring the hungry mourners. "So that's April?"

"Yes."

"Are you happy she came?"

"Yes. She was close to my father. He would have wanted her here. It was nice to see her. She suggested giving the relationship the old 'college try'." He picked up her glass of wine absentmindedly and sipped.

"Will you? I saw the way she looked at you."

"No, that time came and passed. She's gone and Dad's gone, and those things make me sad. I won't dwell on what's gone. It's time to start over. I'm painting again and that's good and you're good. I need good in my life. She did say she liked our work."

"Your work. I just sit there."

"I wouldn't be painting without you, Eve. It's truly our work. I'm ready to get out of here. Want to come with me? Cora will give my regrets to the remaining guests."

"Give me a minute." Eve stowed her apron and grabbed her jacket, joining Baker outside.

"How are you feeling about your father?"

"Not so good. I can't believe he's gone." The two walked slowly down the street.

"When my mother died, I felt the same way. But I was running away. I didn't have time to really grieve before I was on my own. She was buried and then I was on my way here. I thought the ceremony today was beautiful with the horses, guns, and bugle. The party at Union Street was nice, too. I wished we could have done that for Momma, a real party with friends. That's what I've been thinking about today. She deserved to be remembered surrounded by people who loved her."

"She is remembered, Eve, by you, and you're all that matters." They were at the boat. "I'm going to walk Oscar; would you like to walk with us?"

"I have to get ready for my shift. Can I ask you something personal, and if I'm prying, just tell me" Baker nodded. "Do you miss April and being married?"

"A little. We were together and those were important years when I grew up. But I've moved on and it's a relief. I've never said that out loud." Baker looked at Eve with a smile. "I'm sorry I've been so distant."

"It's okay, you lost a parent. It's not my place, Baker, but I'm glad she's not in your life any more. You don't need someone like her." She stopped. "I'm sorry. I shouldn't have said that."

"No worries." He touched her arm. "I'm glad it's you who's here with me. Can we paint again? Monday morning sound good?"

"Yeah, I'll be there." Eve turned and walked away feeling awkward. What was it about them? Their dance was slow, barely moving. It reminded her of junior high school and pining for the boy on the other side of the room to ask you to dance but he never did. Eve kept walking.

Twenty-two

"Good morning, Baker." Eve put down two coffees on the desk and then gave Oscar his treat. "Good morning, my handsome boy." Oscar nuzzled Eve, rubbing his thick torso against her legs.

"Get a room,you two," Baker joked. "Thanks for the coffee. Johnny Walker and I stayed up a little late last night. I need this."

Eve noticed a faded pink gown hanging in the alcove. "What's up with the prom dress?"

"Well, I've got an idea for some fun poses. Today is a close-up of you. But I have some ideas for a couple of portraits and that dress. I want to depict you in a more traditional pose and color. I saw the dress at a secondhand store, and it shouted your name." Eve laughed, pulling the dress out to hold it up in the sunlight. It had seen better days, but the form was good.

Baker painted Eve, the two close while he worked, her hair moussed back, the gold cross on her neck, his breath on her face.

"Are you feeling better today?"

"I guess. I don't need to tell you about life and the empty vessel. Something that was there that's now gone. I can't go visit him anymore." He stared past her. Eve stayed silent and seated, afraid to see him emotional and more vulnerable.

Baker was satisfied with the facial close up. Eve put on the secondhand gown, lying on the small sofa with her bare feet kicked up, her chin in her hands, gazing at a green apple, the small serpent coiled on the arm rest, no longer a tattoo. A candle on a table illuminated a large array of flowers and Oscar, alert on the floor below, his white fur now black, the background dark. This painting took longer, the artist and model were into the second week of work. A second painting followed with Eve on the same couch with the pink dress hanging over her legs, her hands in her lap. The cross hung from her neck and her head was lowered, her mop of hair covering her expression. The small snake lay coiled at her bare feet.

The final painting was a life sized portrait of Eve peeking from behind a heavy maroon curtain. She wore the gown for the third time. Her expression and half of her body was hidden from view, an enigma in a curtain. The snake nested on the bough of a large potted fern near her. Her look was indiscernible, perhaps wonder, fear, or guilt? She seemed to have the hint of a smile, an expression witnessed by the artist on the ridge. Baker stood back from the full-sized portrait, eye to eye with the Eve on the canvas.

"We're almost done. There will be touch-ups, but I'm satisfied." Eve joined him.

"She's or I'm beautiful." She paused. "I know that's me, but it's not me, at least not the way I see myself. Is that how you see me?" Baker didn't answer, lost in thought. Eve studied the painting. "I like her."

It was still morning. "Feel like taking a trip? We've been working hard. I think today calls for a holiday."

"Sounds great to me, but where are we going?" Eve turned her back. "Can you unzip me?" Baker unzipped the dress slowly. She could feel his intense stare, his hand lingered where the zipper stopped at the small of her back, his other resting on her hip. Eve held the front of the dress to her chest with nothing underneath the shear fabric, goosebumps rising where the zipper stopped. She spun around and smiled. "That's all you get to see," then ducked into the alcove to change. Baker looked at the empty set, the faux curtain and potted palm. Eve stepped out in jeans and tee shirt. "You never answered. Where are we going?"

"My favorite place. I go there to get motivated. But I'm not going to tell you. You'll have to wait because I want to see your expression."

The two walked Oscar, leaving him on the boat, then strolled up King Street to the Metro. Baker pointed out several galleries he liked on their walk. Maybe one day his work would hang there. He purchased tickets and took the northbound yellow line toward Washington, DC. Eve played big-eyed schoolgirl, stepping nervously onto the sleek, rectangular car that swept them away. "I've never been on a train." She was amazed as they quickly passed the airport, and then crossed Memorial Bridge and the Potomac River. Spring waited to burst forth; the cherry trees along the river were still light green, preparing for their gaudy, pink show. The two exited at L'Enfant Plaza, walking down to Hains Point, the spit of land that jutted into the Potomac from the Monument Grounds. Residents and tourists were walking, jogging, cycling, and sightseeing like her and Baker. They walked to the end of the road to stand in front of a large hand that rose out of the earth. Eve stood in front of the palm while Baker took her photo. They moved over to the face of the bearded giant and his partially exposed leg.

"Amazing," she exclaimed. "I've never seen anything like it."

"It's one of my favorites. It's called The Awakening. It's good accessible art."

"It's funny to live in a place where little trains take you wherever you want and you can see sculptures like this. All we ever had back home were a few Civil War statues."

"You haven't seen anything yet." Their next stop after a short walk were the Jefferson and Lincoln Memorials. Baker snapped more shots next to the bigger than life statues. They ended their hike at the Washington Monument, looking down the huge lawn to the U.S. Capital.

"I feel like Alice in Wonderland. It's all so big."

Baker pointed to a large, square building in front of them. "This is the National Gallery of Art. I come here to get perspective, or to feel good and to see something special. There is always something wonderful to see." They went in, the building dark and cavernous, taking time to view each piece of art, moving floor to floor, taking their time. Eve mocked Titian's Venus with a Mirror, posing like the chubby woman from the Middle Ages on one of the couches in front of the painting. A small gathering of Japanese students Baker, snapping photo after photo. Eve flashed the requisite peace signs at the end of the impromptu photo shoot, to much applause.

"You are a ham," Baker whispered.

"You know us models," Eve responded happily, leaning in closely.

The afternoon was fading as they exited. She was tired but exhilarated. Baker bought push-pops from the ice cream vendor as they began their walk across the lawn toward the Metro. Eve's eyes bulged at the elaborate amusement just ahead.

"Oh my God, Baker, look! A merry-go-round like the one my mother told me about. Can we ride?" Baker bought tickets. Eve chose a unicorn next to Baker's black horse. They rode the carousel over and over, having grabbed a handful of brass rings by the time they had to leave. The sun sunk over the river. "I could stay here all night." Eve sighed.

"We'd better go. Oscar is going to need to be walked." She didn't protest.

"Thank you, Baker. Today was magical." Eve kissed his cheek as they stepped from the merry-go-round. She didn't flinch when he reached for her hand, enjoying his touch. She slept on the short ride back, her head on his shoulder. The two exited at King Street, following the throng of commuters onto the brick-lined street.

Eve smiled and nodded to Baker when she saw the flash of color from a woman's sundress, the same faded pink she'd worn only hours before. Baker saw her too - the painting subject beside them in the crush from the Metro, visible one second, hidden by the moving bodies that rushed home the next. Eve and the woman were similar in height, skin color, even hair style. She held a Starbucks cup like many of the commuters. Eve noticed a slight tremor as she put her foot down in worn sneakers that didn't match her dress. She almost stumbled, one foot dragging. On closer inspection, she had little muscle tone in her legs and the pattern on her dress seemed strange, her hair a mess of tangles. In a heartbeat, Eve realized that the faint patterns were stains and dirt on her skin; a dress slept in on a bench, in a box, the back of a car. Her arms and legs were smeared with something the color of foundation. She had bruises. Their eyes met, hers glassed over, her pupils large. She looked through Eve, thrusting out her cup that jangled with change.

"Oh, fuck me!" Eve mumbled, her ideal day crashing in around her. She grabbed for Baker. "How much do you have?" She pulled her tip money from her pocket. Baker started to protest. "Shut up. Don't say anything. What do you have?" He handed her a twenty, his wallet empty. Eve ran to catch the girl, dodging commuters. She stuffed sixty dollars in the cup. A smile slid across her face in a practiced way, her eyes shutting with a flutter of her lids.

"Thanks. That's kind of you." She moved on with the crowd in an instant, the transaction complete. Only a few of the hurrying strangers noticed the exchange. The young woman disappeared, once again invisible.

Baker and Eve walked in silence to Eve's apartment. She wiped her eyes several times and sniffled on the way. The two paused outside.

"I know what you're thinking. She'll use the money to get high, but I don't care. That was me not so long ago, not the drugs but the homelessness. That could be me now. She'll know someone cared about her tonight. Maybe it will help a little."

"But she's not you, Eve. We found each other. You made me see you and I'm glad you made me see her. It's not always easy to see someone in need. I know I didn't look at her a second time, but you did. You're a good person."

"Baker, there is more of her in me, than you think. I'm not the woman you've been painting in the pink prom dress. If you wonder why I get moody, it's her. I don't want to be her but this life, everything I have is because of you. I don't want it that way. I want to contribute and stand on my own two feet."

They stood in silence, Baker, Eve and the ghost of the young woman.

He kissed her goodbye, a chaste, quick peck. Eve wanted to pull him close and kiss him back longer. The day had been intense, wonderful, and tragic, but he was already gone. Her world swirled, a maelstrom from the woman in pink and her own unease. Something was unsettled and she felt anxious. She wanted to be his equal, like April, but she was not April and never could be. She had more in common with the young woman in pink and didn't really belong in his world, but it would all have to wait. She needed to get ready for work.

❖

Moving up the parkway path at a steady pace, Eve increased her tempo slightly. She had begun running most mornings before going to the studio. Some days she ran five kilometers and some days, ten. On the weekends when there was more time, she ran longer - for an hour or more. She enjoyed running. It was hers alone and she could feel at peace from the angst that gnawed at her. Running was something she did that others could not. Cora was a chef, Baker an artist, and Eve was a runner once again.

She recalled her high school victories. Her wins had been effortless. She had only gone out for cross country to make friends. The workouts were drudgery, the afternoons hot and sticky her first year. Running hurt and her legs and lungs burned. At the first meet, she wasn't supposed to be with the leaders, but as the finish line approached, she was still there while the other girls fell back. Eve won, and after that came a string of victories and the state championships. She had been a minor celebrity at her high school. The coaches from the University at Huntington and the University at Morgantown came to her races to talk with her about attending their schools.

They wanted her to visit. Reality set in when Daddy told her she couldn't.

Adjusting her lean to mount the hill, Eve moved steadily toward Mount Vernon where she passed two women running in the opposite direction. At the top, she entered the parking lot of the famous mansion, circling the path before exiting the way she'd come in. Further toward town, she caught the two, slowing a little.

"Nice pace," one offered.

Eve smiled. "Thanks." She said, pulling alongside. "Can I run with you?"

Ellie and Sue introduced themselves to Eve. "So, you must be new in town. I haven't seen you running before."

"I moved here last fall. I've only recently started to run again. I used to run in high school."

"Your pace was pretty fast. Did you ever race?"

"Yeah, in high school. I was a state champion in cross country in West Virginia." She had their attention.

"You should run for our club. We have a great group. We run on our own most of the week but get together for long runs on the weekends and track work on Tuesday nights."

"I could do the weekends, but I work nights at Union Street."

"Oh, I like that place. The chef is world class."

"She's my friend." Eve smiled.

"Lucky you. Well, you should join us. We'd love to have someone with your pedigree on our team. There's a 10K race in a few weeks."

"I might do that." Eve ran into town with her two new friends. She'd never had anyone to run with and enjoy their company - normal women who liked to run, like her. The banter made the time pass quickly.

Sue complained about her husband. "I mean I'm trying to get out the door this morning and he's trying to pull me back to bed. You could imagine what he wanted, but I gave him the slip."

"What did you have to promise to get away," Ellie gave Eve a sly glance.

"Wouldn't you like to know? I don't kiss and tell, but actually it does involve a certain type of kissing."

"Eww, too much information." Ellie covered her ears. All three laughed, slowing to a jog. "Well, it must be nice to have to turn sex down." Ellie revived the topic. "I can't find a guy who interests me. Between work and training for Boston, I don't have the energy for a relationship."

"You're training for the Boston Marathon?" Eve asked.

"Yeah, I qualified at the Marine Corps Marathon last fall. It's in the spring so I'm really psyched. Sue is my coach. She used to run marathons at a pretty high level."

Sue shrugged and pointed down. “Bad knee. Can’t do the long runs anymore. But more important, what’s your situation, Eve? Do you have a significant other?”

Eve laughed, looking down. “I don’t know. Maybe?” Something was going on between her and Baker, but it wasn’t clear, and it all seemed so new. She had a lot on her mind with work, the possibility of going back to school, and Baker. Maybe it was time to see how she really felt about him. Sue and Ellie made her feel normal. It felt good to have friends.

Twenty-three

The night's service was over. Eve sipped her beer at the bar pretending to be Margaret Smallwood, The Asp—a single woman alone in the big city. She'd developed a taste for pale ale since resuming her daily runs. She found she craved the piney, citrus taste of the ale, thirsty after the day's work.

"You look lonely." Cora joined her, signaling for her champagne.

"Baker's off tonight." Eve made a casual comment. She wasn't thinking of him, but it was funny how his name was the first thing from her lips. She sounded lovesick.

"So," Cora gave her an incredulous look. "Why are you here? Go see him."

"He might be asleep, or he might want to be alone." Eve knew that statement wouldn't hold up to Cora's cross examination. She was nervous.

“No way, sister. My guess is he’s sitting in that snug little boat wishing you were there. You two are so alike. You both need a shove out the door. Now get out of here.”

“I guess you’re right. I’m trying to get up my nerve. Can I take him a present?” She pointed at the Johnny Walker bottle.

“Take the Red not the Blue or Black. If it’s for the two of you, then it’s on the house. Now get your skinny butt over there.” Eve downed her beer, then fetched the bottle from behind the bar. She gave Cora a nervous smile and walked into the night.

Momma had said, “Sometimes, you have to decide what you want and go get it.” She repeated the statement over and over on the short walk to the boat. Eve texted Baker.

You up?

Yeah, what’s up? You off?

Yeah, can I come by?

Smiley face, thumbs up, heart.

Be there in a minute.

Her heart raced. The funny, warm sensation she’d felt at times in the studio spread pleasantly through her body. She recalled him touching her. She always liked when he moved a strand of hair or placed her hands. What would it feel like when they weren’t painting? What would an actual kiss be like - a real kiss? They’d come so far, their relationship slow and measured as opposed to Marcy and Cora. Those two had been more of a lightning strike and Marcy had been all agush the next morning. Is that what she felt? The words 'next morning' made her stop. She wasn't going to stay the night, and nothing had to happen. "Yeah, right," she muttered.

Her breathing was rapid, her heart thumping in her chest. She rubbed the sweat off her palms. Something stirred inside her, building and replacing her nervousness. She walked between the boats, the night calm and quiet, her step measured on the wood planks. A small light from the boat welcomed her.

Eve knocked on the cabin door. "Baker, it's me," she squeaked, at least one pitch higher.

The hatch opened. Baker's grinning face popped up.

"May I come aboard?" She climbed down the stairs without waiting for an answer. Eve placed the scotch down on the small table.

"Wow, a nautical reference and Johnny Walker. What's the occasion?" Baker took two small crystal tumblers from a cupboard and poured the drinks, neat. Oscar watched through sleepy eyes, looking from Baker to Eve.

Eve took a small sip to calm herself, ignoring his question. The liquid burned the back of her throat. Her heart beats slowed a little. “Do you really like this stuff?” Baker gulped his and poured a second.

“I do. It takes a while to develop the taste. Stick your nose in the glass and breathe the aroma before the next sip. I developed the taste from my dad. He always liked his scotch.”

Eve took another small sip, savoring the flavor. “There’s a smokiness. Is that what I taste?” She knew she was stalling. She didn’t take her eyes off his face, watching him through the amber liquid in her tumbler and pretending to be interested in the scotch discussion.

“Yeah, they burn peat to heat the stills and toast the grain. What? What is it?”

No more stalling. It was time. She held her glass out to him, indicating a toast.

“So, what’s the occasion? Not that we need one. I’m happy you came by tonight.”

“To us,” she clinked his glass. Eve tilted her head provocatively and smiled, batting her eyelashes for effect.

Baker asked, “To us?”

Eve downed her last sip with a forced gulp then slid around to the seat next to Baker. Her thigh pressed against his. She could feel his warmth, touching his shoulder lightly. It was nice to touch him for a change. Her hand slid up his back, his tee shirt soft. She leaned in to kiss his neck, and then his ear. He smelled good - something nautical she guessed. She moved slowly to his lips as he turned to meet her, the warmth inside her building, guiding her movements, her tongue touching his lips. She wanted more, the blood pulsing through her chest, her kisses searching him.

Their lips parted and their eyes met in the candlelit cabin. “Can I stay?” Baker nodded. He finished his scotch, wiping his mouth with his hand. Eve crawled into his bunk, pulling him to her.

❖

The light was bright through the porthole. Oscar lay nearby, watching her. When he saw her move, he got up, tail wagging, and licked her hand. She patted him. Baker was gone. It seemed only moments before that she’d woken next to him with the same intense need from the night before, their bodies twining before falling into a deep sleep in the early morning dawn. Now what? She could wait for him in her current state but felt awkward, naked in his bunk. Maybe she should get dressed? Her clothes were all over the cabin. The scotch bottle and glasses still sat on the table from the night before. Were those her panties on Oscar’s bed? Her bra was nowhere in sight. What if he walked in while she was dressing?

Her phone vibrated, tinkling its location. She stepped out, scooped up the phone and dove back under the covers.

"Marcy?"

"What are you up to, girl?"

"Um." Eve stammered. "No judgment and no questions. I'm in Baker's bunk and he's gone. Should I get dressed or wait for him?"

"Oh my God, you two had sex. I can't believe it. How was it?"

"Marcy, please. This is embarrassing enough. I don't ask for details about you and Cora."

"Want some? I'm happy to share."

"Marcy, I think I should get dressed. I'll call you later."

"Eve, how was it? Tell me."

"Well." She paused for a moment, smiling at the recent memory. "I was nervous, and things happened so fast. It was kind of awkward and not really that great. I think both of us were nervous. But then he was holding me, and we were so comfortable in his bunk just talking about anything and everything. I fell asleep with the boat rocking on the water."

"Whoa." Marcy giggled. "What happened this morning?"

Eve was suddenly embarrassed by her confession. "I'm going to hang up and get dressed. Bye, Marcy. I'll call you later." She hung up before Marcy could ask another question.

There was no way she could tell Marcy about the morning. Eve had a hard time believing herself. She'd opened her eyes to Baker's back in the early light, his breathing steady. She ran her hand down his spine and neck, amazed to find golden hair covering his body. His warmth felt good, clinging to him. Her hand moved down his ribs and across his stomach, flat and hard. Baker rolled over, viewing her with dreamy eyes. Eve slid onto him, controlling their movement, kissing him and taking his hands. She watched him as she moved, their eyes locked in the dawning light. Eve gasped, closing her eyes, collapsing on Baker, her breaths slowing, and then she slept again.

Eve pushed the thought away, and then dressed hurriedly after finding her undergarments in the dog's bed. She shook the white hairs off and pulled them on quickly, then gathered the rest of her items to dress. There was a noise on the deck above. She took a swig from the scotch bottle for her breath, maybe courage. Eve swished several times and swallowed, grimacing, then opened the hatch and climbed up into the sun. "Hi." She felt the flush in her cheeks. A new day had begun.

"Hi." He said softly. "I brought you coffee, two creams. I didn't want to wake you." He handed her a cup.

"You didn't seem to mind me waking you this morning?" She smiled shyly.

"You can wake me anytime you want." He handed her the coffee. She took a sip, looking at the ripples on the water below. Baker slurped a little, then set his cup down and moved to her.

"I need to kiss you now. My breath is probably terrible, but I can't wait. I missed you while I was gone."

"I want you to kiss me. I missed you." Baker pulled her close. The kiss was long and soft.

"Ummm." Baker murmured. "My favorite things; scotch, coffee, and you."

The two sat on deck to watch the sun on the water, warmed by its rays. Both had questions, but neither asked, content in the moment, content with each other, the long dance consummated. Being together was enough.

❖

The restaurant felt different when Eve returned for work after a quick shower and change to set up her station. Baker ran in, seconds before the evening gathering. He flashed a quick smile at her as he slipped on his apron. Cora gathered the staff, preoccupied as she spoke, making the food introductions short. Her eyes flicked from one staff person to the other, always coming to rest on Baker and then Eve.

The first patrons wandered in. Eve felt Cora behind her. "Let me see." Cora examined Eve. "Oh my God." Eve looked down and blushed. "You two? Together? Oh my

God." Cora grabbed Eve in a bear hug. "I'm so happy. I think I'm going to cry." Cora fanned herself. "Okay, I have to get going but you and I will have champagne after service tonight. Have you called Marcy?"

Eve nodded her head. "This morning. She wanted details so I hung up."

"I'm so happy for you, Eve. He's a good man." Cora snapped Baker with her towel on the way to the kitchen. Eve ducked away to her station. It was a close staff, maybe too close. There were few secrets in their little family.

Twenty-four

Her breathing was faster but not more labored. Eve pushed the pace fast for a minute, then jogged, then pushed again. It was her favorite workout, the mini-sprints getting her heart rate up and the rest in between just enough to recover. She wanted to keep up with her friends for the upcoming 10K and had added some of her old high school workouts. She also liked the familiar feeling of fatigue during her workday.

Her mind wandered as she ran, amazed at the changes in her life. She was so different from the girl who left Nitro the previous fall. Then, she ran to escape. Now it helped her deal with stress, but she'd also found friendship with Sue and Ellie. She was a woman now; it sounded funny, but she'd crossed that threshold. She liked her work and had a career with Cora if she wanted. She had money invested from the life insurance, more adult words and notions. Then there was sex. She'd never really considered the physical act, not since her fantasies about Bigun before leaving town. Now she'd slept with a man, a man she cared for and who cared for her. She shivered at the thought of being with him. She liked being an adult and making her own decisions. It should be perfect, but something was out of balance.

At Union Street, Eve moved from serving to the kitchen, spending time with the Marx Brothers. She learned each station: pastry, bread, salad, sauces, and the grill. It was daunting. None of the men spoke much, their favorite form of communication a wink, a nod, a click of the tongue, a whistle, and sometimes a quick shove out of the way to get to the pan. Eve learned quickly, observing and pitching in where she could. Cora told her to be tough, don't pull any punches, and don't sit back. She nicked her fingers from knives, picked up bruises from an elbow or platter that passed too close, and dealt with burns from the grill—all minor wounds encountered on the battlefield.

Today was salad duty. Eve headed for the walk-in cooler. She retrieved a box of lettuce and other exotic greens, going back for cucumbers, spring onions, and tomatoes. Last she took out cooked eggs and cheddar cheese. She washed all the vegetables, slicing the cucumber, onion, and tomatoes as she was shown, and then placed the pieces in airtight containers, ready for plating. The slices of egg were prepared next, followed by laces of cheddar cheese that would go on the plate to complete the house salad. She did the same for the Caesar, tearing the romaine lettuce precisely, shaving the parmesan cheese ribbons, and placing the anchovies in a bowl to complete the preparation. Chico showed her how to make the dressings for each, whisking oil, French mustard, vinegar, spices, lemon, salt and pepper. She tasted each with a clean spoon, then wrote notes in a small notebook she kept snug in her back pocket. Finally, she chopped day-old baguettes with a rough chop, rubbed the pieces with baked garlic and sprinkled it all with olive oil, salt, and pepper, before toasting the croutons under the broiler in a flat pan.

Cora inspected her station. "Okay, you look ready. When the orders come in, listen for my call, house or Caesar, with or without for the anchovy or egg, on-the-side or with for dressing, okay? Plate and dress, then place the dish on the serving station for the server to pick up." When the last salad had been served around 10:30, Eve moved to dessert, the evening flying by. She helped plate the pie and cake, adding ice cream or whipped cream, finishing with a sprig of mint or a berry. The last dessert went out near 11:45.

Eve walked outside for fresh air, exhausted. Baker joined her. "How'd it go tonight?"

"I'm whipped. The pace is grueling. Getting it out the right way and on time for the queen is nerve wracking." Baker smiled.

"She's a tough cookie. What are your plans tonight?" He stood close to her.

"I'm going to go to my apartment. I hope you don't mind but I need to sleep and wake up in my bed before another day in the kitchen. I also need a shower badly." Eve held her arms up to air out. "I need to get my bearings." She snuggled up to Baker. "Tell Oscar I won't be gone too long." She kissed him, folding her body into his.

"We'll miss you, but I understand." The two walked to her apartment, savoring the time together. Eve released his hand at the corner.

"See you tomorrow." She kissed him lightly, holding onto his finger as long as she could, then ran to her apartment.

The rest of her week was similar. Eve woke late, went for a run, showered, and went into work at the salad station, making sure each plate met Cora's and her own standards. She was learning the kitchen rules. Baker gave her space. After Friday's shift, she waited for him.

"I'm so tired. Who knew this is what real life is like?"

"Can I walk you to your apartment?" There was disappointment on his face.

"I said I'm tired, but not tired enough to spend another night away from you. I'm catching my breath. I caught myself thinking about us together on my run today." She shivered visibly then found his hand.

"I know what you're feeling. Cora let me try my hand in the kitchen once. It was a disaster, and I was completely wiped out. I know how tough it is and I also know it's not for me."

"I don't want to wait for anything. Take me home to the boat. I need you. I want to wake up with you, have coffee, and hear the gulls." She put her head on his chest.

Baker led her to the boat, the warm spring night to the harbor and the small boat that rocked gently on the still water.

❖

Sue and Ellie led while Eve struggled to stay up with her friends. "Can we ease up, guys? I'm hurting today."

"That time of the month?" Sue asked, the question more of a statement.

"No, it's work. It's kicking my butt. I'm learning the kitchen stations at the restaurant. The pace in the kitchen is hard to keep up with. I come home and fall asleep, then do it all again the next day. How do you do it with a family, job, and still find the time and energy to run?"

"This is the only me time I get." Susie answered. "If I didn't get out here and run, I'd go crazy."

"Yeah, me too. I have to run all the shit that happens at work or home out of me. Welcome to real life."

"Hang in there, kid. You'll catch your breath. Is anything happening on the boyfriend front?" Ellie grinned.

"It's all good. He's great. We started as friends and now it's more. I think about him and us all the time. It's distracting."

"Wow, new love. Now we know what the problem is. You're having sex all night." The two hooted. "I remember what that was like. The sex was nonstop, and we couldn't keep our hands off each other." They slowed to a walk.

"Well, it's not all about the sex, but that part is pretty good. He's got a boat in the harbor, just the two of us and his dog. It's romantic when you think about it. He's an artist - he paints."

"Has he painted you?" Ellie asked. They were stretching out in the park.

"That's how we met. I modeled for him. He drew me at first but then painted some abstracts and portraits. They're really beautiful."

"Any au naturel?" Susie had a wicked smile. Ellie giggled. Eve joined them.

"Funny, you two. Last weekend he sketched me with charcoal while I was taking a nap. It came out nice. He's got it hanging in the cabin." Her two companions shook their heads. Ellie fanned herself.

"So romantic. Do it all now. When the kids start coming, all that mushy stuff goes away with the diapers and crying." Susie chided.

Kids weren't even on the radar. Once again Eve had to chuckle at the conversations she was having with these ladies.

❖

Harpo showed Eve the sauce station. She helped him make the stock, the white sauce, the brown sauce, and the hollandaise. She minced shallots, chives, mint, and other herbs that were set aside to be added to the sauce or stock with a pinch of salt, slab of butter, or squeeze of lemon. After each adjustment, he'd hand her a fresh spoon to taste, nodding or shaking his head. Their station moved faster than the salads, keeping everything warm without overcooking and plating the sauce either before or after the piece of meat or fish came off the grill. Eve took elbows to the ribs and arms routinely in the scrum, the heat from the stove her compass. She traded her Danskos for Crocs after spilling veal stock on her foot the first night. By the end of the week, she had adjusted to the pace and held her own.

"You smell incredible. You're like a short rib that's been cooking in wine all day, completely edible." Eve lay on her stomach in Baker's bunk, her eyes closed, savoring his massaging touch down her spine. He kissed her neck.

"Cora calls it the perfume of the kitchen. I think I'm adjusting. I'm not as tired, but I'm anxious about working the grill and the main courses."

"You'll do fine. You're a competitor, Eve."

"Like I said, I'm not as tired." She rolled over, attaching herself to him. "I might be the steak, but you're my cake, and I want dessert." She put her lips on his with an audible sigh.

❖

"Not bad, rookie. Keep your eye on Groucho, do what he does. Watch his timing for each entrée. Watch the orders as they come in so you know when to get each entree started. I think you're ready."

"I didn't grow up with food like this. It's all new to me. Some things I like and some I don't."

"That's okay, there are a lot of things I don't like, but most of our food is good old American comfort food. Get the proper heat, salt, butter, and acid and that's all there is to it. Watch and learn. When you go to culinary school, you'll have the basic techniques and a frame of reference for the French and other styles they'll teach you. Do you like cooking now?"

"Yeah, I like it. It's insane, but I like working on the team with the guys. I don't cook at home at all. Baker does all of it and he's pretty good."

"He's not bad. How is Mr. Baker?"

"Good. I think he's gotten his father's things settled. He's also trying to get the drawings and paintings we did together shown at one of the galleries uptown."

"That's really cool. I always knew he had the talent. He'll find a place to show his work and it'll be a big hit. But enough about him. I want you to keep seconding the Marx Brothers in the kitchen and me in the office. You can be manager when I'm gone and run both sides. It will make a big difference to me to know you're in charge. The way you handled that boy with the gun, I have no doubt you can run my restaurant."

Eve smiled. "There are so many moving parts, and each piece has to be perfect. There's the food order, the setting, and staff. I don't know how you do it but I'll try my best."

"I know you will. I wouldn't offer you this opportunity if I didn't think you could do it." Cora put her hands on Eve's shoulders. "Like I said, I was impressed with the woman that took charge in Nitro. I was happy she was there to protect me. We all have talents. Mine was spotting you and getting you to work here. Everything else is just fancy food and a talented chef." She winked.

Twenty-five

Baker and Oscar snored in tandem. It was still dark, but light would fill the cabin soon. Eve wanted to sleep, but something bothered her, a constant feeling as of late. A man slept beside her and she knew him, or at least she was learning to know him. She'd seen his moods and what he liked and didn't like. Baker was an open book and held little back from her. He loved his mother, his father, his dog, and the boat. He loved her apparently and said so quite often. There had been another woman once, someone from his past. Eve had memories too—Momma and Daddy, her grandparents, and her home in West Virginia. Baker's life and hers were so different. The differences in their lives mattered, causing her to wake her in the early morning.

She was kidding herself about being a woman. She was nothing like April in her pearls and heels. She'd experienced nothing in her life while April and Baker had been to Europe, Mexico, and California. She'd only been to Alexandria and Charleston, the one in West

Virginia. Baker had graduated from college and painted in an artist's colony. Eve had a bad apartment and was an apprentice at a local pub. They both lost their parents, but his father and hers were worlds apart. The life she and Baker had together, the little world they'd created was easy, but she realized she lived in his world more than her own.

Eve turned away but Baker pulled her to him. She scrunched away again, crawling in the sheets. He pulled her back. Eve resigned to his touch, feeling his heartbeat against her back. He began to snore. Eve sighed, waiting for dawn to walk Oscar.

❖

"I have to go home tonight. I haven't seen Kitty and need to check on her." The two stood outside the bar, the evening shift over. They began to walk, hand in hand.

"Bring her down to the boat. She can live there with us."

"Us?" Tired and confused, she asked. "What are we? I love being with you, Baker, but I have an apartment and you live on a boat. I get confused and don't know where I live anymore." He frowned. "What are we doing and who am I trying to be? It's all so fast, everything that has happened."

"Don't overthink it, Eve. I love you. Okay, I said it first, but I do. From the moment I saw you I was attracted to you and every minute together has only made me love you more. I want to be with you, however or wherever. We can go as slow or as fast as you want."

"And I love being with you. But it's new and I've never known someone like you or a life like this. We're new, work is new, and Alexandria is new. I'm struggling, Baker. I'm still not over seeing that girl coming back from the metro that could have been me. This is your life and that was mine. She haunts me and I miss the ridge, my home." She exhaled, hanging her head.

"I get it, Eve. It's hard to escape the past. However much time you need, you take. I'll wait."

"I don't want you to wait. I want you now. But I want to see the things you've seen. I want to be your equal, not someone you saved. You're an artist and I'm a runaway, a dropout. There is such a difference between our two worlds. I want you to love me because I have something to give that's valuable. I don't want to be some poor homeless thing from West Virginia that's your project." She turned away.

"Eve, I fell in love with the woman who came to my studio to work with me. The past doesn't matter and where you're from doesn't matter. I love the woman who introduced my best friend to her best friend. I love the woman who came on my boat with a bottle of scotch and kissed me. I've known love before, but never like this.

Now that I've found you, I'm willing to do anything to keep you close to me. You are my world." She buried her head in his chest, his jacket open and warm.

"You don't make it easy for me, do you?" She smiled, wiping tears away. "Let's go get Kitty."

❖

Kitty liked the freedom of the waterfront and dock, walking the planks between the boats, watching the birds and fish, then snuggling into a warm berth at night. Oscar put up with the feline's presence, an annoyance not unlike a large flea. He had the floor, while the cat moved out of reach on the countertop and seats.

The little ginger completed their family, giving Eve comfort and having something from home onboard. When not at the boat, she spent her time learning the restaurant books - revenue and deposits, weekly groceries, accounts receivable, and worst of all, payroll. Cora was a good teacher with most of her lessons in her head. Eve researched and quickly set up software to run the day-to-day finances. The program was basic but made the tallying of evening sums, payroll, and bill paying easier. She also organized the office. Cora stayed away, preferring the kitchen, nodding and pretending to understand while Eve explained.

"Cora, I need to show you how to use this program and the passwords."

She raised her hand and rushed off. "You've found your art, Eve. Make it work, keep the ship sailing and we're good. I have filets to sauté." Eve groaned, also preferring the kitchen's hustle and bustle as her employer.

❖

"So how was work tonight?" Baker asked, raising his scotch. Eve held her wine glass lightly.

"It sucked. Books and bills. I'll take the action in the kitchen any day, burns and all."

"You know you're the first person ever allowed in that office, other than the accountant. She has big plans for you."

"She knows I prefer the kitchen. It's not fair, just because I'm new."

"Two more Vouvrays, Larry, plus whatever Walker Mr. Baker's enjoying." Baker mouthed the word "black." Cora joined the discussion. "So how you doing, champ? Still loving me and my little establishment?"

"What happened to training in the kitchen," Eve asked cautiously. "You don't think I can do it, do you?"

"No, I do think you can do it and do it well. But learning the kitchen is going to take a while. You can't become a great or even good chef overnight. If that is what you want, I say great. We'll work you in and you'll learn the whole kitchen and fill in each night. But learning the back office - the menu, ordering the food and groceries, setting the work schedule, getting payroll out is also important. Someone has to be able to do it if I'm away. Check your paycheck. I'm making it worth your while. I need time off with Marcy. We want to get away and you are the glue that holds this place together. It takes a certain talent to be able to manage all this and keep the wheels turning. Do this for me and if you still want to become a chef when I get back, we'll start the training in earnest."

"Okay."

"And check your paycheck. I think you'll be happy." The three clinked glasses.

"Thank you, Cora. I didn't expect you to do that for me."

"I'm doing it for me. You're my investment."

"So where are you two going?" Eve asked, satisfied for the time being with her new station.

"My family's beach house in New Jersey. I want them to meet Marcy." The chef was bringing her date home and positively glowing.

❖

The top males took the front line, Eve settling in a couple rows back. She'd forgotten about the nervousness at the start. The jittery feeling swept through her, and she felt she needed to pee again, even though she'd just gone to the nearby port-a-potties. Her breath was rapid.

She wiped sweat from her brow, her mouth dry, and underarms soaked. She jogged in place beside her friends.

"Let's take the first mile at a reasonable pace and not get sucked out with the guys. After that, we run as we feel. First one across the line buys the beer." Ellie laid out the plan. Eve nodded. She had no voice.

The gun popped. The crowd surged. Eve felt a hand on her shoulder, pushing her forward. She jogged a few steps to start, not wanting to run into those moving slowly in front of her before picking up her normal stride. She ran with Ellie and Suzie near the side of the road where there was a little more room. The first mile went by in a little over six minutes and felt fast, her breath still rapid. Eve's friends dropped back but she continued without slowing, her head down, her arms moving in sync with her legs. There were younger men on either side, their pace comfortable. The turnaround point came quickly, and she could see it just ahead. Eve leaned to make the U-turn around the pylon and headed back toward town and the finish. Only three miles to go.

"Looking good, Eve. You got this." The voice broke her concentration. Susie yelled as they passed on opposite sides of the street.

"What?" She wondered what Susie meant, focusing on her pace. The early nervousness had passed and she felt strong. Eve ran toward the finish mildly tired but with energy to burn. The streets were now crowded with onlookers. The mile markers and split times flashed by but meant nothing. Eve raced, picking off the runners in front of her. It felt good to go fast though the effort was accumulating, a dull sensation in her quads. Another voice and a loud woof broke her concentration.

"Beautiful, Eve. You're in first and the finish is just ahead. You got this, babe." Baker shouted. The dog bounced beside him, woofing at the passing runners. She could see the finish line, the large timer placed above the scaffolding, hearing him but racing on. The clock ticked away. She could see the numbers, thirty-seven minutes, ten seconds, twenty seconds, twenty-five seconds, twenty-nine seconds. She crossed the line and stopped, exhausted but happy to finish. There were maybe a half a dozen men in the brightly ribboned chute in front of her. She stood alone in the women's lane, hands on her hips, and breathing hard. Baker and Oscar ran toward her on the sidewalk. Susie came into view on the horizon with Ellie not far behind. Both were laboring in exaggerated sprints. Someone pulled her down the chute to move away from the finish line. She broke away waiting for her friend's to finish.

"Go, Susie. Go, Ellie." It was all she could manage, her breathing still labored.

Susie staggered into the chute, throwing a sweat-drenched arm around her neck for support. "You were amazing, Eve, sub-forty?" Susie struggled for oxygen between words.

Ellie agreed, also grabbing onto the pair, a trio of support. "I knew you were good, but sub-forty in your first race, oh my God." The three women labored, breathing deeply and holding on to one another as they recovered. Eve nudged them into a walk toward the end of the chute.

"You ran great, guys. I didn't know what I was doing out there."

Baker arrived with Oscar and gave her a hug and kiss. "Fantastic, Eve. Did you have any idea you were going to win?"

Eve smiled. "I had no idea. Training's felt good. But no." She shook her head. Her two friends, somewhat recovered, were making faces at her and nodding at Baker. "Yeah, he's the boyfriend. Ladies, this is Baker. And this is Oscar. Baker went to shake their hands but was immediately ignored as the two women fawned over Oscar. "Baker, this is Susie and Ellie. We're going to the Oyster House. I owe them some beers. Want to come?"

"I'll take Oscar home and meet you."

"What's the big grin for?" Eve asked as Baker turned away. He stopped and turned around to face her.

"You were so beautiful out there. I see something new every day with you." He gave her a second kiss, this one on the lips. Susie and Ellie smiled.

❖

The runners had donned their race tee shirts with large medals dangling from their necks, gold, silver, and bronze. A trophy with a female runner perched on the top sat in the middle of the bar, surrounded by schooners of lite beer and bowls of chowder. The three were enjoying themselves, posing with the trophy and their medals for Baker's pictures.

"No comments about the tee shirts and medals, Baker. I'm going to be a big old nerd and wear them all day." The large beers and post race fatigue were kicking in.

"And what do you plan to do with that?" Baker pointed to the trophy.

"It's a little gaudy. I think my dresser will be fine." The whole scene was surreal. The win, her friends in the pub—a perfect day. Eve took a deep breath and realized she was thankful, a prayer of sorts. Baker interrupted her reverie.

"Watching you run today was amazing. You're a natural. When's the next one?"

"Not so fast, Baker. This was for fun and I have no plans. Running is casual for me and a stress release. I want to keep it fun."

"So how good is she?" Baker asked the other two women, not satisfied by Eve's answer.

Susie chimed in. "Thirty-seven puts her among the best in the Metro, and they're all youngsters like her, college age or just out."

The comment caught Eve off guard. She took a big gulp, hearing her name and college.

"She's good," Ellie confirmed. "She can win the short races if she wants but she could probably run one hell of a marathon. The word marathon, the legendary Olympic distance, rang another bell.

Baker's oysters arrived. Eve politely said no when he offered her one. He doused the bivalve with horseradish and hot sauce then slurped it down. It looked disgusting and she had to chuckle at his delight.

Twenty-six

Eve sniffed, moving a hand to her eye to wipe the tear, her morning routine of late.

"What's the matter, babe?" Baker snuggled against her, wrapped in the sheets.

"I don't know. I'm upset all the time and I don't know why. I'm such a mess."

"You're not a mess. Tell me what's bothering you. I can tell you've had something on your mind for a while now. Talk to me."

"I think I miss home. I love what we have, this boat, Oscar, and Kitty. I love work, and Cora. I enjoy running with my friends. Everything is so good, but I'm sad all the time. I miss Momma, I miss Marcy, and I miss home." She wiped her eyes, accepting a tissue from Baker, and blew her nose.

"It'll be dawn soon. Let's get up and get some breakfast at the cafe. Something warm will make you feel better, then there's something I want to show you."

They dressed quickly, walking Oscar and settling in at the pastry shop. Baker returned from the counter with coffee and croissants. Eve peeled an orange and gave Baker half. The two ate silently, Eve's funk had been temporarily replaced by whatever Baker was planning. Maybe it was the booth, the same booth they had sat in when he'd brought her in off the street. Eve couldn't wait any longer. "What is it? What do you want to show me?"

"Come on. It's a short ride and Oscar can come." They drove out of Old Town in the old Bronco to the south side of town, pulling into a small townhouse community.

"This is my dad's place," Baker announced.

"I didn't know he had a place."

"It's been rented out, so I haven't thought about it much. It needs work."

The townhome sat in a nice block overlooking a golf course. Jaguars and Mercedes dotted the driveways. The end unit was faded brick, with peeling paint on the shutters and trim. The shrubs were either overgrown or dead.

"This is where I grew up - my old home." The two walked up the steps to look out over the golf course, the haze lifting with the sun that rose over the tall oaks.

"I thought the view at Malone Ridge was nice, but this is gorgeous." She could see the river and Old Town in the distance. "So, you must play golf?"

"Not since Dad went to the home, but we used to play every Sunday. I think my clubs are still in the garage. I had a couple of junior championships at that club."

"Wow, Baker. I didn't know you were such a jock." She smiled for the first time that day.

"Coming from you, I'll take that as a compliment. It's good to see you smile. Come on inside." He opened the door. Oscar barged ahead into the familiar home. "The floors need to be redone. The kitchen and baths need to be replaced. The garden needs to be replanted, not to mention the whole house needs paint. It needs a lot of work." The two wandered, each taking a separate path. Eve went downstairs to the den that looked over the fenced garden. She let Oscar into the backyard where he found his spots, relieving himself here and there with a happy look. There was a small koi pond in the back corner near a shed. It was empty of fish, the water murky and green. A dilapidated patio table and chairs sat neglected. It could look nice with a little work. The two met in the kitchen.

"I want to put in new tile, cabinets, and appliances."

"Will you do the work or hire it out?"

"I don't know yet. I have to save some money first. I'll work on it in my spare time most likely. But I have an idea. The boat is cramped. Why don't we move here and work on the place together? You can pick out the upgrades. It needs a woman's touch after my dad and me living here for so long without my mother."

"You never talk about her. What was she like?"

"She was perfect - PB&Js for lunch, Cub Scout den mother, soccer mom. She was always there for me—clean clothes, school projects, and rides to friends or scouts. She drove me to all the golf matches and walked the course with me. She was wonderful."

"So that's where it comes from."

"What? What comes from where?" Eve walked into his arms and put her head on his chest.

"Gentleness, you're kind and gentle. I love that about you most and I wish I knew her, but in a way, I guess I do." Eve paused. "Are you asking me to move in with you?"

"Yes. I want us to live here together and start a life. We can take our time and fix it up. If it's too small, we can sell and move somewhere else. There's an extra bedroom for Marcy when she comes, though I doubt she'd stay here." Both laughed. Eve nodded in agreement. "You make me happy, Eve. This will be wonderful. We'll keep the boat, but you can let the apartment go. It's close to work and to where you like to run. It will be perfect."

Eve didn't answer.

"There's one other thing I need to show you." Baker locked up and led Eve around the side of the house. An

Airstream trailer was parked on the side lot with a canvas cover tight around its body.

"Your father owned a rocket ship?"

"Yeah, he did. I used to pretend that's what it was as a kid, sitting in the seat and playing with the wheel. We took our family vacation in this baby every summer. We went to the beach, to the mountains, and even cross country."

"That sounds so wonderful. I'd like a vacation like that one day. I've never had a vacation and I feel like I could use one now." The tears burst forth again. "I can't do this anymore. I need to get away. We are so different. You do everything for me, and I don't know who I am anymore."

"Eve, you won a race. You're going to run Cora's restaurant while she's gone. You helped me out of my artistic slump. Most important, you came into my life and gave me something I never thought I'd have again."

"But what happens when the next homeless girl walks by?" She pouted.

Baker pulled her to him and held her tight. "I only want you, Eve. Let's get away. Let's take a vacation in the Airstream to find out who we are. Tell Cora you need time off. Let's go before you get locked down, to take care of the restaurant for her. Let's take some time for ourselves."

"Where would we go?"

"Malone Ridge to begin with. I know you're homesick. We'll bring Oscar and Kitty. You can visit Marcy." Eve jumped on Baker, kissing him urgently.

"You make me so happy." The dark mood vanished. "Take me back to the boat right now. I think there's enough time for a few hours of bunk time before work." The two walked quickly to the car, starting the engine and pulling out to the street. Baker quickly shifted into reverse and backed back up the driveway. He applied the brakes and ran back into the house. Oscar ran out happily when the door opened.

❖

JJ pulled up to the curb outside the beauty salon. Patsy waited inside, coming out when the beat-up Trans Am rattled to a stop.

"This thing's a piece of junk." The car door squealed in time with her comment as she opened it. "We should have sold this crappy old thing and kept mine."

"Can't sell old Red Betty. She's been good to me." JJ pushed in his Doobie Brothers cassette tape. "How was work, hon?"

"Uncomfortable. What do you think, having to carry this thing around inside me? It's kicking all the time, I'm always sweaty, and I always gotta pee."

"Did you find out anything about my sister?"

"I did. Take me back to the apartment so I can shower. She's in Alexandria. It's about a day's drive. We need to go soon. The money from my car ain't going to pay for the apartment for long and I'll be having this baby come summer."

"We can go whenever. I'm ready." JJ pulled out the pistol from under the seat. He laid it on the dashboard, pulling up to the one stop light in town. The deputy drove by slowly in the opposite direction, JJ staring him down.

"You can go cause you ain't got nothin' else to do. I got work."

"I'll show you what I'm going to do when we get home. I'll join you in the shower." He smiled a hopeful smile.

"Oh, no you ain't. You ain't touchin' me till you get that money. That's how we got this baby. You do what you need to do and get that money, then you can touch me." JJ put the gun under the seat once again and drove the rest of the way home in silence. People didn't know how hard it was being the man.

Twenty-seven

The old travel-trailer was hooked up to the Bronco. Eve bought groceries and stocked the cooler. She made the bed in the cabin, ready for occupation. Kitty was loaded in with her box and a bowl of water. Oscar took his back seat in the Bronco and Eve sat beside Baker.

"My first vacation. I'm so excited." She slid on her shades from the glare.

"I'm excited, too. It's been a while and it makes me think of Dad. He would have been happy to be with us and on the road again. It's great to get the camper up and running."

Baker and Eve took their time on the journey back to Nitro. There was no rush. The two headed south, ending up at the State Park just inside the West Virginia border. The park offered something for everyone with hiking, golf, or rafting. They set up camp, or glamp as Baker called it. The Airstream was well-fitted with a spacious bed, efficient toilet, sink, shower and decent galley. Baker rolled out the awning, setting the camp chairs by the fire pit. Eve and Kitty explored while Oscar lay under the picnic table in the shade.

A cheery fire crackled in the pit. Baker popped the top on a Guinness and poured Eve a pale ale, the two beers icy from the cooler. She placed the cornmeal-dressed trout in the sizzling pan on the small camp stove, dropping a few cherry peppers in for color. The cat mewed at her feet. Eve checked the succotash on the other burner, adding a lump of butter.

Baker took a deep breath. “Ah, Union Street West. Nothing like bringing a chef on vacation.”

“Don’t get too used to it, buddy. I’m on vacation, too.” She sipped her ale. “Oh, that’s good, so cold.” They ate in front of the fire in their chairs. Baker cleaned up at the campsite facilities. Kitty followed him, exploring the brick structure in search of mice or crickets.

The stars were bright against the blackness of the mountain. “Just like the boat,” Baker said, pulling up the cover on the double bunk. Eve locked the door and crawled in, snuggling close. The windows were open, and a mountain breeze cooled the small space. An owl hooted somewhere nearby.

“I can feel it. I’m close to home. This reminds me so much of Malone Ridge. It’ll be good to be back.”

The next day the two hiked the trails down to the river before taking the gondola ride up to the top of the

3,200-foot peak. They picnicked on the mountaintop, surveying the valley below. Baker held Eve's hand on the descent, finally confessing his fear of heights as the valley floor rushed toward them, his eyes shut. Eve was wide-eyed and Baker's scaredy-cat confession added to her enjoyment of the ride down. The two grilled burgers that night, the weather once again perfect for outdoor cooking.

The next morning, Baker made coffee. He took out croissants, butter, and cheese, and poured black cherries they'd purchased at the farmers' market in a bowl. A light rain fell. Eve came out in her running shorts, top, and shower sandals.

She stretched and yawned.

"Hey, sleepyhead." Baker lifted his mug of coffee to signal one for her.

"It's the air. I slept so well. I could go back to bed and sleep more."

"You should. That's what vacations are for." She picked up a mug, sipping her black coffee. "Want to head up to Nitro today?"

Eve nodded. "Yeah, I'm anxious. Looks like it's a good day to travel."

"Or you could try your hand at golf?"

"Some other time. I have a feeling it might require a little bit more concentration than I'm willing to give the task right now and I have to say, chasing a little white ball around all day doesn't really get me excited."

"Okay, we'll save golf for another day when you feel like being frustrated. We'll head out after breakfast."

Breaking camp took next to no time. Kitty was loaded in the trailer while the other three hopped in the Bronco. The drive was pleasant in the light drizzle, rolling down the turnpike and through the mountains toward Charleston.

"So how do you feel, coming back home?"

"It's strange. So much happened here. I'm different and I've changed. Alexandria is my home now, but it will be nice to be back. I'm not sure what I feel. I was so unsettled before we left. I meant what I said about us, about being equal. The two of us need to finish working things out. I don't want you rescuing me or giving me everything. I need to bring something to this relationship." The gold dome of the state capital appeared around the bend, the wide river running alongside the highway. Eve smiled, knowing her family home was just up the road. "And don't worry about me and my crappy moods lately, Baker. I'm looking forward to working with you on the house. I think we can make it ours."

Baker smiled. "That's my girl, and anyways, I need to figure a way to finance it first."

The drive up to Malone Ridge was slow going with the Airstream and the narrow switchbacks but they eventually cleared the last turn to see the shabby trailer, the lone sentinel to their arrival. Baker parked the RV near the old homestead on a slab between the two chimneys, and then unhooked the silver tube.

"I'm going into town to take care of business if you want to set up camp. I'll give Marcy a call so we can get together." Eve skipped off to the truck, waving out of the window as she drove out, happy to be home.

She came back with groceries and ice. "I paid the tax bill and had the electricity turned on. We should be able to hook up instead of using the generator." The camp was comfy. Baker built a fire pit with stones from the rubble. The Airstream fit in the flat space that was once a foundation. Eve ran her five-mile loop each day and they cleaned the lot and trimmed the weeds around the burial plot. The junk man came to tow the trailer away, and JJ's garbage was removed by the county. Malone Ridge hadn't looked so good for many years.

"I'm happy, Baker. I'm really happy. You, me, Oscar, Kitty. I don't know if this is a typical vacation, but I couldn't imagine a better day." The fire had burned down to orange embers, Baker sipping a single malt, his legs stretched out, Oscar nearby.

"You know I could sell the house and we could move up here and build. I could paint here, and you could follow your nursing school plan. Cora would be the only casualty."

"You'd do that for me? You'd move up here?" Eve moved closer.

"I'm going to go where you go, and I have no one to keep me in Alexandria now. It makes sense that we live somewhere that makes you happy." Eve moved to his camp chair, sitting in Baker's lap unsteadily. She put her arms around his neck.

"Whoa." She balanced them. "Why are you so good to me?" She kissed him.

"Because of kisses like that."

"That one was nothing. Let's close up for the night and I'll give you a much nicer kiss," Her face glowed from the embers.

❖

Marcy was a daily visitor. She loved the Airstream, shiny and efficient. The three ate dinners outside on the ridge or drove into town for pizza and beer.

Eve met Marcy after work. "So where did you want me to go with you?"

"Take me to Ridge Works. I know you know the dude there. It's a present for Cora."

"Oh my God, Marcy. You have gotten adventurous since we were here last. You're gonna let Bigun tattoo you?"

"Not without gloves and not the way you wanted him to." She stuck her tongue out.

"What are you getting?"

"I want a little mermaid, like Cora's. I'm thinking upper back, sundress view?"

"So, you two are serious."

"Yeah, we're serious. We talk almost every night. We're going to the beach to meet her family later this summer. I think I'm going to transfer to school in Northern Virginia. We want to be together."

"I'm so happy for you. You're going to live near me. Perfect." Eve hugged her friend. Both wiped their eyes quickly. "Come on, I'll drive." Eve drove to the parlor. Bigun seemed happy to see her. The two hugged and she told Bigun what Marcy wanted. He flipped to the page in the book with the mermaids.

"So how are you and Baker? You two seem happy," Marcy asked. She had changed into a stretchy tank and sat backward in the chair so Bigun could work on the small area beneath her hairline on her upper back. He applied the stencil of a small curvy mermaid, then picked up the tattoo gun. It started with a whir. He dipped the nib in the black ink. Marcy gripped Eve's hand tightly and shut her eyes.

Eve avoided looking at Bigun, uncomfortable with the question. Bigun didn't acknowledge, concentrating on his work. "We're good, Marcy. But I've been unsettled and kind of a mess. I was missing home and you all. But it's more than that. I want to be his equal, not the runaway homeless girl. I don't want to be rescued."

Marcy relaxed her death grip, a fishtail visible on her neck. Bigun wiped away the extra ink. "Hang in there, Eve. He's the real thing and the right guy. You're back home now and he came with you. That's special. I can see you both working on his father's house until you're old and gray." Both laughed. The tattoo artist stopped, changing ink color. Their small talk was awkward.

Bigun started again, Marcy leaning forward while the gun whirred, wincing. The mermaid's head appeared along with the long, wavy hair that covered her curves. Eve continued.

"The trip's been good for me. Everything's falling into place. I love working for Cora. The house I'm not so sure about. I think I needed to calm down. Did I tell you I won a local 10K race?"

Bigun stopped and looked at Eve. "You always could run, Eve. Good for you and keep it up." He started again, smiling a little.

"Thanks, Bigun. Yeah, I have some good friends I enjoy running with. Maybe I'll try a marathon one day. Things are good and I'm finding myself and might consider college again." The tattoo took shape, the little mermaid's hair dark, her body full-figured like Marcy. Her emerald tail curved around and up. She had a coy smile below two dark eyes.

"And now you're a mermaid. Cora will love it. I love it." Eve held the hand mirror so Marcy could see the back side of her neck. Bigun put transparent tape over the tat and gave her instructions for keeping it clean. "Let's go show Baker. See ya, Bigun. I'll be back to catch up before I leave." Bigun settled into his chair with the newspaper. As Eve was closing the shop door he spoke.

"It's good to see you and I'm glad you're happy, Eve. I miss you." This time he turned around, looking directly at her.

She paused, considering how to respond. "I miss you too, Bigun. I'll be back, I promise." For some reason she fluttered her eyelids and blew him a kiss, quickly shutting the door, her face flushed.

Baker had a fire going when the two women pulled up. Eve opened a bottle of red wine, slipping on one of Baker's old hoodies to calm herself with Baker's presence after seeing her old friend.

"Look what Marcy got for Cora." Marcy spun and lifted her thick hair, so the little mermaid became visible.

"She'll love it. Do you?"

"Well, aside from the fact that I can't really see her, yes, I do. It's empowering, doing something I was always told not to do. Did Eve tell you I might be moving down to Virginia? I'm thinking of transferring to NOVA."

"That's great. Looks like everything's falling into place."

"Eve tells me you're going to be working on your father's house?"

"It'll be our house. There's lots to do, but it will be something we can do together."

The three sat around the fire enjoying the evening. Eve cleared her throat. "I had an idea while Marcy got her tattoo, Baker." Eve paused. "Think about it before you answer. You know how you want to sell the Airstream?" She paused. "I want you to sell it to me."

"What? Why would you want to buy the Airstream?"

"Because I can. I want to use some of the money my mother left me. We don't need it in Alexandria, but it would be perfect here in Nitro. Sell me the Airstream and we'll park it here. This can be our getaway home. If we want to go somewhere else, we drive here, hook up and go. But if this is mine, then we're equals, and I'll feel better about helping you with and living in your dad's house. You'll also have money for the renovations. I'll give you $24,000 for her and the Bronco. I Googled the value. You can use your Dad's Lexus."

Baker was amazed. He glanced at Marcy. "I'd do it, Baker. It'll make her happy."

"Well," he started slowly. "I was thinking of selling the Bronco anyway. I hadn't thought about leaving her here. I guess we could hook up security cameras and get a property management company to keep the hunters and kids out. It's a wonderful place. It could be our vacation home."

"So, sell it to me. The offer's on the table." Eve walked over to the stray-dog patch that now bloomed with wildflowers, sipping her wine. She smiled.

Marcy turned to Baker. "She's proud and stubborn. She's always been that way since I've known her. But I'm sure you know that by now. Make her happy."

Baker followed her to the gravesite. He pulled Eve to him. "I guess you own yourself an Airstream." He kissed her growing smile.

A second bottle of wine was opened, this one celebratory. Eve grilled a pizza on the hot stones. An opossum moved closer from the old tree toward the food while an owl hooted further above, the moon hanging over the ridge.

❖

The cocoa butter Eve rubbed on Marcy's fresh tattoo smelled good. She'd spent the night, the galley converted to a spare bed. "It's going to get a little scabby, but that will peel away before you show Cora. Keep the lotion on it. When do you see each other again?"

"As soon as you all go home and take over for her so she and I can go to the Jersey Shore."

"Sounds serious, bringing you to meet the family."

"It is serious. We're committed and she's talked to her parents. They know about us and they're happy. Look at what a difference a year makes. I told you we'd make it out and find true love."

Eve hugged her friend. "Yeah, I have to admit. I wasn't so sure. I know one thing, though, it's good to be home."

❖

Eve had one last task before leaving for Alexandria with Baker the next day. She maneuvered her new truck down the road to the highway and headed west to Huntington, on her own and hopeful. She was making her own decisions.

Twenty-eight

“They’re here, JJ. Your sister’s up on the ridge in some fancy RV. You need to go get that money she owes you.”

“You come with me?” He looked at the pistol on the small table nervously.

“No, I gotta work. I want you to take care of this today.” She’d just come from the shower in a towel that barely covered her baby bump. She waddled across the room, settling into a tattered armchair. “And pick this place up. The bathroom’s a disaster. Make the bed and clean that kitchen. We’re not animals.”

JJ slunk to the kitchen while eyeing the gun. It was his friend. It made him the man. He’d wait till she left, then take care of business.

❖

JJ cleaned the gun good. The bathroom and bedroom could wait. He loaded the chamber and spun the barrel, then snuggled the pistol into his belt, grabbed his favorite camo hat with the big fishhook, and pulled it on. He was careful not to touch his ear that still hurt like the dickens. He was the lone stranger in a western movie, the loner wandering into town looking for a gunfight. He needed a cheroot to chew, like Clint. His steed, Red Betsy, waited for him. He slid the gun under the seat, explaining gently, "you're not a shotgun so you ride below." The engine rumbled to life with the turn of the key. He was saddled up and ready. He'd get what his Daddy left him, sister or no sister. JJ drove toward the Ridge.

❖

There was a pull-off just below the homestead where he parked, hoping to sneak up on the campers. Surprise would be important. The aluminum trailer and open sunshade amazed him. The metal glinted bright in the morning sun and the smell from the fire pit hit his nose. His ear throbbed and he felt a little unsteady, the medication long gone. He'd be able to remedy that problem soon. Whatever, he put the pain and doubt aside, stepped up to the door and opened it quickly with his left hand, the revolver drawn in his right, near his hip. For a split-second, he thought about fanning the hammer to let the lead fly and scare them a bit. Eve, Baker, and Marcy sat in the comfy galley with mugs of coffee, expressions of shock on their faces. A big white dog growled. Baker grabbed the dog's collar.

"N-N-N-Now, you hold that huntin' dog back and don't take another step, fella. I don't want to shoot him, but I will and that goes for you too and anyone else who moves at me. No throwing stuff, sis." The gun went back and forth between the four.

"JJ, you ass. What are you doing?" Eve stood slowly and took a small step forward, partially blocking his view of the others.

"Getting what's mine. I heard you got the insurance money from our Daddy. I want my share. We're half brother and sister so I get half." Eve rolled her eyes.

"It doesn't work that way, JJ." Her tone wasn't nice.

"Shut up. I make the rules." His eyes bulged, his skin pale and greasy. "You going to the bank today, Eve. I'll hold them here. I want half and Patsy says that's near $12,000. You come back and I let them go and no one gets hurt. You don't come back, or you send the sheriff and it's all over. This place has a gas canister. I saw it when I came in. It'd be a shame for a fine vehicle like this to blow up with everyone inside."

"That means you go too, JJ."

"Maybe, maybe not. Don't really care. Life ain't that great."

"JJ, you don't know me, but this is a major crime. Think about what you're doing." Baker tried to move to Eve's side. She waved her hand to stay back.

JJ waved the gun towards Baker. “You’re right, mister. I don’t know you, and you didn’t know my Daddy. But even if I go to jail, I’ll be warm and get three meals just like he did.”

“JJ, you’re an idiot. You remember the hospital and how hard that was on you. Jail would be worse. They’d eat you alive in there. Think about Patsy and the baby. They need you.”

“You shut up, sis. Now get to the bank and don’t come back without the money. I’ll keep an eye on these two. If I see or hear a cop car coming up here, I’ll shoot the gas tank.” Baker nodded to Eve to leave. Marcy hung her head in her hands at the table, trembling. Eve patted her friend’s back gently. There was foam around Oscar’s jowls. His eyes darted from Eve to JJ, his teeth clenched and lips quivering.

“I’ll be back. Don’t worry, Marcy, or you either, Oscar.” Eve and Baker’s eyes met briefly, saying everything.

“No cops, sis. I’ll take everyone out.” He wiped his forehead and leaned back.

Eve walked out in a panic. The sheriff’s office was down the road in town near the bank. That was the smart play. But Marcy, Baker, or even Oscar could get hurt. JJ would die or be gravely hurt. She couldn’t risk it in the small space of the Airstream. She climbed in the Bronco and pulled out. Gravel spun from the back tires.

Eve found herself at the bank after an unsettling drive down, her memory foggy. It was only money. She filled out the withdrawal slip, showed her ID, and held out her backpack. The bank could only give her half of what she asked for, the other half to come in the next day courier pouch. Six thousand dollars would have to do. Eve walked out to the Bronco with her pack heavy, spotting Patsy smoking out in front of the beauty parlor down the street. pulled out and drove slowly to the shop, She waved to Patsy and rolled down her window.

"What are you doing here?" Patsy looked embarrassed.

"Getting money from the bank. You should know. This seems more like your plan than his. JJ doesn't have an original idea in his head."

"Well, at least he'll have what he's due."

"He's not due any of this. My mother bought that policy. That means she owned it. I'm her beneficiary and that means it comes to me. She owned a policy on Daddy and one on herself. That's all my money. Do you understand?" Patsy started blankly. Eve got out and walked over to her.

"Listen, Patsy. I have to get back. JJ doesn't look well, and he's holding the people I love hostage. He's got a rotten ear, too. That's gotta hurt." The silence was uncomfortable. Eve made up her mind. "There isn't much I can do but give him this, but he's gonna go to jail. If you were there it might help calm things down and make him see straight. I'll help you two and give you some of the money for the baby and his meds if he backs down, then he won't have to go to jail. Stealing it from me and hurting my friends isn't the way. Think about it, I'm willing to help if you come with me?"

"I don't know." She put out the cigarette and stared at her belly.

"Think of your baby and your life. They might make you an accomplice if something bad happens or I press charges. You'll lose your baby and your freedom. Come help me and I'll help you."

Patsy sighed. "I'll see if they'll let me take my break." Patsy went inside reluctantly, then came back out with her purse.

"Has he been taking his medication?"

"It ran out."

"How about you, have you seen a doctor for that baby? You know you shouldn't be smoking."

"I know, but life's been stressful. I have to work a lot. I figured we'd take care of the birthing ourselves when the time comes."

"You're a brave lady." Eve shook her head. "Come on, let's go. We can talk about all this later." Eve helped Patsy climb up and into the truck. The two made the short trip to the ridge in silence. Oscar barked as Eve opened the door.

"Here you go, JJ." Eve placed her pack slowly on the table near Marcy, touching her hand gently. "It's six thousand. They don't keep that kind of cash around here with all the drug problems. Let us go now, I kept my word."

JJ paced. "I said twelve and what's she doing here?" His eyes flicked back and forth between the bag and Patsy. "What you think, Patsy? She telling the truth?" He waved the gun at Eve.

"Yes, she's telling the truth, JJ, and we were wrong. It's her money, not your Daddy's. It'd be wrong to take it."

"Not after all this. I'm taking what's mine. Money came from his life. We shared him as Daddy, we share the insurance." JJ stood directly in front of Eve, the pistol in front of her chin. She didn't flinch. He moved her blouse collar with the gun. Eve shut her eyes. She could smell the gunpowder but also the rot from his ear this close.

"Well, I guess I'll take this as my other half." He lifted the fine gold cross with the gun barrel, then used his thumb and forefinger to grasp it and lift the chain over her head. Eve exhaled. JJ made an awkward toss of the necklace to Patsy, but it landed on the floor. "I reckon that's about equal to what we's due. Pick it up, Patsy."

Patsy reached for the cross with a grunt and set it down on the table. "No, JJ, we're not robbing these folks. They're family, or at least she is and we're not highwaymen."

"This says I am! I'm taking what's mine and nobody can tell me anything different! We need the money for us and the baby - you said so!" JJ became louder, almost shouting. He picked up the back pack to look inside. "This will have to do. Come on, Patsy, let's git."

"No, JJ." Eve stood in the way. "You and I are going to get something straight. Now you listen to me. I'm going to give you this money. Do you understand? I'm giving it to you on a couple of conditions."

"You ain't giving me shit, sis," he snarled, leaning toward her, threatening. Once again Eve stared down the barrel. "This says I make the rules. I'm the man."

Eve stood her ground. "You do as I say, and you'll get to see the birth of your child and Patsy will get to be its mom and see it grow up. I'm not having jailbirds in my family anymore. One was enough. You take this money at gunpoint and you, and Patsy end up in jail. Baby goes to foster care, and nobody wins."

"Please, JJ. She's real smart. She knows what she's talking about. Listen to her." Patsy begged.

"I'm listening." He was breathing hard. His tee shirt clung to his chest, wet with sweat. JJ lowered the gun a bit.

"I'm going to give you some of this money, and I won't go to the cops. But first thing when you leave here, you go get your prescription refilled and take your medication. Have them put it on monthly refills. All you have to do is pick it up every month. Number two, you get an appointment for Patsy's baby. It's called a prenatal check-up and you can do that while you're at the clinic."

"That's going to cost a lot."

"I'm giving you money to pay for everything and I won't go to the cops as long as you do what I say and get healthy. You need meds and she needs to see a doctor and prepare to have that baby and quit smoking." Eve glanced at Patsy. "There's one other condition. You leave that gun here tonight. Tomorrow you and I take it back to the gun store and ask for your job back."

"Gun's mine. Make's me a man."

"The gun makes you a criminal. You have a chance to become a man by the decisions you make today. Be a daddy, a good daddy to that baby and a husband who works, takes care, and fixes things for Patsy. That's a man, but neither of us ever knew one like that. You got a chance to be that man. Now put the gun down and head on down to the clinic with Patsy. They can look at your ear and take care of the infection. The smell is making me sick. They can also get you your meds." Baker had to hide a smile.

Patsy walked to JJ. She took the gun gently from his hand and laid it on the table next to the necklace. "We're leaving these. Tell her thank you for helping us. She's done right by you. More than your Daddy ever did."

Tears welled in JJ's eyes. He wiped his face with his tee shirt. "Th-Th-Th, thank you, Eve. You've only been good to me, even when I wasn't to you." His bravado drained away with the tears.

Eve counted out $1,500. "Here, take this. It will get you started. If you need more, text or call me."

"I'll come by tomorrow morning," JJ mouthed. Patsy took his hand and led him out. The cat ran in when the door opened.

"Well, I'll be. You still got the dang cat."

"Kitty is family. We take care of our own, JJ. See you tomorrow."

Marcy stood with an exasperated exhale. "Oh my God. I am so glad that's over. I have to pee so bad, excuse me." She shut the small door behind her.

Baker went to Eve. The two touched foreheads, both focused on the pistol. "That was nice of you. Lord knows I wouldn't have thought to get the pregnant girl and handle things that way. You never cease to amaze me." He picked up the cross and opened the chain to place it around her neck.

"I'm exhausted." Eve slunk to the sofa.

"Who needs a glass of wine? I know I do." Marcy returned with glasses and a bottle from the refrigerator.

"Make mine a scotch." Eve pointed to the bottle and Baker nodded, joining her on the sofa. Oscar wedged in, tail wagging. Marcy poured the scotch and then her own glass of white wine. All three looked at the bag of money.

"I'm not sure," Marcy held her glass out to toast, "but my guess is that something good just happened up here on Malone Ridge. The spell may finally be broken, Eve. Here's to new beginnings."

❖

Eve rested with Baker in the cabin of the RV, their bodies warm. Baker breathed deeply, her head next to his chest.

"Why'd you give him the money?" Baker asked quietly.

"Everyone needs help sometimes. You helped me. I helped them. It all comes around," she murmured. "Momma always said we take care of our own." Eve snuggled in. "I'm so tired. I have to close my eyes."

❖

JJ knocked on the Airstream's door.

"Come in," Eve called out. "How did your visit to the clinic go yesterday?" She could see the fresh bandage on his ear, the ridiculous bandana gone. He stayed in the doorway sheepishly.

"Good, I guess. Patsy's due a month from now. We got to see a picture of the baby in her tummy. That was cool. They said the boy's gonna look like me." He grinned, looking up for the first time.

"That's very cool. Can you unload that thing and we can go?" She pointed to the pistol. "Baker, you coming?"

"No, you two go. Oscar and I will wait here." Oscar lay in his bed, his eyes never leaving JJ.

JJ picked up the gun. He took out three bullets and placed them in the box of ammo, then spun the chamber, checking to make sure it was clear.

"I feel bad I caused you to lose your job when I threw the gun away. Let's see if we can get it back." JJ followed her into town. They parked by the loading dock of the gun store. Eve followed JJ through a door next to the bay. A big man came out of the office.

"JJ, I'm surprised to see you. You a Daddy yet?"

"Doctor says next month. I brought this back for you. All clean like you gave it to me." The man checked the gun, holding it up to the light.

"Well, I'll be. This will get me out of a fix. I had to file an insurance claim. Suppose you'll want your job back now."

"If you'd have me, s-s-sir."

"Don't know that I need anyone now at the dock. I do need a custodian. You'll keep it clean in here, the showroom, office, and the john. If you do a good job, we'll make you full-time later before your baby comes. That work for you?"

"Yes, sir. Thank you."

"You can start today. Haven't had anyone to clean for a while. We've all had to pitch in. Bathroom's a disaster. You might want to start there and show me you really want to work here." He laughed.

JJ shook the man's hand. "You won't be sorry, sir. Thank you." He hugged Eve. "Thank you, sis. This will help us."

"Stay on your meds. Do what your boss says to do. Take care of Patsy. She's a good woman and she's going to really need you when the baby comes. Go to one of those classes they offer at the clinic for what to expect. It will help you get ready for everything."

JJ had a quizzical look. "Everything?"

"Changing diapers, feedings, baths, and watching the baby while she sleeps. You will have to be able to do all those things while she's at work. That's what a good

Daddy does. He helps the mother." She smiled. "You can do it. Oh, I got one other job for you. Can you check on the Airstream for me after we leave? I don't want hunters and kids messing around up there. We'll turn off the water and electricity, but if you'd go up a couple times a week to check, then we'll call everything even and I'll pay you a little something as the property manager. I'll get you a key so you can keep everything up and eventually we'll get a camera so you can watch from home." Eve held out her hand to shake, but JJ lunged to give her an awkward hug. Eve smiled. The boy was now a man.

❖

Eve felt like she was leaving a piece of herself on the ridge. She wanted to stay. The Airstream glistened as Baker, Oscar, and Eve pulled out without her. Eve was happy to return to Alexandria but it was more difficult to leave the Ridge this time than the last.

The three made it to the interstate, leaving small town West Virginia behind. The turnoff for Huntington and the large billboard for the university featuring campus life with students studying, the football stadium full of cheering fans, and the girls cross country team running in their signature dark green. Eve waved to them with a smile.

Twenty-nine

The Athena chugged away from the dock, a bluish smoke wafting from the engine. Oscar joined Eve on deck, happy to be in the sun with the breeze in his face. He lifted his nose.

They entered the channel, moving smoothly south on the wide river. The interstate bridge rose above them, its cold cement covering them in shadow. "I don't know if I've ever seen something so big up close."

"Think about what's underneath that we can't see. Probably three times the size." Eve hugged the dog and shivered.

The three cruised down the river, their destination a half-hour south. The pastoral scene unfolded, grand houses, eagles fishing from the air, and herons along the shore. After a while they crossed the river to the eastern side. A dilapidated building and dock came into view. She could make out "Captain Billy's" on the numerous Bud Light banners that hung from the pilings. Boats were moored alongside and southern rock blared from the speakers. Two women waved from a picnic table along the water's edge.

"Take your sweet time, Baker. We're already one pitcher of margaritas ahead of you. By the way, we're counting on you driving back today. Bronco's out front." Cora helped Eve up onto the dock. Baker gave Oscar a chew bone and water bowl in the shade below.

"I'm definitely thirsty." He ordered a pitcher of light beer and two mugs. The hot crabs arrived, dumped in a pile in the middle of the table covered in brown paper. Their pungent, salty scent blended with the vinegar, the swampy water, and gas fumes that was the trademark for the crab shack.

Eve was doubtful. "You eat these things?" She picked one up by the leg, letting it hang limply.

Cora laughed. "I'll show you how to peel one, honey. You watch too, Marcy. We'll eat a lot of these little critters at the shore. It's a family tradition and one of my favorite meals with corn on the cob, coleslaw, and hush puppies. Baker, let's show these dainty West Virginia ladies how we eat crabs, Jersey Shore style."

Cora took a good-sized crab and removed the two claws. She peeled the outer shell back exposing the insides. Eve made a face as Cora scraped away some gooey yellow stuff along with the gills, and then broke the crustacean in half. "See, here is where all the meat is."

She sucked on the crab, working the meat from the shell then held the other half to Marcy, who nibbled reluctantly.

"Looks like a lot of work for a little reward." Eve sipped her beer.

Baker showed her how to get the meat from the claw, crushing it with a wooden mallet. Her face lit up at the taste from the tender morsel dipped in butter. "Ummm," Eve murmured. Something caught her eye. She nodded to Baker toward Marcy who dabbed her lips with the napkin.

"What?" Baker looked from face to face.

Eve gave him a second, more serious look, and touched her ring finger.

"What?"

"Baker, are you blind? Marcy, do you have something to tell us?"

Radiant, Marcy held up her hand, the silver band glistening in the sun. Eve jumped up, moving to hug Marcy first, then Cora. Baker caught on finally, noticing Cora's matching band. He sat back and smiled, raising a mug to his oldest friend.

"Well, I'll be, congratulations."

"You all are the first to know. We want to be more than dating when we go to visit Cora's family," Marcy beamed.

"They're going to love you as much as I do." Cora pulled Marcy to her, kissing the petite mermaid on the back of her neck.

"What do you think of her ink?" Baker came around the table to hug the two women. He held onto Cora.

"Lovely, like the owner." Cora smiled ear to ear.

The afternoon slipped away in a celebratory manner, eating crabs, summer sides, along with the beer and margaritas. Baker paid the bill, got Oscar out of the boat and walked him to the truck, upsetting a mother osprey in her nest on the telephone pole across the lot. He handed the keys to the boat to the mechanic who motored her to the nearby shop. The drive home was drowsy that afternoon, crossing over the same scary bridge to arrive in Old Town.

"I want you to promise me, Cora. No worries while you're gone. We'll take care of Union Street. You enjoy your family and celebrate. We're so happy for you two." Eve had to move Oscar's head to talk to her friends, the dog leaning forward to lick her salty face.

"I promise and I know you'll do a great job. We'll see you in two weeks." Baker dropped Cora and Marcy off, then drove to his Dad's townhouse, parking next to the big dumpster filled with old cabinets, wood, sheetrock, and appliances from the renovation.

Eve still felt strange walking into the house, not yet her home. She came to Alexandria with a backpack and now she had a closet full of clothes. The small frame holding her mother and grandmother greeted her from the mantle living room. Oscar ran out to the garden. A koi splashed in the newly filled pond.

The following day was different. Eve showered after her run and changed into work clothes, donning a black smock with her name stitched on the front. She climbed into the Bronco, feeling small on the bench seat without Baker and Oscar. It was hers now, delighted by its size and power for the short drive to the restaurant. Eve parked in the space reserved for Cora and took a deep breath before entering. She reviewed the menu and checked stations, moving about to make sure everything was ready. Satisfied, she called the staff, standing tall like Cora with Groucho, Harpo, and Chico behind her in a sign of support. She made eye contact with everyone but Baker. This was her night and she wanted to do it on her terms.

"So, let's start with tonight's specials. First the soft-shelled crab." Eve described the treat in detail, passing it around with the sauce and garnish, then the appetizers, also passed to the staff to taste. The soup-of-the-day and main courses came next with their wine pairings. Finally, she finished with dessert, a homemade peach pie a la mode. The staff moved off. Eve took a deep breath and drank most of a sparkling water, relieved the night had begun. The first guests arrived. Water and drinks were served, followed by bread and butter. Eve floated through the kitchen and dining area, assisting where she was needed to help get the plates to the servers, pouring wine, or assisting with desserts. The night flew by.

Baker was in bed when Eve arrived home, the house quiet. Oscar didn't move. His tail thumped against the floor from his bed. She flicked on the kitchen light. Tile was half installed. She smiled; the renovation had been partially funded from the Airstream sale. The transaction enabled Baker to start on the house. A sample cherry cabinet door sat in the corner. Backsplash and granite countertop samples lay on top. She held them together. It would look nice. Decorating had been fun, choosing this and that, matching color schemes and patterns for paint, tile, and wood. It didn't seem possible that this was her house and her kitchen. Baker had finished the outside paint and landscaping. They'd tackle the bedroom last, converting an extra room into walk-in closets and expanding the master bathroom. Eve turned off the light but did not go to bed. She poured a glass of wine and looked over the backyard, illuminated by moonlight. She was exhilarated, the moment almost perfect. As invigorated as she was, she couldn't say she was content. The purchase of the Airstream and Bronco on Malone Ridge had changed the dynamics, but the desire to be on her own and equal still bubbled just below the surface. This house was not hers and it never would be no matter how much she contributed. She knew what she wanted after talking with the coach. He still wanted her on the team. She'd be in Huntington in the fall, finally in college. The only thing was how to tell Baker.

Eve slept-in the next day. She took her normal run and showered before a light breakfast of coffee and toast late in the morning. Later, she'd eat something more substantial that the Marx brothers would throw together before the dinner service. Baker came home from the studio. He took her in his arms.

"What are you up to?" she asked. Baker never could keep his feelings a secret. "You seem to have a spring in your step."

"The gallery on King Street is going to show our work." His grin slid across his face. Eve hugged him back.

"That's fantastic, which one?"

"Chastain's, up by the metro stop, the really nice one. It's perfect. We'll open at the end of August."

"That's so wonderful, Baker. But that means people are going to be looking at me, doesn't it? I'm not so sure how I feel about people seeing me like that, so vulnerable." The late summer show and school crossed her mind. The timing was perfect.

"They'll look at you, but they'll judge me. I'll get you some of those big sunglasses so you can be incognito." He paused. "What are you thinking about? You've been preoccupied lately."

"I was thinking about August and how time flies here." She gathered herself. "I'm proud of you. I'll see you later tonight and we can celebrate after work." She kissed him.

"Love you, babe."

"You too, babe." The statement was her typical response to Baker's profession. What she loved was that he didn't pester her for the same response. "Just say the damn word," Eve chastised herself as she left for work, threading through traffic. She turned off the parkway to make her way down to the river. Love was a funny word, more difficult to say than show. She'd said it a few times when they were in bed in the throes of passion. It was almost impossible for her not to, saying almost anything in those moments. But to toss the word around casually was difficult. Baker seemed satisfied with her affection and use or lack of use of the word. She hoped he was satisfied.

Thirty

The evening gown slid up and on, the sapphire sequin fabric spreading to cover her torso. Eve slid her arms through the thin straps and turned her exposed back to Baker. "Zip me?"

The quarters were close in the boat's cabin. Their boat clothes were piled on her bunk. Baker finished threading his cufflinks, pausing to wipe his brow before zipping her dress. The boat was warm. He picked up a tie but thought better, tossing it back on the bunk. "I keep wondering why we're not in our new bedroom dressing in air-conditioned comfort. Our walk-in closets are bigger than this space."

Eve laughed. "You forget, we have no water or electricity, and most important, no A/C." Baker stood before her, tall and lean in a dark suit and white, open collar shirt, his hair pulled back. "You look fantastic by the way. Are you ready?"

"I look fine. You look fantastic." Her hair was moussed like the portrait they'd soon premiere. Bangles hung from her wrist to complement her ears. Her nails were emerald, like the her serpent. “And, yes, I’m ready.”

“One thing first.” Eve moved close. “Before everything gets crazy, I want you to know something on your big night.” She paused. “I love you, Baker, and I’m glad I get to share this moment with you.”

He held her, their faces close. “Do we have to go?”

“Our friends will be waiting and it’s your show. It’s what you’ve worked so hard for. We’ll be back later, just us on the water. Let’s go.”

“I love you too, Eve.”

“I know,” she smiled a wicked little grin. “You tell me all the time.” Eve slid on her sunglasses and stepped out of the cabin to the waiting limousine, oblivious to the tourists milling about. The chauffeur helped Eve into the big black sedan, a gift from Cora complete with iced champagne and crystal flutes. The ride was only a mile up King Street, but Cora insisted that the artist was to arrive in style with his muse. Eve held Baker’s hand while the limo moved through the tourist crowd and up King Street.

❖

A string trio played light jazz. White wine was served in plastic gallery glasses and small plates of canapés were passed—crab cakes, stuffed mushrooms, chilled shrimp in cocktail sauce. The stern but approving faces of the Marx Brothers supervised the catering staff, and the restaurant closed for the night. Baker's art hung from the two long walls of the gallery. It began with the sketches—a hand, a face, a long torso. The sketches were spare like the surroundings, black and white, the only color, the flower sprays strategically placed. Paintings followed midway through the gallery: an abstract, the woman painted in black and gray in various poses, the burnt-orange woman standing out alongside an angelic figure in pale blue, the setting cloudlike. There was seating in the back near the bar where the musicians played. The portraits in that area had more wall space and room to view, beginning with the doorway portrait and then the playful couch scene, followed by the young woman with the unseen face. The large portrait of Eve in the faded pink gown hung on the far wall, the focal point of the room. People moved through the gallery to view the work. Baker and Eve mingled, noting the double takes of onlookers from the painting to Eve and back to the painting. She smiled a smile not unlike that of the young woman in pink leaving the Metro, still with her and not forgotten.

"It's a big success. Are you happy with the turnout?" Eve turned to Baker.

"I am very happy with the turnout. But best of all, the review was good. That's a relief and honestly the thing I feared most. I've been told there is interest in some of the pieces and offers are forthcoming. I won't sell the Woman in Pink." He looked at the portrait, then to Eve, his face blank.

"Are you okay? About what we discussed?"

"I'm happy for you, Eve. It's what you've always wanted." Baker forced a smile. He gripped her hand. He'd taken her news as well as he could. It was her life after all.

Cora came by with a tray of white wine. Marcy joined them, glowing after the summer beach trip. Cora toasted her friend.

"Here's to your success, Baker. Your work is fabulous." They clinked glasses.

"Thank you, Cora. It seems like another time, when I painted those." Baker continued to hold his glass. He looked at Eve. "One more toast. To Eve - good luck at university. You're going to love it, and though I'll miss you, I want you to know how happy I am for you." The four clinked glasses, Baker's face a mask while Cora and Marcy looked shocked and happy all at once.

Eve blushed. "Thanks, Baker." She gave him a quick kiss on the cheek.

"What's this about college, Eve?" Marcy's mouth hung open.

"I've been offered my old scholarship to run at the University in Huntington." Eve gushed, hugging Marcy, then Cora. Cora took the hug begrudgingly.

"Well, I'm not exactly happy about this news," Cora pouted. "I'm losing my best employee - sorry, Baker. Why can't you go to school here, Eve?"

"Cora," Marcy answered for her friend. "She has to choose her own course. This is her life and a chance to do something she's always dreamed about. I support you, though I'll miss you, Eve. And Huntington isn't that far. We made it work after all." Marcy grabbed Cora's hand tightly.

Eve looked at their faces, each different in expression, unable to hold back any longer. Her hands shot up in the air and she spun around, squealing, "You guys, I'm going to college!"

MALONE RIDGE

Thirty-one

University life felt like something from another planet. Eve knew Huntington from growing up nearby and from her recruiting trips. Somehow the campus had grown, and everything seemed foreign in a little over a year's time. Classes were a bonafide whirlwind. Like every other freshman, Eve struggled to find her way through the maze of brick buildings, to get her books from the bookstore, and finish assignments that came rapid-fire starting the first day. The assignments made her time in the kitchen with Cora seem like a vacation. Unlike most of the other freshmen, she had cross-country practice in the afternoon, too.

On the first day, Coach gave her a locker, a large wooden box with a comfortable green cushion that she could sit in. MALONE was printed in block letters above the shelf, with hooks inside to hang her gear and bags. Freshmen lockers were near the showers, across from the upperclassmen. The room was elaborately decorated in the school's colors—various shades of dark green plaid with comfortable couches, chairs, a big screen TV and sound system. Arriving for practice one afternoon during the first week, Eve was taken aback to find a huge travel bag filled with running gear stuffed into her locker. The bag held a thin lycra racing top and shorts set, medal-stand sweats, a hoodie and tights for cool weather running, socks, headbands, workout shorts and tees, and a university backpack with her name embroidered on the back. There was even a travel parka for the winter months, all embellished with the school's name in distinctive cursive letters and the omnipresent shoemaker's swoosh. There were also several boxes of new training shoes, cross-country racing spikes, and shower sandals. It was better than any Christmas or birthday she could remember. Eve tossed her old gear into the garbage bin with no regrets.

Coach had them dress out for the school photographer and the obligatory head shot, team photo, and action shots of the team running over the golf course, all for the university website. Eve's teammates helped her with makeup with great delight, applying blush, mascara, and lip gloss. She wore her hair as she always did, spiked with gel. After the shoot, Eve stood in front of the full-length mirror in her racing shorts and top with her spikes knotted, hanging over her shoulder. She couldn't believe the haul. She posed in front of her locker with a slight head tilt, her shoulder to the camera, pouting with the obligatory duck lips. She snapped a selfie for social media and texted one to Baker and Marcy.

❖

The workout the previous day was an easy jog after pictures, or as the team crabbed, a waste of good makeup and hair dos. Today's practice would be much harder, the team running single file over their home course on the nearby golf course. The women were remarkably similar in size and shape, and difficult to tell apart from a distance. Eve stood out, slightly taller and thinner, her hair short and white. She'd added a short braided rattail in the back, a concession to her teammates' french braids. Her tattoo also stood out, a source of much fascination among her teammates. The team glided across the grass at a moderate pace, Coach keeping pace on a mountain bike while barking encouragement. At a designated marker, the leader sprinted away for 100 meters then jogged slowly till the others caught her, dropping to the back of the line. The next runner then took off, the team continuing the drill, sprinting one at a time, then recovering over the five-kilometer course, a simple but exacting routine.

It was Eve's turn. The acceleration felt good after the slower recovery pace, her arms driving, leading her knees and feet in syncopation. Her respiration was quicker and deeper but without stress. Eve knew she was good, and not just the best freshman, but perhaps one of the best on the team. She'd arrived on campus in shape that August. On the first day of practice the coach had them run the River Road ten-mile loop, meeting them at the halfway point with small cups of water. Eve and Kate, her senior captain, had separated from the rest early in the run. Eve waited for her at the turn around, jogging in place while Kate had a second cup of water. Coach observed quietly. At the finish back on campus, Eve was alone, setting a new team record for the hilly, ten-mile run, the first to ever break sixty minutes. Kate straggled in two minutes later.

"Sorry, Kate." Eve apologized to her captain, handing her a cup of water.

"Dang, Eve. Never apologize for feeling good." Kate was red, bent over with her hands on her knees and trying to recover.

❖

Eve eased off, having hit the 100-meter mark, slowing for her teammates and taking the last slot at the end of the line. This was fun. At the five-kilometer where they'd finish their races, the coach called the group over.

"I want Kate, Eve, Mary and Samantha to do one short loop, 2,000 meters. Hit your marks and keep the pack together. Make sure you recover between sprints since there are only four of you, and remember, it's not a full sprint but an acceleration and efficient stride. The rest of you run the same loop at recovery pace. Everyone is looking good for this early in the season. I can see some of you have been training." The whistle blew and they were off again.

After the run, Eve sat in her locker, tired from training but more so from classes. She was soaked in sweat, a towel around her neck. Her teammates moved to and from the shower, but the ice bath was her next destination. There was a loud knock on the door, followed by, "Coach coming in, cover up." Eve counted thirty seconds when the door opened and Coach and the female assistant entered the room. Teammates pulled on sweats for the most part, but a few had to grab towels and duck into the bathroom. Eve studied the paper Coach handed her, the meet schedule for the season. Charlottesville in October was the closest meet to Alexandria. Baker would be able to drive down to see her. There were other meets across the east coast. She'd get to travel. The dream kept getting better.

"Okay, ladies. Good work today." Coach moved to the center of the locker room. "We have a strong front four, maybe five. Our next five are looking good, too, and if we're patient, we'll be ready for Conference. That's the goal. We need seven scorers for each meet. He wrote CONFERENCE in all caps on the whiteboard. If we run together, then who knows what we can accomplish; Regionals, maybe Nationals? Take it easy the next two days to recover from today. I want everyone to do a long run on Saturday, ten to twelve miles, but no more. Take Sunday off and get a good meal tonight. Oh yeah, don't forget to do a little studying, too." Eve only heard part of what he said. Her eyes scoured the page to Conference Meet, Tulane, New Orleans, LA, and the last line, NCAAs, Eugene, OR, the fabled track town.

❖

The microwave beeped. Eve took out a chicken dinner, carrying it to the table next to a green salad. With the weekend off, she'd driven to Malone Ridge to relax and study in the Airstream. She'd toyed with the idea of going home to Alexandria but needed to catch up on sleep and her reading assignments. The ridge was the perfect study hall. She'd promised several of her teammates they could come up later in the fall for a getaway. JJ, Patsy, and Joe III had come over the first weekend when she arrived before the start of school. She'd enjoyed holding baby "Tre" and feeding him his bottle. JJ looked as good as he could, notched ear and all, his complexion and teeth still a mess though he had filled out some and wasn't wearing any rebel flag shit. Patsy was good for him, and more importantly, she was good to him. She'd be a good mom and he had a chance to be a good dad, breaking the trend for parenting on Malone Ridge. The little family made her smile. She appreciated that he'd kept an eye on the camp when she was at her dorm and fed Kitty, too.

Eve filled a big plastic cup with water and ice. Kitty pranced at her feet, mewing for a treat. The Airstream was home - quiet with no distractions. Her phone buzzed.

"Hey, Baker, I'm so glad you called." Eve tried to sound excited, her voice was thin from the day.

"How's my favorite college girl doing?"

"Your only college girl," she corrected him. Both laughed nervously. "I'm good - tired, but good. The workout today went well but afterward I felt like I was looking up from the bottom of a well. I'm going to study for a while and hit the sack. I'm beat." She yawned, slowly chewing a bite of chicken.

"Do you like the team and coach?"

"Yeah, my teammates are great, and Coach is cool. They all want to come up here for a training weekend soon. I think Coach likes that I'm in good shape and our locker room is nice. Oh, did you get my pic in our gear we got this week? It was Christmas in September."

"I loved the track star pose. I blew up a copy and hung it at the gallery next to the Pink Dress portrait for contrast. I'm happy it's going well for you and that university suits you. I'd hoped you'd be home this weekend. I can come up if you want since it's a holiday on Monday."

There was an awkward silence. Eve took a breath. "Believe me, I thought about coming home this weekend. I miss you and the gang in Alexandria so much but I need to catch my breath and catch up on schoolwork. I'm not used to studying." The conversation died again. "Oh, our schedule posted today. We race in Charlottesville in October on a Friday. Why don't you come to that race and we can drive back to the Ridge? You can spend the weekend here with me and I can show you around school. Maybe I'll invite JJ and Patsy over and you can meet baby Tre."

"Uh, the last time I saw JJ, he had a gun pointed at my head. I don't know, Eve. Baby Tre?"

"Baby Tre. You know, Joe the third, Dad, JJ, and Tre. Give JJ a chance. He's really doing well and watches the trailer and Kitty when I'm at school."

"If you say so. Can I bring my 'huntin' dog?" Baker did his best JJ imitation.

"Don't make fun or I'll make you wait even longer." She teased. "But yeah, bring Oscar. I miss my boy and so does Kitty. I want to introduce him to the team."

"Make me wait? I wonder what for?"

"I know exactly what you miss and I do too. I miss you and us being together." Eve's voice was lower and soft. "But you know what Marcy says. Abstinence makes the heart grow fonder."

"Is that how it goes? I think that's a Marcyism." Both laughed. "I really do wish it was October and I was there with you by the fire pit. I miss us, too. I miss waking up with you, baby." The silence spoke volumes. Eve looked at her new watch.

"I'd like for you to be here tonight with me, too, but I wouldn't get any studying done. I've got a ton to read. Give me time to adjust to school and the team. October will be here before you know it, followed by fall break, and then it will be Christmas and I'll be home with you. Did I tell you we get to race in Birmingham? If we do well there, there's a chance we'll go to Eugene, Oregon for NCAAs. Eugene is Mecca for runners."

"That's so cool. How are the classes?"

"Kicking my butt. I just need to get used to being in the classroom. I almost forgot to tell you; I'm taking an art class. It's introductory and all, but between you and Bigun, I think I might like to study art. The building is really cool, and I met a few of the teachers." She yawned. "Speaking of classes, I need to get started. I'll call you tomorrow, okay? I can't wait to see you in October and to come home on break."

"You said home, Eve. That makes me happy."

"You are my home, Baker. Give Oscar a hug and I'll talk to you tomorrow. It's good to hear your voice." She paused then added a quick, "Love you, bye."

The phone clicked. Eve picked up her drink and walked out to the garden with Kitty in tow, her tail in full bristle mode in the night air.

The late summer katydid chorus was at high volume as she walked to the garden. "I'm doing it, Momma. I'm in school. College is wonderful and I get to travel with my teammates. They're my new family, and I'm home on the Ridge." She fingered the cross on her neck. Despite what she had just said to Baker, she knew Malone Ridge would always be her home.

Thirty-two

Eve chose art as her major. She wasn't sure what form her art would take on, the creative seed had been planted by Baker, Cora, and Bigun, giving her a leg up on many of her classmates. She chose construction management as a minor, eager to learn how to design, build, and dream about rebuilding the family home.

Eve's roommate, Cassie, was the second fastest and firmly on the second team. The first night on campus, Cassie's parents took the two roomies to dinner at the local steak house. Not Cora's cooking but easily the best meal either had had on campus. Cassie ended up filling in for Marcy as friend and confidant. Practice over and Friday night possibilities lay ahead of the two.

"Want to get some pizza and go clubbing with the team later."

Eve was noncommittal. "I don't know. The pizza sounds good, but I don't know about clubbing. I might stay in, call Baker, and have an early night. We have that ten-miler in the morning."

"Don't remind me. I'm still recovering from this week's workouts. My legs are dead but I need to dance tonight. The boy's team will be out, too. The one from Tennessee is cute. We could go have fun, nothing serious." Eve didn't respond. "So how old is Baker? You said he's out of college."

"He's six years older than me but it's no big deal. You'll meet him in October. I think he's going to come back to Nitro with me for the weekend."

"You two alone all weekend in the mountains. It sounds serious." Cassie was sitting cross-legged on Eve's bed.

"We are, kind of, but I don't know. There's so much to get used to here. He's busy traveling with exhibitions of his work. He's an artist. We have a place in Alexandria that we fixed up and his studio is there. He'd like more commitment, but I can't yet. I want to experience college life and give the team my best. I'll wait and see how things go over the holidays. I told him to be patient and let me have some space." Her face reddened.

"You used the "L" word yet?"

"He does all the time. I have a couple. It's difficult for me."

"But you're together? You know, doing it - the smash?"

Eve sat up. "Geez, Cassie. What kind of question is that and what the hell is the smash?"

Cassie made very obvious motions with her fingers.

"Yeah, we are "doing it" and I miss him a lot."

"Sorry, I didn't mean to be nosy but we were all wondering. I've never been with a guy." She shrugged. "You have such a cool life with your homes in Nitro and Alexandria. What about family? I mean, I know about your parents. That's so sad. Do you have anyone else?"

"It's okay, yeah, I have a half brother in Nitro. He's not all bad. My best friend Marcy lives in Alexandria, too, with her partner. They're my best friends and family." Eve decided to change the subject.

"Okay, I am officially hungry after that talk. Let's get that pizza, Cass."

❖

It was clear Kate and Eve were the top two on the team. They finished most workouts together, well ahead of the rest of the team. Kate had grit and wouldn't let Eve's talent and summer training get the best of her. Eve dutifully stayed behind her captain in the first couple of meets, finishing just a few steps behind. Coach noticed, calling the two to his office.

"Eve, I know you're only a freshman and that you respect Kate. That's good, but I expect you to give your all. Don't hold back. Kate is a big girl and will fight back. She can handle it."

"Yes, Coach." Eve looked shyly at Kate. To her relief, Kate gave her a thumbs up and smile.

The next race was Charlottesville. Baker would be there. Eve's nervousness clicked up a notch.

The day was drizzly and wet, the turf and conditions more like Ireland than Virginia. The team warmed up in tights and jackets, jogging nervously together. Eve was deep into her pre-race thoughts when coach called them over to their chalk box at the start and gathered their warm-ups.

"Kate and Eve, full out today. No holding back. The top three will be from Virginia, Tech, and Wake Forest. Run with them but stay within yourself and be ready for the last kilo to make your move. Mary and Samantha, keep them in sight. Everyone else mid-pack and make your move according to how you feel. I want a tight first five."

The team put their hands together like spokes on a wheel. They did a low, slow-building West Virginia, "Yeeee-Haw!" Eve jogged out, shaking loose. She spotted Baker behind the tape about 100 meters down the track. She waved with both hands and blew him a kiss, which he returned. She had a race to run before she could think of him. She gathered herself on the line, staring at her spikes while the official gave instructions. Her stomach fluttered.

The gun fired and 70 collegiate runners, all capable of running six to seven minutes per mile, raced through the muddy grass. Eve latched onto the Wake girl who was right behind UVA. Baker yelled to her with his cupped hands. "Gooooooooo, Eve!" The large pack raced out toward the end of the mowed field and began a large circle of the estate. Coming past the start for the end of the first loop, Eve heard her coach say she was fourth, then heard him call out seventh place for her teammate. "Good," she thought, "Kate's just behind. Stick with me."

The second loop was shorter, an inner loop with a long hill. Eve struggled to the top, catching mud on her face from the girl in front, holding onto her place. They were headed back in reverse of the way they started and nearing the last kilo straightaway where Coach wanted her to move. The UVA runner was pulling away for the win. That left Eve, Wake, and Tech running three abreast. Eve's legs and lungs screamed at her as the meters flew by. Six hundred, five hundred, four hundred meters to go. The finish line clock was visible. Eve had nothing left, conscious of driving her arms and barely getting any response from her legs. Coach and Baker were screaming as she flew past. Fifty yards and no one had broken. "Come on." She willed herself to the line, all three arriving at nearly the same time. Hands grabbed bodies to sort the finishers—VT in front and Wake behind her, pushing her toward the exit. Coach greeted her excitedly.

"Third, Eve. You got third. Nice job. I knew you had more in the tank. Your sweats are over at the tent. Jog over, dry off and get warm. Kate's in the top ten just behind. Gotta go." He jogged off. Eve had never seen him smile so big. She laughed, happy to be finished. Baker appeared.

"Eve, my God, what a finish. You were amazing." He put his coat over her shoulders and wiped off mud splatter from her nose. Eve shivered. "Want me to get your sweats?"

"I need to wait for Kate," Eve answered breathlessly. More finishers came across in various states of distress. Someone fell, another runner was bent over vomiting, everyone bedraggled and covered in muck. The numbers flashed by, the clock ticking away. Seventh, eighth, ninth place, then Kate. Eve whooped.

"Go, Kate!" Kate staggered across, dropping to her knees. She was speckled all over. Eve held her teammate up, helping her walk out of the other end of the shoot, Baker following outside. The three meandered to the water table where the teammates recovered a little. The two entered the tent to gather their gear, followed by Baker.

"You ran great, Eve." Kate said. "I knew you could handle it up front with the best today." She shook her head in disbelief.

"You were great, too, Kate. I would have held back but Coach said to go."

"Naw, don't hold back for me. You have talent. I'm glad you ran your own race. We're here to score points. You gotta go if you have it." Eve and Kate hugged in agreement.

"Oh, Kate, this is my boyfriend, Baker." He'd followed the two into the tent.

Kate rolled her eyes at Eve. "Great, Eve. You bring your bf in here and I look like shit! Nice to meet you, Baker. Now turn around so we can change into something dry." Kate and Eve pulled off their wet, muddied outer garments and slipped on dry tees, hoodies, and sweat bottoms.

"Okay, you can look, Baker. We're decent." The ice was broken. Eve led Baker back to the finish to cheer and to introduce him to her coach and teammates.

❖

Baker followed the team van back to Huntington. Eve climbed into his car with her travel bag at the University athletic center parking lot. She acknowledged Oscar first, allowing him to give her several sloppy kisses. She then squeezed next to Baker, taking his face in her hands and kissing him deeply while her teammates paraded by, hooting and cheering. Eve didn't care.

"Um, you taste so good. I can't believe it's been since August. Take me back to Nitro so we can get naked, and I'll tell you everything on the way."

Baker smiled, happy to be together. "I've missed you," was all he managed, putting the car into drive for the ride up to Nitro.

The weekend passed mostly in the Airstream, except to run out for food. Baker's phone rang Sunday morning. He stepped out to answer, walking the perimeter of the property, returning after a few minutes.

"Something important?" Eve asked, looking up from her literature textbook.

"Oh, the gallery. One of my patrons called. I'm going to have to head back today if it's okay with you?"

"Sure, I need to study anyways and get back to campus tonight, plus Cassie will want a full report of our visit here." Eve smiled, sipping her coffee watching Oscar keeping an eye on his people, the scene familiar.

"I don't want to leave, Eve." Eve sat in Baker's lap, her hand running through his hair. She kissed his neck while he massaged her back. "What will happen with you beating Kate this weekend? Will she be okay?"

"Kate's chill. She'll be fine. We both push each other and I'm sure she'll rebound and probably beat me next time."

"I'm glad you have friends on the team. So, what's your favorite class?"

"I like my art classes - go figure. There's a big studio where we can do all kinds of fun things with wood and metal and casting. I really like the construction management classes, too. I want to learn how to build. I want to rebuild Momma's house one day."

"I have no doubt you will. Now, how about you put that book down and study me for a while.

❖

Baker dropped Eve off at her dorm. After a long goodbye she walked into her room to find Cassie ensconced in a pillow-chair, doing homework in bed. Eve flopped on her bed and crawled under the covers fully dressed, covering her head with the pillow.

"What, no hi Cassie, how was your weekend?"

"Ugh, I need sleep, a shower, and then to study. Catch up later, okay?"

But Eve didn't sleep. A thought crept into her mind. Something was different between her and Baker. Something had shifted, her more than him, a minor change or feeling. She'd felt it as Baker talked about her being "home" for the holidays. Eve really didn't want to be away from home, JJ, Patsy, Tre, and Cassie in December. Maybe he would come there. Alexandria seemed a world away, though Marcy and Cora were there.

Eve took her shower, enjoying the hot water on her race-sore muscles. She threw in a load of laundry and tried to decide what to do about dinner with Cassie later.

She called her old friend. "Marcy, it's Eve."

"How was your weekend?"

"I ran really well, third place overall and first on my team." She teased Marcy, knowing she wanted to hear about Baker's visit. "I got in five easy today to recover a little."

"No, not running. Your visit with Baker. How did that go? You went back to the ridge, right? I want every juicy detail."

"Marcy, it was great, like nothing had changed. We stayed in a lot, but ..." Eve stopped, unsure what to say next. "Something was different. I love him, Marcy, I know I do. But I'm not sure I want to come home at Christmas, and I don't know if we're going to make it for four years if I feel this way now. I may stay here and tell him to come up. I want to see you, though. He's so excited about the holidays and I'm not."

"Calm down, Eve. No decisions now. Finish your semester. You have a lot going on. Plan to come back to Alexandria, but don't put any pressure on yourself.

There's no need to make decisions for the future right now. Give it some time and space. I miss you."

"I miss you. Call me." Eve hung up, feeling better but just as confused

Thirty-three

Cross-country and the semester wrapped up in December. The team finished second at conference with Eve second overall to a Kenyan runner from South Alabama. She finished eleventh at regionals in South Carolina, missing qualifying for nationals by one place. It was an off race, battling a cold. She finished her classes with a solid 3.8 average and made matching rings of copper and enamel for her and Baker as a Christmas gift. Marcy and Cora were getting bracelets and earrings.

Eve tentatively walked into their house in Alexandria. Baker had put up a tree and decorated it with lights, garlands, and ornaments. Underneath were presents, all beautifully wrapped. On the new stove, was mulled wine that filled the house with the scent of cinnamon and spice. The Union Street staff party was later that evening.

"You've been busy, Baker! This will be my first Christmas with a tree since I was a child. I can't tell you how happy I am and how stupid I've been. I've been dreading coming home and I don't know why. How do you put up with me?"

"This is only the first of many wonderful Christmases. I love you, Eve, and it's my job to put up with you. Shall we go?" They drove the Bronco in the direction of the river through a lightly falling snow. "Do you mind if we stop by the boat first? The engine compartment has been leaking."

Baker stepped onboard and flipped a switch to light the cabin, disappearing into the engine compartment. Eve sat on her old bunk, moving her hands across the comforter and taking in the cabin. As her eyes adjusted to the dim light, something odd peeked from behind Oscar's bed. The leopard print of the fabric stood out. Curious, Eve reached into the space between the dog bed and the wall with the tips of her green fingernails. The silk panties slid out from under the dog bed. She dropped them on the table in disgust.

Baker popped back into the cabin. "Ready to go?" The smile fell from his face at the sight of the undergarment. "Did you leave those here?" he joked half-heartedly.

He was pathetic. "I don't wear leopard print or granny panties, Baker. Who is she?"

Baker stammered, turning away and pacing across the cabin and back. "It's not like that, Eve."

"Like what? I'm not even gone a few months and you start fucking someone else on the boat, our boat. Did she pose for you, too, or did you meet her at one of the exhibitions?"

"It was once, Eve." He confessed, looking down.

"Was it once? If I check around the house will I find more panties? Besides who leaves their underwear behind? Is she the one who called after Charlottesville and told you to come home? Goodbye, Baker and don't follow or call. I thought there was a reason I wanted to stay home and now I know why." The boat, once special, now meant nothing. She wouldn't let him see her cry or glimpse her pain. She was leaving.

"Don't leave, Eve. I'm sorry. It won't happen again."

"Go to the party, Baker. I'll call Marcy so we can get my stuff packed. I'm heading back to Nitro for the holiday. I'm sorry things had to end this way but you've made it a lot easier for me. I'm going to spend the holidays with my family." She walked out, dialing Marcy in her anguish.

Marcy left the party to meet Eve at the townhouse, fretting while Eve packed her things. Luckily, she didn't have much other than the clothes she'd brought down. She took the charcoal nude that Baker had done of her sleeping on the boat. She wouldn't let him see her like that again, vulnerable. She picked up Baker's Christmas present from under the tree and stuffed it in her bag.

"Eve, please come stay with me and Cora," Marcy pleaded.

Eve held Oscar's face, kissing the big dog and shedding tears freely. "I'll miss you, boy." She loved the big dog. "It's too hard to be here, Marcy, and Baker works with Cora. I won't get in between their friendship."

"But you should be with us for the holidays. I don't want you up there all alone."

"I'm going to stop at Cassie's house and stay there a few days. Then I'll go home and spend the holiday with JJ and Patsy. I won't be alone. I've got Kitty, too." Eve gave a hopeful smile. "I'm relieved, Marcy. Something wasn't right and I really wanted to be home for the holidays. I'll miss you. If you hurry, you can catch the end of the party." She handed Marcy her and Cora's presents, each in a gift bag and wrapped in tissue. "Give Cora my love. Merry Christmas, Marcy." She hugged her friend tightly.

"Merry Christmas, Eve." Marcy sniffled. Eve walked out to the Bronco, driving toward the interstate. Tears flowed freely, closing one chapter and opening another. She'd be at Cassie's in a couple of hours, surrounded by her family and warm home.

The trip to Cassie's seemed quick. Eve cursed Baker over the course of the drive, replaying him and the other woman on the boat over and over, the woman distorted, old and gross, a perversion of everything she'd shared with Baker. Eve fell into Cassie's arms, her friend waiting at the front door. The refuge was perfect to dispel the blueness Eve felt from her loss. The house was full-tilt Christmas, decorated to the hilt and full of good smells, good food, and family and friends. Cassie had two sisters and a brother. Eve ate, slept, and ran with Cassie each day, the two taking it easy and doing just enough to work off the food Cassie's mom fed them when they weren't sitting in Cassie's room discussing how crappy men were.

The sun tried hard to break through the gray of the winter afternoon. The two roommates jogged in their matching shoes, tights, and hoodies along the park trail that circled a lake. The Blue Ridge Mountains were framed in the ice-patched water beside them.

"I can't believe the skank was wearing leopard panties." Cassie shook her head in disgust.

"It was so gross. I mean you would know if you left without your underwear. I think she left them on purpose."

"For you to find, no doubt. Bitch was marking her territory." Cassie lived vicariously through Eve's sex life. She'd confessed that her only sexual encounter up to that point in their lives had been a fumbled attempt at second base by one of the boys on her high school team on prom night.

"Yeah, one of his patrons no doubt. Whatever." Eve waved the whole thing off.

"Fucking panty dropper." The two slowed, walking along the shore and laughing for the first time. After a while, Cassie asked, "Does it hurt, leaving him? You two were really in love, weren't you?"

"I don't know. Something changed when I went away to school. Maybe because I wasn't dependent any longer, and on my own, and I had you and the team. Baker was always saving me and providing for me, and I didn't want that anymore. I want to do things on my own. I love our team, and you, and school. I love my trailer in Nitro. Hey, why don't you come up after Christmas and spend New Year's with me?"

Cassie's face lit up. "Really? We'll have so much more fun there than at my place. That'll be lit." They began to jog.

Eve spent Christmas day with JJ, Patsy, and Tre at their apartment. She had stockings filled with snacks and little goodies for all three. She helped Patsy with Christmas dinner. Eve enjoyed the day, Patsy once again pregnant and JJ preparing for a new job.

"Yeah, I like welding. I'm making things like you do in art school, though I'm making trusses and beams and such. It's hard work but the money is good. I can take care of Patsy and the kids."

"I'm proud of you, JJ. You have a lovely family now and you're doing so well as a man. Promise me you'll show me how to weld. Not big stuff, but how to use a torch and cut metal and stuff. When I get the house done some day, I want to have a studio and maybe make metal art, suns and moons—stuff people can hang outside."

"That sounds cool, Sis. I'll show you. Take care going home, it's slicker than a 'possum's a-hole' out there." She hugged him goodbye, an act that seemed impossible only a year before.

Eve drove up the ridge past the Minimart and Ridge Works. The lights were on and Bigun's car was out front. She had a bottle of wine, a gift from Patsy and JJ. Eve pulled in the lot automatically.

"Merry Christmas, Bigun." Eve burst in the door with her arms wide and big smile.

"Well, look who's back. Where's your boyfriend?" Bigun checked the parking lot with a glance.

"Do you care? I'm back and he's not. Besides, I came to see you." Eve had no idea what she was saying. Her emotions were getting the best of her, but she wanted human contact on Christmas.

"Come to see me, huh? Guess we can catch up and it's Christmas anyway. Want me to open that?" Eve was shocked when Bigun came up with a corkscrew and real wine glasses, the stemless kind. She told him her story sitting in the chair next to his. Bigun listened, nodding occasionally. Eve finished in tears, sobbing quietly.

"I didn't think love could hurt like this."

Bigun went to her and held her gently. She clung to him, his embrace soothing. She wanted him to carry her back to the mattress and forget everything, to erase the memories of Alexandria, the boat, and Baker. "Can I stay tonight, Bigun?" Eve looked into his eyes, vulnerable and open.

"Not like this, Eve. You know I've cared about you since your home burnt down and you were hanging out here all day as a little thing. You're all I've dreamed of since you left the ridge to go back to school. I could tell you about the million times I've dreamed about you staying over or going home with me. But I want you free and clear and because you want me. You're in pain right now and it wouldn't be right. Go home tonight and rest up. Come back New Year's Eve and we'll sort things out." He hugged her, kissing her gently on her head. Eve finished her wine in a gulp, suddenly embarrassed.

"I better go before I start crying again. I feel a mess." She'd just asked her friend to sleep with her and he'd said no.

"You didn't embarrass yourself and you're not a mess. I'm glad you stopped to see me. Having you here tonight and sharing the wine is the best Christmas present I've ever received. You were my wish, if you really want to know. Come see me for New Year's and we'll really celebrate." Bigun winked, putting his arm around Eve to walk her to the door. She felt better getting in the truck, but what the hell had she been thinking, asking him for a hook-up? She shook her head and breathed in the cold air to wake up, turning on the Christmas station. She turned it off quickly when Wham began singing, Last Christmas and her tears began once again. Eve drove the rest of the way up the mountain slightly confused over what just happened. She sighed, nothing else to do but look forward to the new year.

Thirty-four

New Year's Day came but Eve never went back to Ridge Works. Cassie came up and the two ran or did classwork, hitting all of Eve's old haunts, namely the pizza parlor and Walmart. She didn't take Cassie to meet Bigun, scared of having to follow through on her feelings. He was right, she wasn't ready. As they drove back to the Airstream, she looked at the small shop and forlorn car, knowing Bigun was waiting for her. She should call him, but let her apprehension get the best of her. And then she was back at Huntington and in classes.

Second semester started off well. Eve won the indoor conference title for 3,000 meters, qualifying for nationals. The circus that is the NCAA Indoor Championship caught her mentally unprepared. Coaches and athletes, men and women, high jumpers, pole vaulters, weight throwers, and sprinters of all shapes and sizes warmed up and competed on the tiny indoor track. Eve took in the spectacle, rooming with Shelly, a long jumper and the only other qualifier from her team. The coach had a room next door in the Sheraton in downtown Boston. Seeing Harvard across the river for the first time blew her mind, not to mention the track was small, two hundred meters of rubber on a raised wooden platform. Indoor was confined after the wide-open fields of cross-country.

Eve qualified for the finals, finishing fifth in her preliminary heat. The finals were set for two days later. The race went out fast from the start, the dry indoor air burned her throat and her legs were unresponsive after her heat earlier in the week. Eve finished last, humiliated and in a position she had never found herself before.

Coach scooped her up off the track, helping her to the warm-down area where she could put on her sweats. He brought her an energy drink to recover and ease the dryness in her throat.

"I'm sorry I let you down, Coach." He came to her with her bag.

"Eve, no worries. You ran in the finals of the national championship as a freshman. Chalk this one up to experience and learning to run through heats to make the finals. We'll work on that in practice, and you'll be ready for outdoors." Coach believed in her and always made her feel better. Eve smiled despite her distress.

Outdoor nationals in May were different. The team had multiple qualifiers travel to Indianapolis. Eve ran the 5,000 meters and Kate the 1,500 meters or metric mile.

Once again Eve moved through her heat to make it to the finals. She warmed down and hydrated afterwards, sitting in the shade while cheering on Kate. She ran well but was the first non-qualifier in her heat.

Eve felt ready for the final with two days' rest, stretching and jogging with Kate, just like in Huntington. Coach met with Eve for breakfast. The final would be at six that night.

"Rest today, eat a light lunch and get to the track by five to warm up. Stay mid-pack for the first eight laps. It should be a steady pace. Move up or hold on as you feel but be ready to go with the leaders with three laps to go. It will get really fast with the 1,500-meter girls doubling back in the race."

The whole day was a blur and then Eve found herself on the line with fifteen athletes from across the US, all as fast as she was. It was daunting and close quarters - elbow to elbow. The gun fired. Bang. Eve ran to the middle of the pack and tried to stay calm, biding her time. The pace felt incredibly fast. With four laps to go, the familiar fatigue began to set in - thighs, hamstrings, calves, and arms all deadened by the heats and pace. The two 1500 meter competitors, one from Oregon, and one from Stanford, moved to the front. Eve went wide to cover the move with several others following her, leaving six in contention, strung out along in their collegiate colors. The front five were moving very fast, all elbows and knees to drive their bodies forward. The lap counter clicked - two laps to go. Eve maintained her third place, not daring to think about a podium finish. She was aware of the footsteps behind her. Coming down the straight for the final lap, the official with the small bell rang it frantically. Ding-ding-ding-ding. Eve was on her toes, sprinting with everything she could muster. The first two runners were away. Purple and gold went by and then another wearing powder blue. She was struggling toward the finish, her gait awkward. Just past the line, Eve collapsed, one of several to fall onto the forgiving Tartan surface. Eve lay on the track, her chest heaving and the sweat rivulets from her head, neck, and torso, forming a puddle silhouette around her on the warm rubber surface. It felt so good to be finished, her body exhausted.

Coach helped her up to walk, her legs wobbly like a toddler's. "Fifth place, Eve. You're our first All-American and you were the first freshman finisher. She tried to smile but only managed a dry retch from the effort. Despite her state, she was ecstatic. She was an All-American.

❖

Eve picked up where she'd left off for her sophomore cross country season after a summer of training in the Allegheny mountains. She easily triumphed at conference and regionals, this time taking Cassie and her team to NCAAs in Florida over Thanksgiving. Eve finished third, her first podium and second All-American honor. By indoor season, she was a fixture, winning races on the small tracks up and down the East Coast. Eve moved up in distance, winning the 5,000 meters at Nationals decisively. She wanted to double back in the three-kilometer, but Coach stressed patience. He wanted her to enjoy the victory, the university's first national champion. At the outdoor championship, Eve galloped away from the pack of twenty-five qualifiers in the 10,000 meters, running easily for the first twelve laps then taking the lead and upping the tempo, dropping the competitors one by one until she was alone. At lap twenty-three, the bell clanged with one lap to go in the six mile race. Despite her lead, Eve sprinted, charging down the inside lane and passing the slower runners who were all a lap down. Eve broke the string with her arms held high, smiling broadly. It had been the easiest race she'd ever run. She pulled on a long-sleeved tee shirt and warmed down several laps with some of the other competitors, basking in their congratulations and banter. At the awards ceremony, trackside, Eve stood proudly on the top step, the champion's medal on her neck and the trophy that would later go in the school trophy case in her hands.

Eve and Coach were having dinner that night at the hotel. He excused himself to take a call from the athletic director back on campus. A man at the bar had been watching her. He was tall with longish hair, new Nike trainers, and the ubiquitous jeans and sport coat. He had a trim beard and she had to admit he was handsome. He approached her, holding out a card and the evening edition of the local news with her picture on the cover crossing the finish line. Huntington's First Outdoor Champion.

"Nice race, Eve. I'm Mike Kelly with Athletics East, a Nike-sponsored team. I'm an agent and national team coach. You ran an incredible race tonight."

"Thank you. I've never run so easily, and it was a championship. I have a great coach who seems to know how to get the best from me."

"You do; he's one of the good ones. I won't keep you long but take my card. If I can do anything for you or if your circumstances change, call me. I'd love to have you on contract."

"Contract? I'd have to leave school and lose my eligibility. I think you're wasting time. I plan to run four years and graduate."

"Counting up all those All-American honors and championships between now and graduation? I believe you'll have a bunch more. But sometimes circumstances change. Keep my card so you have options. You're good now and we could make you great as a professional. You're going to get an invitation to run Nationals and a chance to represent the US in Europe and the Pan Am games. I hope to see you there. I'll be a coach on the team." His eyes sparkled and he smiled not unpleasantly. "Tell Coach hello." He left quickly.

Eve turned the card over. Money, shoes, and travel on a professional contract. The thought intrigued her, but she loved school, her coach, and teammates. She'd stay and graduate and then, maybe go pro.

Coach sat back down and looked from Eve to the man disappearing across the room. "Do we need to have the 'talk', Eve?" He leaned in. "He's an agent and agents only want what's going to benefit them. Once you go pro it will always be about your last effort. I hope you love the university enough to stick it out and mature. I will help you get there and be ready for the pro ranks after graduation. Deal?"

"That's a deal, Coach." Her smile was all teeth. A championship, an agent trying to represent her, and the prospect of travel with the Junior National Team. It was all a bit surreal.

The 5,000 meters was a completely different race from the earlier 10k. Eve had to qualify, which would be her third race of the week. The fatigue was wearing on her body. Eve ran from the back of the pack to conserve her strength and stay out of trouble, wanting no trips or falls. She only exerted herself with a few laps remaining, moving up quickly to take the lead and qualify first in her heat. In the final, Coach wanted to try a different strategy.

"Stay in the middle of the pack and move up slowly. The two who earned silver and bronze in the 1,500 meters will try to control the pace to keep it slow so they can use their speed at the end. With two laps to go, move to the front and push the last two laps. It will be an eight-hundred-meter race instead of a sprint."

Eve wasn't sure what to say other than, "Okay." She gulped under the pressure and the thought of those two oxygen-draining last laps.

The race started out as Coach told her it would, with a slow early pace. The pack practically jogged for the first six laps, tightly bunched together. On the seventh, the girl from Stanford took over and the pace increased, stringing out the pack. Eve moved with her, sitting in third. The laps ticked off with the eighth, ninth, tenth laps passing - two to go. Eve sped up to pass but the other runner put in a spurt to hold her place. The two were a contrast - Eve tall and lean with shocking white hair and the Stanford girl, also lean, but shorter, darker, and more muscular. Eve kept up the pressure, pushing down the back stretch and into the bottom curve, all the while increasing the pressure. She wouldn't break. Eve pushed harder, the two now away from the other competitors. Neck and neck they raced with the bell jangling for one lap to go.

Eve couldn't get past, her every move covered by the other runner. Stanford's head dipped and she heard a gasp, ever so slightly. That was all Eve needed, rushing by one, two, three strides to cut to the inside, the pass made. Eve was in full flight coming out of the last turn. She sprinted up the straight, the filled stands screaming. Eve leaned awkwardly to break the string. She'd won.

It hurt. Eve doubled over, the girl from Stanford grabbing her and holding on, the two hugging, sweating, sliding off each other's limbs, while grasping for any breath they could gather. She'd won the classic distance double, NCAA Champion for the 5 and 10k.

The whirlwind began as soon as Eve arrived back on campus. An impromptu student cheering section, mostly teammates gathered at the airport to greet the double NCAA Champion and All-American. Eve made appearances on localTV and answered calls for interviews on the radio and with the running magazines. After a week, Eve and Cassie packed up before Eve headed for Nitro and the seclusion of the Airstream. Life almost came back to normal for the moment, but Eve would head out soon for most of the summer.

"So where are you off to first?"

"San Francisco for Nationals. Coach arranged for me to go on tour in Europe after that. I have a race in England, then Ireland, and one in Switzerland. Then I come back for a few weeks before Brazil and the Pan Am Games, if I make it. It's crazy."

"I want a postcard and tee shirt or hat from each stop, okay?"

"Anything for you, Cass." Eve was happy her roommate was with her.

❖

A weary, world-worn woman returned in August to Malone Ridge. She wasn't a girl any longer, having visited foreign countries, dealt with jet lag, new food choices, friendly and not so friendly spectators, foreign languages, coaches, and fellow athletes. She'd also seen the money that flowed to big-time athletics that funneled to the agents and teams, the athletes always on the short end and begging for handouts. She was happy to be home and to rest, going over the plans for the house and avoiding Ridge Works. "Not yet," she told herself, though she did think of Bigun often.

Thirty-five

Cassie's ring tone tittered. "Eve, did you hear the news? We have a new coach."

"Who'd we get?"

"Some chick from out west somewhere and a bigger program. That's all I know."

"Well, they wouldn't have hired a bad coach. Not after all we accomplished last year."

"All you accomplished you mean. Three national championships and four All-American awards plus bronze at the Pan-Am Games. I'm sure she wants to kiss your sweet little ass."

"Uh, as I recall you're the one with the sweet little ass."

"Yeah, you totally want it." Both giggled.

"Yeah, I do. I'll see you in a few weeks." Weird, Eve thought after hanging up. She remembered the agent talking about change. She had that same feeling when Momma told her about her father's return home long ago.

❖

The locker room was full to meet the new coach in late August. The stocky sprinters and jumpers, tall powerful throwers, and skinny distance runners filled the room, the noise and energy level high after summer break. Their dress was casual, in shorts, flip-flops, tee shirts with various slogans or signs and of course the dark green college track gear. Eve and Cassie sat in their lockers, happy to watch the show. Someone turned up the music, the beat thunderous, the dancing suggestive, accompanied by clapping, hooting, and locker room suggestions.

Coach Morris walked in, taking off her aviator shades. Her hair was silver and swept back military style. She wore Adidas sweats and shoes with a green university polo shirt. The chatter abruptly stopped, her silence and gaze commanding. The coach walked the circumference of the room, turning off the music before stopping in front of Eve's locker, her back to Eve. The bottom hovered inches from Eve's face. Eve looked to Cassie while trying to scoot further into her cube. "Embarrassing," she mouthed.

"Listen up, ladies. I'm Coach Morris. You'll get to know me better over the semester. I have a few rules. When you're in this room you'll be in uniform, tops and shorts. Shoes are to be worn or shower sandals. We will be wearing Adidas this year. I don't want to see any swoosh stripes on clothing or shoes in here once the order arrives." There was murmuring and a few s-bombs escaped. "Quiet. I'm talking." She hushed the group. "You'll arrive early for workouts and many times leave late. There will be no jewelry worn at practice or at meets." The groans were audible, and several hands went up. Eve touched her new hoops, one for each city she had visited overseas. "My team, my rules." The raised hands disappeared quickly. She turned around to meet Eve's gaze. "And you must be our All-American, Eve Malone. Congratulations on last year's accomplishments. Please stand." The team began to clap and call Eve's name but stopped when Coach put up a hand to silence. Eve stood slowly, the coach not moving. The closeness was even more awkward. The coach took out a roll of thick white athletic tape. "Hold out your arms." Eve did as she was told and held them out. The coach wrapped the tape around her wrist to cover the green serpent, her face was blank as she wrapped. "There now, that shouldn't slow you down too much. No tattoos. When you represent the university, it's the college logo and our shoe sponsor only. Cover up any tattoos with tape, a shirt, or tights before you enter school property. Does everyone understand?" The coach looked past Eve to make eye contact with the rest of the team. Eve felt heat rising in her head, embarrassed in front of her friends as an example.

"You can't make me wear this tape." Eve spoke quietly.

"You're right, I can't. But I can prevent you from competing for the university for breaking team rules." Eve smelled the mint from her breath, but she held her ground, not moving. "Now, those of you on the track team can leave. We'll regroup in late fall. Call me or schedule an appointment if you want to talk. Cross-country, stay so we can go over the season ahead and today's workout." She broke her gaze with Eve, a slight smile on her lips, following the other girls out of the room.

❖

Cassie was in the ice bath. Eve waited her turn, sitting on the trainer's table and hugging her knees. She was wearing a long-sleeved tee shirt and training shorts. The team had just finished a workout consisting of 20 times 300 meters on the track.

"I'm wasted." Cassie mumbled. "Third day in a row of repeats. Whatever happened to cross-country and grass running?"

"I know. My shins have been sore like in high school. I don't know if I can keep this up. We're all going to get injured. I hate her." Eve rubbed her shins with an ice cube.

"What are you going to do?"

"Honestly, I've been thinking about taking a break to work on the house. I run because it's fun and I love my teammates. I love my team, but I hate our coach. I don't know what to do."

Coach stood in the doorway. "What's that Eve? Hating isn't Christian now, is it? We're all supposed to forgive and give second chances. Now you might not like my training program, but you'll adjust if you give it a chance."

"But I won under Coach's schedule with longer runs and grass drills. At least let us run our repeats on the grass behind the stadium."

"Maybe if you'd run my way, you'd have won cross-country nationals last year instead of finishing third."

"Or I would have gotten hurt and quit the team."

"Your choice, young lady. I have no room for prima donnas on my team, even if they are All-Americans. It's your choice." Coach Morris spun and left the training area. Cassie climbed out shaking her head. Eve handed her a towel and slid into the ice bath in her shorts and tee, massaging her shins. She gasped as she submerged.

❖

Eve drove back to the ridge on Friday, sore, tired and unsure of the future, an idea forming as she drove. She needed counsel. Her old coach had meant everything to her, and she'd thrived under his guidance. She'd been so sure about her junior year when she arrived home from overseas at summer's end. Now mid-Fall, she wasn't running well and very unhappy. She hadn't even competed this season, her tendonitis too acute to race.

Eve had a list of things to do. She checked her voicemail and saw Marcy's call. She dialed the number.

"Hey, Marcy. What's up?"

"Cora's selling Union Street and we're moving to Charleston in a few weeks. She's going to open a new place on the river. We'll be close by again."

"Wow, what brought that on?"

"I need to be closer to Mom. Cora's tired of the grind. We want to adopt and start a family. Here, she can tell you."

"Hey, girl." Cora began. "I've missed you. We're going to be mamas and you're the first to know."

"Aw, you are so sweet! You'll be the best mommas, and I'll be an auntie. I'm so happy for you two. You made me smile for the first time in weeks."

Marcy took the phone. "What's the matter, Eve?"

"The new coach is a bitch and she's ruining me. I'm sore, I hate the workouts, and she's banned my tat. It's not fun anymore. I'm thinking of quitting. But then money's going to be an issue."

Cora grabbed the phone back. "Come work for me. I've found a place on the river, the Kanawha Café. You can stay with us when you're not at school. It'll be like old times."

"That sounds great. I'll get right back to you and anyways, I need to see you both. Bye, Cora." She waited for Marcy.

"Call me back, Eve."

"I will. Love you, Momma Marcy."

"Love you, Auntie Eve." She hung up feeling much more hopeful. Friends and a job solved a lot of issues. Eve checked her text messages. There was one from Mike Kelly. The header said CHANGE.

Eve thought I'd check in with you and see what was happening. I know Coach Morris from her days at the Academy. She can be a "tough cookie" to say the least. Anyway, this is a reminder that if things don't work out there and you don't transfer, I can get you a contract with a guarantee, signing bonus, and performance incentives based on last summer. There are other ways to pay for college! I can also get you in with a new team if you want. Olympic Trials are coming up next year. You should be there! Call me. Mike" She called him and within a few minutes, agreed on money-saying yes at the first amount he offered-the contract arriving by FedEx the next day. Eve was now a professional. She took a walk outside to get a grasp on what she'd done.

JJ had cleared all the burnt remains of the old home. The cement foundation, the basement meth lab and the two bookend stone chimneys was all that remained of the old house. She walked the perimeter, now marked with ribboned stakes, her project for construction management class. Eve felt the urge to start, the house coming alive on the blueprint paper. What was running compared to a home, family, work, and her art? The old stone siren sang her seductive song, urging her to commit.

Eve ruminated the rest of the day. Change came at the most surprising times. She'd run in a few road races this fall and maybe a marathon in early winter. That's where the money was. She could also help Cora for a regular paycheck and be close to Marcy in Charleston. She'd finish school the next year and begin to build her house. It was a plan, though much different than the one she'd started with as a freshman. She'd miss her teammates, but she'd see them in class or at meets. Relief and a direction cleared her mind.

Looking over the ridge in the warm fall air, with everything seemingly settled, Eve realized something was still amiss, a promise not kept and an important friend waiting for her. She needed him in her life, whatever happened between them.

Thirty-six

Dolling-up in the tight quarters and shower in the Airstream was a challenge. Eve put on a pair of cute shorts, strappy tank top and sandals. She applied eyeliner and lipstick, then ran her hand through her hair and dabbed on a little cologne behind her ears. She hadn't worn a Friday night date outfit in sometime, psyching herself up to leave. Eve walked to her truck, apprehensive for the short drive down the hill. She parked in front of the Minimart.

To come bearing gifts was always a good idea. Eve purchased a twelve pack of lite beer, chips, salsa, and cheese dip. She stood outside of the tattoo parlor and took a deep breath. Time to face the music.

Bigun barely acknowledged her arrival. "I'll be finished in thirty minutes or so. Waiting room is over there." Gone was the carefree welcome of old. She'd hurt him and deserved the response. Eve walked to the waiting room, amazed by a new mural that covered the wall. There were green mountains with an eagle soaring in the blue sky above a winding road. A lonely young woman ran toward the stately log house on the ridge. He'd painted the folk-art mural for her, the details of their side of the mountain amazing. It must have taken him months, all the months she'd left him alone, dreaming of her return. Eve snapped a photo on her phone. She wandered over to a corkboard covered with articles and pictures of her exploits from the previous year. Local Girl Finishes Third at NCAAs for Huntington, Garners All-American Honors; Malone Wins NCAAs Indoor; Malone, Double NCAA Outdoor Champion; Malone Represents USA in Brazil. The room was a shrine. Bigun's customer was paying and getting instruction on care for the new tat. She was breathing like her race was about to start, her emotions flooding the room.

Bigun sat in his barber chair with a small groan, paying her no attention. He picked up his newspaper. "Can I offer you a beer?" Eve walked over with two cans. He looked at her sadly, the hurt visible. "The mural is lovely, Bigun."

"What can I say, I was inspired. That and I didn't have anything else to do while I waited." Ouch. Eve winced. "What's it been, a year and a half? If you hold out another six months, you can come see me for New Year's like you promised." He accepted the beer and took a gulp.

"Oh, Bigun, you know the turmoil I've always had in my life. I've always been a mess. I was running, running a lot. You know." Eve nodded to the board in the other room.

"Yes, Eve, I know. I read the articles about Nitro's golden girl and her exploits in Europe and South America. I cut the clippings. I painted that mural thinking of you all those days that you ran by or drove past, but you never stopped. I knew you were around." She winced again; his pain much harder to take than she'd anticipated. "You were coming home to the ridge all that time and couldn't stop by or call me?"

"I won't lie to you, Bigun, I wanted to so many times, but I wanted the time to be right and my running career just took off." She stopped, then added a confession. "I won't lie to you, I was scared to come back."

"Scared of what? Me?" He laughed long and hard, finishing his beer. He popped a second. Eve took a sip of hers and set it down. She walked over to him.

"I was scared of what I felt and what might happen. With school and running there wouldn't have been much time." Eve hesitated, "Time for us. Can I tell you something? Running all those miles and traveling to those races, I was always thinking of you and me and our home on the mountain. " She placed her hand on his and gazed into his watery eyes. Eve moved his leg with some effort to make a place to sit next to him. She squeezed in, leaning back with her head on his chest, then pulled his free hand and arm around her stomach. "I'm sorry, Bigun. What can I do to make it up to you?"

"Come with me to Hawaii." Eve pushed up his tee shirt sleeve to find the hula girl tattoo and traced her curves with her finger. "It's been my dream since I was a kid. It would be a dream come true to go with you. I've thought about that trip a lot. It got me through the tough times when you weren't here."

"That sounds wonderful, let's go. I can't wait." His strong arm gripped her lightly, his fingers moving to her hair.

The two sat in silence. Eve felt at peace for the first time in forever, his heart beating with hers. Bigun finished his beer. Eve initiated their first kiss, long and slow, looking up at him as she'd once daydreamed. Eve then pointed to the back room. Bigun locked up while Eve lit candles, the evening warm, magical, and fulfilling.

Eve felt the sleep that comes with weighty decisions, exhausted from emotion, and bliss that flooded her body. "I don't ever want to leave, Bigun. I love you." Eve whispered.

"I love you too, Eve and I never want you to leave." He pulled her closer.

❖

Morning came with a rush, neither wanting to leave the enclave of the mattress and tangled sheets and blankets. Bigun had to run errands and check on his mother and sisters before he could open for the day. Apparently he had a huge extended family in town and Charleston. Eve had to sign and mail her contract and call her friend Susie in Alexandria for coaching advice. Last, she needed to check out of her dorm room and tell Cassie she'd quit the team.

❖

"I'm relieved, Cassie. I'm going to miss you and the team more than anything, but I'm going to stay in school and graduate. I'll see you on campus. And you can always come up and stay with me anytime in Nitro."

"Eve, are you sure about leaving the team?"

"Yeah. I can't tolerate that woman. She wants to break me and that won't happen. I won't let her. Besides, I'm a pro now. I signed a contract."

"You signed a contract? Oh my God. That's amazing."

"I know, right? Who would have thought that a year ago? It will pay the bills and tuition, keep me in shoes, and allow me to travel to races."

"I'm going to miss you, Eve. I'm happy for you and a little jealous." Cassie pouted while Eve pulled her into a hug.

"I'm going to miss you, Cassie." Eve gathered her things and loaded the Bronco. She stopped at admissions to change her status. She'd get to keep her scholarship for the year because of her injury and the coaching change. After all, she was the school's only NCAA champion and All-American. She'd have to finance her senior year on her own.

❖

Cora's new restaurant was lovely. Unpretentious and casual, it had a patio for drinks and small plates that looked over the big, slow river toward the gold-domed state capital and city skyline behind. Business people walked down for lunch, boaters motored over for wine and cheese at day's end, and dinner was served in the dining room for sunset and river vistas.

Eve worked as server, hostess, and assistant manager when she was there, usually four days a week between classes. Most of her running took place on the grass and dirt towpath along the river and up in the suburban hillsides. Her legs were healing and the old training improved her fitness. Eve finished a workout, took a quick shower and arrived to work at the Kanawha as hostess for the night.

"So," Marcy joined Eve in a lull before service. "You and Bigun are finally an item." Marcy was doing her best to be supportive.

"Yep. I let him use his tool on me every night." Eve delighted in the joke, but Marcy shook her head. "I can't even fathom how it's possible. He's so big and you're so tiny."

"I know, he is big." Her grin was wicked. Marcy smacked her, the two on the patio under an umbrella with sparkling water late in the afternoon.

"Eww. Stop, Eve. I'm happy for you, and I know he's a good man, but this is one time I don't want any details. I guess you two were inevitable. I'm happy if you're happy."

"I am so happy, and it feels surreal. We're talking about making it official and going to Hawaii. Bigun has some money saved and I have my shoe contract. We have to figure out when. Oh, and he has to ask me first." Both laughed. "But enough about me, how's the adoption coming?"

"The birth mother is coming from Korea and will have the baby here this winter and have the baby here at our hospital. Everything will change. I'll cut back at work and Cora can keep everything going here. I want Mom to know our baby before she slips away." Marcy already had a motherly glow, despite the frown from her mothers state.

Driving back to Bigun's that night, Eve was shocked at how happy she was. His apartment was a complete surprise, clean and tidy with lots of light and a nice porch where he had a small garden that looked up toward the ridge. The plants were his children, each one tenderly cared for. His bed was huge and luxurious, a king that she swam in at night and late mornings when not in his arms. She kissed the slumbering man and snuggled in, content.

At school the next day, Eve attended Industrial Art class, fiddling with the torch and her metal sculpture. Her phone rang. She lifted her mask and walked out to the hallway.

"Susie, thanks for calling me back. I have a favor to ask you."

"Eve, it's good to hear your voice. What's up?"

"I'm not running for the college any longer."

"I'm so sorry, Eve. What happened?"

"Don't be sorry. Onward and upward. That's where you come in. Will you help coach me? I want to run a marathon and qualify for the Olympic Trials."

Susie squealed into the phone. "You want me to coach you for a marathon? Eve, I've been following your career. You really have been running great since you went back to school. We couldn't believe the NCAA's and Pan Am Games last summer. Who knew? But I can't coach you. You're way out of my league. Tell me what happened first."

"We got a new coach and the bitch tried to make an example and hurt me, so I quit. I've signed a contract with Nike. I want to run a winter marathon and qualify for the

Olympic Trials next spring. My sponsor will help with your coaching stipend and travel as well as equipment. What do you say?"

"Holy moly, Eve. You want me to coach you for the Olympic Trials? Like I said, out of my league."

"You know me, Susie and you've run marathons and coached Ellie for Boston. Just advise me so I do enough but not overdo and get hurt. We can get more help from Mike, my agent if we need to, but I'd be comfortable working with you, picking the race, and well, going for it."

"What can I say? Of course, I'll work with you. You still come to Alexandria to see the guy?"

"No, that didn't work out. I have a new guy here in Nitro and I'm going to get my degree. Oh, I'm also working in Charleston for Cora, normal life." The two laughed. Eve was happy to hear Susie's voice, as comfortable and familiar as on a training run. "We can do this via email and phone. I'll email the workouts I've done since last summer. Let me know how to adjust and I'll come see you when I can."

"The big thing will be the weekly long run. We'll want to get you up to two to three-hour-long runs and I might join you for a couple. Everything else will stay pretty much the same I imagine, as if you were training for a 10K. I'll get a list of races you can choose from and send to your agent." Susie paused to gather her breath. "I'm honored

Eve, but we have work to do. I'll rearrange my schedule and do some research. I can't wait to get started."

"It's not too much is it?"

"Are you kidding? I wouldn't give up the chance to work with you for anything. Talk soon."

Eve hung up. She'd put the last piece of the puzzle in place.

Thirty-seven

Eve finished the twenty-miler on the canal towpath in a little over two hours. She then jogged and stretched in the shade, waiting for Susie to finish. It felt nice to be back in Alexandria and to be with Susie. The two started the run together, chatting easily at eight and then seven-minute pace for the first ten miles. Eve gradually quickened her pace to low-six, her last mile a 5:35. She was adapting to the weekly long run.

Eve had their water bottles when Susie arrived. "Good run, Eve. It amazes me how easily you acclimate to the longer runs."

"I like the long runs. The dirt path and shade along the canal is nice. I really felt good today and enjoyed having company. I'm hungry. Let's go get some bagels."

"Let me catch my breath. You can finish warming down and hydrating."

Over bagels and coffee, the two talked strategy. "I think you should consider the Richmond Marathon." It's in late November so you'll have time to get in the training. They also have prize money as the National Championship. I doubt there will be a stacked field since it's after New York City. It's a well-run but low key, perfect for your first race. You should be able to get an OT qualifier there."

"Okay, Richmond it is. I like that it's not far. Besides, my contract has a bunch of incentive clauses for top finishes at Nationals. I'm anxious to see how this training is going and want to race soon before Richmond. The Charleston Distance Run is coming up. It's a 15-miler in September so it's longer than I'm used to but it will give me some clue of what I'm getting into. What do you think?"

"Okay, sounds great. I'll check it out and get you entered."

❖

The normal 2 mile jogging warm-up put her into race mode. Eve then strided out for 100-meters fast, then 100-meters jogging back to the start. She repeated the stride, returning to the start to take a sip from the cup Susie handed her, swallowing half and spitting the rest out. It was a warm, humid Charleston morning in late September along the old river. Eve was nervous even though it was a local race.

"Relax, you're the class of the field today. Consider this a long training run. Run the first ten miles at a six-minute pace. Once you come off the mountain it's five miles flat back to the stadium and you can race as fast as you want. This is the same strategy we'll use in Richmond. Hold back and relax then open it up."

Eve shook her head but wasn't really listening, the adrenaline buzzed through her body and in her head too loud. She stepped to the line and stretched, her uniform new, crisp and white with the swoosh seemingly everywhere. She was the only woman on the front line.

The pistol fired and a thousand runners surged off the line. Eve dodged the men and boys who sprinted past, wary of being tripped. After two miles the course moved out of the city toward the small mountain on the outskirts, the early sprinters falling back. Eve passed each, one by one, working her way to the front. It wasn't much different from all her runs up Malone Ridge. She leaned into the pitch, concentrating on relaxing and breathing. It was hot but at least trees on either side of the street provided some shade. At the top of the hill, she grabbed a cup of water from the table and poured it on her head and chest to cool down, opening her stride as she coasted down the back side of the mountain on the serpentine road. She was largely by herself, a couple of top men out of sight and everyone else behind her.

On the flat road, the heat crept up with no shade. Her singlet and shorts clung to her body. She dumped two cups of water at the next aid station and had enough left in the cup for one sip to wet her dry mouth. The time on the clock at the ten mile mark showed 59-minutes, 50-seconds. She was happy to be on pace, but her legs felt dead due to the long downhill run and the rising heat. She tried to increase her pace. She began to question why she was out here racing in the heat when she could be home on the cooler mountain with Bigun.

Eve's misery was disturbed by screaming. Marcy, Cora and all the patrons of the restaurant were on the street as she approached. She'd forgotten they would be at the thirteen-mile mark. They handed her a water bottle - heaven - the two screaming and jumping.

"Top woman, Eve," Marcy yelled.

"You catch those boys up ahead, Eve," Cora chimed.

She passed them in an instant, spraying her burning head and quenching her dry, cottony mouth. Feeling better, she began to move faster with a mile to go.

Eve tossed the bottle as she entered the stadium. She could see herself on the big screen, the clock at one hour and twenty-nine minutes. She'd run sub six, her normal 10K race pace for fifteen miles. The training was working, and she let a little smile come to her lips. The announcer welcomed her. "Ladies and gentlemen, let's give a big applause for third place overall, Eve Malone, one of our own from Nitro, West Virginia and Huntington University, NCAA Champion and All-American." There may have been clapping and a few cheers from the small crowd in the stands. Eve was just happy to finish, stepping across the line and walking directly to the drink table. She continued to dunk herself and drink, eventually finding shade on the other side of the stadium. She picked up Marcy's bottle.

Susie jogged over. "How was it?"

"Sucked," Eve replied and stuck out her tongue. "If Cora and Marcy hadn't handed me the water bottle, I don't know if I would have finished." She picked at her clinging top and shorts. "I'm covered in salt and sweat, my head hurts, I think I'm getting my period. I feel like shit and need a cool shower. Do you have my towel?" Susie tossed her a towel from her bag.

"Hydration is important, and we'll practice drinking on the run. You'll need to take fluids during the marathon. Glad you figured that out today. Let's get you moving and stretch a little, then you can dry off, gather your winnings, and head for the shower and your friend's café. Third place in the open division and first place female. You also averaged under six-minutes per mile on a super hilly course. Add another eleven miles and you'd have run a marathon." Eve shook her head. "No worries today. Come on, we have some celebrating to do."

"After I change. A shower, dry undies, shorts, a tee-shirt and flip flops are all I can think of right now."

❖

The training miles added up, mostly along the Kanawha so Eve could do her quality work on the asphalt path. She ran her easy miles at home in Nitro through the mountains, well cared for by Bigun. She was very fit and anxious for her future dance with the mythical marathon distance.

❖

The day of the National Marathon Championship dawned cold and breezy; a raw November day so different from her last race in Charleston. Eve chose a long-sleeved lycra top, plus the new Nike team singlet, and shorts in light blue. She had a pair of knitted gloves and a headband to protect her ears and forehead from the wind as well as her sunglasses - the day was bright. The outfit should keep off the wind but prevent her from overheating. Her anxiousness came in waves at the start. She jogged in place.

Susie held her warm-ups in a parka, gloves and hat. "Okay, the competition is the Russian and the Kenyan runners. Run with them if the pace is moderate. If someone takes a suicide run, let them go and we'll play catch up at the end. You know what splits to hit at 5, 10, the half and 20 miles. You want to be one-hour-fifteen to seventeen at the half marathon and two-hours flat at the twenty-mile mark. Run like we did in training, easy the first fifteen to twenty miles, then see how you feel and bring it home. I'll be on the course on my bike, and I'll check in from time to time."

Eve nodded, nervous for the experiment to begin. She had no words. She'd done training runs for three hours but racing would be a different story.

The cannon fired with 12,000 runners, joggers, and walkers moving across the start for their 8K, half-marathon, or full marathon races. Warm clothing, hats, and gloves were tossed aside from the mass of humanity as it began to surge. Eve was at the front of the wave, running among the elite men and focusing on her two fellow competitors. The three formed a pod within the men who broke the wind as they wound through Richmond. The road was flat, but Eve found it difficult to get comfortable, her lower back tight. Her stride felt funny, holding back and racing at what felt like training pace despite the adrenaline surging through her body. Susie had said to hold back.

The half went by quickly, the three women running alone as they crossed the James River Bridge. The big clock read 1:20, Eve knew she was on perfect pace for a 2:40 finish and OT qualifier. She was running well within her comfort zone. Eve's back still ached and now her right hamstring was tightening from her shuffling stride behind the other two women. Eve willed both areas of her body to behave.

Nearing the twenty-mile mark and only six miles to the finish, Eve could feel the accumulated miles and cold, the road punching back at her with each step. Susie cruised beside her on her bike, handing Eve a water bottle. "Drink up, Eve. 1:58 at 20 miles. You look great. Time to pull the string and show them what you got." Susie rode away toward the finish.

Eve could see Bigun ahead. He'd holed up for the race with a friend at a pub in the quaint Carytown area. He and an old friend of the same size from a local tattoo parlor were playing Māori Warriors, dressed only in shorts despite the temperature. Their faces, chests, and arms were painted with black ink in tribal design. The two clapped and stomped as Eve came by, tongues wagging and eyes bulging, performing the traditional Haka war dance like his relatives from the South Pacific islands. He was more than amped over his and Eve's wedding the following week in Hawaii.

"One step, one step, " the two men shouted, clapping in unison. "Another upward step, Ugh!" Clap and step. The two circled their arms above their head, their stances wide. "The sun shines. Ugh." Clap. The two hopped toward the runners, shaking their heads, hair, and hands wildly. The Russian moved across the street, the Kenyan in tow. Eve smiled; he could be so cute sometimes.

With Bigun and his friend as a diversion, she took the lead, changing her pace and lengthening her stride while the other two runners dodged her dancing boyfriend. She felt better instantly, the stronger tempo more comfortable. She did not look back, the footsteps behind her fading. Eve caught several elite men who were struggling as the miles ticked by. She felt warm for the first time that day, the sun on her back and no breeze in her face. Eve arrived on Monument Avenue which led straight to the finish. She dared to look back briefly as she made the right turn. No one in sight. Someone shouted, "You got it, Eve," but she didn't see who it was. Now in the final mile, Eve was moving quickly on the slight downhill. She barely noticed the stately homes and statues, nor the blisters on her toes, painful from the cobblestone street. Despite her body's condition from the two hours of racing on cement, she pushed on, fueled by her desire to win.

The finish was just ahead. The digital clock on the scaffolding ticked off, 2-hours 31-minutes, the seconds flying by, 2:32, people lined up two and three deep and cheered, 2:33. It felt like she would never arrive. Eve's agent, Mike, came out of the crowd to urge her on.

"Go, Eve. Beautiful run, you have a big lead. Enjoy this and let 'em know how good this feels." He was swinging his arm in a big circle.

Eve cracked a smile, knowing relief was just ahead. Her arms were up, waving to the crowd. She blew kisses to each side, becoming emotional. Almost there, a few more steps, she told herself. She ached everywhere but ignored the pain, the goal just ahead. Eve crossed the line and broke the thick red, white and blue paper ribbon, the tails draped around her shoulders. She was exhausted and stopped her watch at 2:33:45. She bent over holding her knees. Someone draped an American flag around her. She could make out the Kenyan coming toward her through squinting eyes. Mike held Eve up, handing her one of her water bottles. Susie jogged over with her warm-ups. Eve drank and dressed, still breathing hard, congratulating the others as they came in. Bigun had her finishers' blanket which he wrapped her in, before giving her a bear hug.

"You ran great, hon. Damn you looked cold and thin out there, but you won, amazing."

Eve grinned. "It was amazing, but now it feels like my legs are going to fall off. Help me walk a little. I think I have some serious blisters." Her white shoes bore red blobs around the toe area. Eve leaned on Bigun to walk around and get her legs back underneath her, then jogged for five minutes slowly and stretched a little before washing up for the awards ceremony. Team Eve then gathered at a nearby brewpub that had a fire going. Burgers and fries were delivered and devoured, the feast washed down with local ale. Bigun made suggestions on the local brews, having spent much of the early parts of the race at the pub with his friend, whose tattoo shop was next door.

"We had a good day, Eve." Mike looked from Eve to Susie. "You did a great job getting her ready, Susie."

"She did the work and has the wheels. I didn't have to do much, honestly."

Eve smiled a worn smile, tired and sleepy after the food and race. She was completely wrapped up in her sweats and college parka, her medal dangling around her neck.

"So, here's what you won today. You get $2,500 from the race as first female. You get $10,000 from Nike for the win and $50,000 from USATF as national champion. You also get another $10,000 from Nike for qualifying for the Olympic Trials. I think that works out to about $72,500 for the day's work. Not bad. How are you going to spend it?"

Eve looked at Bigun and beamed. "Most of it will go toward the house. But first, Bigun and I are flying out tonight for Hawaii. We're going to meet Marcy and Cora there, and get married - destination wedding and honeymoon. We saved for this trip but now we can upgrade and pay for Marcy and Cora's room." Bigun's hug caused her to disappear in his 3X sweatshirt. He'd removed his war paint but still wore shorts and new Nike slides despite the cool day. Everyone toasted the couple.

"Sounds wonderful and congratulations, you two! I wasn't sure about the timing but it's perfect. Enjoy the time off and relax to heal up from the race today. You're going to be incredibly sore tomorrow and flying won't be fun, Eve. When you get back, we can start getting ready for the OTs." Susie held out her mug. "To the bride and groom." Despite the fatigue that coursed through her body, Eve had never been happier.

Thirty-eight

The flight from Richmond took the happy couple to Dallas. After a short layover and late night Tex-Mex dinner, Eve and Bigun upgraded to first class and flew directly to Honolulu. A twin prop brought them from the Big Island to Maui where they checked into the oceanfront Sheraton. Their suite overlooked an infinity pool that blended into the Pacific Ocean. The view was like a dream. The air was warm and fragrant from the bougainvillea on their balcony. Eve slept for most of the first two days with the sliding doors open, taking in the air, ordering room service, and luxuriating in the big tub. She was recovering, the stiffness in her legs slowly dissipating.

Eve left the cozy hotel bed to shower and eat, joining Bigun on the balcony on their third day on the island. She had on one of his tee shirts that served as a dress. He handed her a mug of the island coffee.

"How do you feel?"

"Better. I'm not as sore. I've never felt that way after a race. I felt like a car crash victim. Now I'm ready to sightsee."

"Are you up for some swimming? There's a snorkeling tour today. Might be good for your legs to get in the saltwater." Eve nodded, feeling she'd been transported to another world, taking in the vista and while savoring the sweetness of a slice of mango. There was a knock at the door. Bigun welcomed Marcy and Cora into the room, both in flip flops and Hawaiian cover-ups.

"She awakens. Hey, sleepyhead." Marcy gave her friend a hug. Cora patted her shoulder.

"You both look great. I guess you'll be poolside today?"

"Yep, it's a tough life." Cora said. "Margarita or rum punch, I can't decide. Maybe both." She smiled.

"I'm so glad we can all be here together. Thank you both for joining us."

"We wouldn't miss it." Marcy hugged her friend a second time, burying her face in Eve's hair. "Upgrading our room and taking care of the charges was too much."

"Hey, we had a good day in Richmond. We wouldn't all be here if it weren't for you two. This is my way of saying thank you for everything." Eve and Bigun snorkeled that day, joining Cora and Eve poolside afterwards. The rest of the week was spent taking excursions to the coffee and pineapple plantations, the volcano, and some of the small towns to shop.

Friday was the big day. Bigun dressed in pressed khaki shorts, new leather sandals, and a white linen Hawaiian shirt. He'd trimmed his beard and pulled back his hair, island style. Eve wore a simple, long white gown with a scoop neck and back, and pearl earrings and matching necklace that Bigun gave her as a wedding gift. Marcy and Cora had on blush gowns, similar to Eve's.

The wedding party gathered under a small portico on the beach at twilight. A native minister led the service and witnessed their vows under a blazing pink sky over the purple water. Bigun and Eve exchanged rings they'd purchased in the town of Hana. Eve's was made up of silver serpentine strands. Bigun's ring was also silver strands but with black titanium woven in for contrast. With the setting sun, the luau began with music, costumed dancers, a roast pig, and flowered drinks. All four were presented leis that matched their attire, Bigun's colorful and Eve's white. The wedding party feasted and drank well into the night, the moon bright on the far horizon of dark water.

"I think Marcy and Cora enjoyed Hawaii. Hope they made it out okay." Eve lay on Bigun's chest late the next day. The morning breeze off the ocean caressed her body.

She paused. "I know you always wanted to come here. Is this everything you hoped for?"

"It is," Bigun answered from far away, "and then some. I always thought I'd come here, drink a few Primos and check out the tattoo and surf shops. But I also thought I'd be alone. I never dreamed I'd come with my bride. It seems like a dream."

"I loved watching you hula with the dancers last night. Who knew you had those skills?"

"You could have joined Marcy and me."

"Not the way my legs feel. I would have snapped in two and been laid up in the hospital instead of here right now. You two represented Nitro well."

Bigun laughed. "What do you want to do today since we leave tomorrow?"

"I'm fine staying here all day, maybe a walk on the beach later and a quiet dinner."

"I hoped you'd say that." Eve snuggled closer, kissing his chest as she worked her way up to his lips. "No time, no agendas - just us today."

❖

The newlyweds returned to Nitro and a cold winter rain. Eve picked up her training. After a few weeks of easy running, the build up to the Trials began. In between training runs and classes she continued her work on her home on the ridge, lining up contractors and ordering the supplies she'd need. Her winnings from her marathon victory were timely. The house would rise in the spring.

The only setback came in January when back-to-back snow and ice storms made running impossible. Eve drove down to Marcy's to work out on the treadmill at her YMCA, staying in their cozy home over the restaurant. Marcy was busy preparing a nursery when she wasn't at work at the hospital.

"So, when are you due?"

"Late summer, we hope. The birth mother is living in town. She'll deliver here, then go home to Korea. I didn't tell you but she's carrying twins." Marcy's face lit up.

"Oh my God, Marcy. Are you ready for twins? How does Cora feel?"

"She's so ready. Eve, I can't wait to be a mommy." She shrugged with a faraway look. "How about you and Bigun, any plans now that you're married?"

"Oh, he's all about getting started on a family. He loves kids. I had to convince him we needed to wait until the Trials are over. However, it goes, good or bad, I'm going to retire and then we can start. Maybe it's the house, but I'm ready for a family, too. I know how you feel and it's funny. I would never have thought I'd want kids. But as soon as he said he wanted children, I did, too. Who knew?"

"Look at us, Eve. We've going to be moms. My, how times change."

Thirty-nine

Atlanta shined in the distance as the plane banked to prepare for landing. Eve gripped Bigun's hand more from what lay ahead than the wind that buffered the small jet on the cool spring day. Eve was restless.

"What's the matter, babe?" Bigun pulled her close.

"Just the finality of this race. The focus on making the team. I've never run to place before. I've always run my best and it usually works out. Mike can't talk about anything else but making the team and the pressure is getting to me. I'm a little freaked out."

"You're going to do fine, Eve. In the end it's us, and I'll be at the finish line to wait for you."

"It's just so far and so hard - what I have to do." She snuggled in, finally finding comfort.

The plane touched down with a jolt, rousing her Eve with its arrival. After exiting, and a short train ride, the two found the baggage area and transportation. The shuttle driver held the sign up with the Olympic rings. They headed toward him after collecting their bags.

He would take them to race headquarters in downtown Atlanta. Susie and Mike were waiting in the lobby of the swanky downtown hotel to greet them. Mike had special Olympic Trials gear from Nike for all of them that included the typical athletic gear but also casual wear for interviews and relaxing. He held up the special kit that all Nike athletes, including Eve, would don for the race. She had a few days to relax, which was hard with all the big-name runners, shoe companies, the runner's expo, and interview requests and reporters. With preparations complete, Eve and Susie jogged parts of the course to de-stress and get ready.

Eve was number twenty-five. "It's going to be crazy with twenty-five women faster than me, not to mention the other one hundred and sixty behind us and all wanting a shot." Her crucible would be daunting. Eve's lunch was not sitting well during her strategy session. She was holed up in a corner of the lobby with Susie and Mike.

"Only five have run in the low 2:20s. Most are closer to your 2:30 or slower and remember, that was your first. Only two have run as fast as you for 10K so you have the speed advantage. Don't worry. The course is rolling and should favor a strength runner like you. And then you use your speed and youth for the last six miles. No sweat," Mike stated.

"Easy for you to say, Mr. Positive." Eve smirked.

"Same plan as last time, Eve," Susie joined in. "There will be a pack of 15 to 20 up front to start. Let them set the pace to save energy but don't lose contact. It's murder to work your way back up. Stay back and pick up spots as people drop off after ten miles. The real carnage will happen around fifteen to twenty miles." Susie looked grim.

"Oh great, I love running through carnage. Way to psych me up, Coach."

"The pace will grind people down, but you should be fine. Relax the first fifteen miles, work through twenty, then race the last six with whatever you have left. Easy-peasey." Susie's grin did not help. The distance was daunting, but the pace that she'd have to run to be a contender would take the stakes up another notch.

Eve shook her head. "Okay. I have nothing to say after the carnage and being ground down by the pace talk." Eve mocked. "I'm ready I guess." Her stomach did a little flip. She patted her belly and smiled.

"Are you okay, Eve?" Mike looked concerned, leaning closer.

"Don't worry, just nerves. Your racehorse is ready to go." Eve laughed his concern away.

❖

Eve laid her gear out on the other twin bed for the next morning's race. Bigun paid the room service tab and wheeled in the cart. Eve ate part of her steak with blue cheese crumbles but pushed the salad aside. The iced tea was all that was appealing to her. Bigun worked on his cheeseburger and fries.

"You can finish my salad, Bigun. I'm not hungry and my stomach is so unsettled. I'm nervous about how hard it will be tomorrow. I've never done anything like this."

"You'll do fine, Eve. First or last, you don't have anything to prove. Want some fries?" Bigun tossed her one which she ate. She then buttered a roll and put a slice of her steak with blue cheese in it to make a sandwich. Eve prepared a second roll, this one with ketchup, her appetite growing. She finished Bigun's fries then ate his pickle.

"Okay, enough. I'm done. I don't know why I'm craving pickles and fries." She made a sweet face. She popped open one of the IPA's on the cart.

"I'll buy you all the pickles you want after tomorrow." Bigun smiled attentively.

Eve was up early the next day. "I'll see you after, my love." She kissed him one last time, his hands on her waist. It was difficult to leave the cozy room and his embrace. The thought of not competing crossed her mind when Susie knocked on the door.

Eve nibbled her buttered toast and scrambled her eggs further with her fork while sipping a cup of coffee in the athletes' and coaches' lounge. She and Susie remained silent with nothing but the day's work ahead. Mike approached but at the last moment steered clear to take his breakfast to the other side of the room. The apprehension in the room was palpable. The trip from the hotel to the start was short. Eve checked in, showing her numbers, one pinned to her front and one on her back. She jogged a mile easy, then came back to stretch out in the big tent. She made one last trip to the restroom for nervous relief. Twenty minutes before, she stripped down to her navy-blue shorts, red singlet and white shoes. Her sunglasses perched on her head. She sipped a little water, spat it out, and jogged out into the sunlight.

The starting numbers were painted on the road. She had the middle position in row three, the twenty-fifth space. Get out and to the side without a trip-up, she told herself. Spectators screamed and clapped with the patriotic, hip-hop, and workout tunes blaring from the speakers. Copters zoomed overhead. The welcome came over the loudspeaker, followed by introductions, the Star-Spangled Banner, and a few instructions. Eve leaned forward, anxious to get things over with and go home. Boom. The cannon sent the two hundred female elites down the street. She started her watch with a flick and stepped into the melee.

The first five miles were manic, Eve moving here and there in the human traffic, dodging bodies in front and behind her. The ever-annoying thought she always had at the start, played with her psyche. Why are you doing this? Why don't you quit? It's too hard and too long. You could be home planting flowers in the garden and building your home. You could be sleeping right now. The list of things other than running at top speed for two hours and twenty-some minutes was endless. She finally broke to the side of the road, still shadowing the front pack. Someone took the lead ahead, opening a ten-meter gap. Not a serious move, not yet she told herself. A mile later, the pack absorbed the impatient runner. At the ten-mile mark Eve was feeling good but pensive, having to hang off the back of the fifteen women lead group. At sixteen miles, a tall runner with a long ponytail began to open a gap. A second runner chased her and Eve's group, now five runners, covered the third spot. The pace was steady, but the real issue of the moment were the rolling hills, a veritable bacon strip of asphalt rolled out ahead causing the carnage Susie had spoken of, and one-by-one, her fellow competitors fell off pace. "Ugh, that last one hurt," she grimaced. The race had suddenly gotten real.

Eve took her water bottle at twenty miles, grabbing the green bottle off the table and swigging down several gulps. She tossed it to the side of the road, a spinning souvenir for one of the screaming crowds. They'd exit the last loop soon and the real race would begin on the five miles straight to the city center and finish at Centennial Park, the setting for the 1996 Olympic Games. Eve thought she was in seventh or eighth, running well but not knowing what she had left in the tank and not willing to push harder for the finish yet. Her twenty-mile split was 1:51, somewhere around a 2-hour 25-minute finish. Yeow, that's fast. Eve was in unknown territory.

Eve's calf muscle cramped, a twinge, a longer twinge, and then the real thing, locking her stride with a jolt. She'd been trying to cover the pace of the women around her, all thinking of that third spot. She eased a little, trying a faster tempo without getting up on her toes, the cramp easing. She was in the front of her group and surprised to not feel much distress outside the normal marathon road induced fatigue and fading cramp in her calf. Third place and an Olympic berth was within her grasp and for the first time she dared to hope, adrenaline kicking into her bloodstream. She passed the 5K-to-go marker, just 3.2 miles to the finish - her college race distance. Eve snatched her last water bottle, took two sips and tossed it away. That little bit of water would have to do until she reached the finish. First place was no longer in sight, and she could just make out second place 200 meters ahead. The course was packed three deep on both sides of the road, the cheering loud. Her group would have third, fourth, fifth, and sixth, the order still undecided. Eve tried to move out and solidify third but was covered by another runner, one of the favorites and an Olympian from the last games. She'd recognized her at the start. The rookie and the pro would duke it out for the final stretch. The two-mile marker flew by, both women racing and in full flight, their struggle to best each other real, one spot on the podium and the team for Tokyo up for grabs.

Spectators and helicopters disappeared. Eve ran down a dark tunnel, the course narrow and spectators close, screaming encouragement at the two racers. One would make the team and one wouldn't. Eve struggled to pull ahead slightly, battling, sprinting with everything she had, but then the other runner fought back and opened a small gap. The finish was in sight as the two came around a bend in the road. Eve dug in but could go no faster, falling back with each stride. She struggled toward the finish, the crowd and noise fading. She crossed the line, overjoyed at the sensation of not running - finished. The time flashed but she didn't care, 2:20-something. She let her watch run. For the moment, Eve had no idea where she was, her legs wobbly and uncooperative.

The scene came into focus. Three finishers in front of her staggered about, draped in American flags. They were waving to spectators and posing for pictures in between recovery breaths. All three came to her, patting her gently and offering hugs. The rest of the field streamed across the line in various states, some sprinting, some jogging in, a few crawling. She felt lost and disoriented, a woman with no flag, no country, no friends. Bigun called her. She walked over slowly on uncooperative legs, her stomach cramping. Eve threw her arms around Bigun and hung on, tears and sobs coming forth from her exertion. She had finished. He covered her gently with her college blanket to stop the shivering that convulsed her body. The blanket was her flag. It was appropriate and made her smile.

"I'm finished, Bigun, I'm really finished. Let's go live our lives."

"Hon, you did great. I'm so proud of you. Fourth place is incredible. I'm with you. Let's go live. Do Mike and Susie know?" Eve shook her head no. Bigun handed her a water bottle. Mike came through the crowd.

"Eve, so close, fourth place. I'm sorry." He shook his head. "I know that's not what we wanted."

She smiled. "No, it's okay and the first alternate is fine. The other girls were better today." She smiled unconvincingly. Photographers were snapping her photo.

"But you're the first not to make the Olympic team." He looked at Susie who had just crossed into the finishers corral with Eve's sweats. He gave her a funny look. "She's okay with fourth place. I don't get it?"

Eve wanted to pack and leave but Susie told her she needed to appear at the press conference. Eve donned her sweats and joined the top five finishers on the elevated stage in front of the reporters and fans, the top three in new USA warm-ups. Eve wore her college sweats and parka, fighting the chill from her fatigue in the spring weather. The press had two rows of chairs in front and multiple cameras from ESPN and the networks to the sides. The carnival roared around the five elite finishers.

The questions went to the top three qualifiers for the first half hour, discussing their races and expectations for the Olympics. Eve stared at her microphone, counting the minutes until she could step down. Her stomach quivered. Finally, a question was directed to Eve.

"Eve Malone, you've had quite the year. You were NCAA champion, competed in Europe, won Bronze at the Pan Am Games in the 10,000 meters, and won your first marathon at the national championships. Today you finished fourth, just off the medal stand and not on the team for Tokyo. They say fourth place is the worst spot to finish, worse than last. How do you feel? And as a follow up, what's next? Might we see you at Boston or New York?"

Eve smiled broadly. "Well, as for the first question about how I feel being forth? I'd say I'm the happiest person in the room." She looked at the other four who returned quizzical glances. She paused.

"Did I hear you correctly? You're the happiest person in the room? Can you tell us why?" The reporter looked perplexed.

"Well, I should say that my husband and I are the happiest people in the room." Eve corrected herself and cleared her voice. "The reason that fourth will be fine is because I'm pregnant and I'm pretty sure they don't make a maternity size for the Olympic Team outfits. It might be a little tough to get around the course in Tokyo in nine months."

Oohs and ahhs came from the women on the podium with her and the crowd. Her fellow competitors jumped up, hugging and congratulating her. Eve's smile was ear to ear as tears erupted again from fatigue and the surprise announcement of her pregnancy. Eventually, they sat. Eve still had the mic. "I want to thank everyone here who's supported me. My agent Mike, my coach Susie, and my husband, Bigun." He waved. She saw Mike toss his phone at a garbage can in the back. He missed. "To answer your second question, I won't be going to Boston or New York. This is my last race. I'm going to retire and go home to West Virginia, get my degree, finish building our home and raise our family." The rest of the presser was anticlimactic. Eve stepped off the stage to a bear hug from Bigun. Runner's World Magazine and Women's Running asked if they could do a story, passing Eve cards and exchanging dates and times to do the interviews and photo shoots.

Mike paced back and forth across the lobby, yelling into what was a badly damaged cell phone while Eve signed autographs. He walked up still shaking his head. "Did you have any idea, Susie?" Eve's friend shook her head no. He looked at Eve, then Bigun, then back to Eve. "Well, you sure I can't talk you into staying on the roads for a while? I just got off the phone and legal says we can keep you on salary through the pregnancy for a couple more seasons. World Champs will come around and New York or Boston would love to have you, in shape or not. You could make a lot of money."

"How much today?"

"I figure with a top five finish, $100,000 plus or minus, depending on the magazine stories and anything else I can round up for you."

"That will do just fine. I'm sorry, Mike. This just happened. We found out about the tadpole in my belly right before we left." She looked at Mike. "Running has always been a way to express myself. I ran for my school and my friends on my team. But now all I want is to be a mother, a wife, and to build my house and studio. We can finish the house now, Bigun." She hugged her husband then walked to her agent. "Thank you for believing in me." She tried to shake his hand.

"Aw heck, come here." Mike hugged her, wiping a tear. "I'll miss you."

Eve hugged Susie next. "Thanks, Susie. You've been the best." Both cried openly.

"Go have fun being a mommy, Eve. You're going to love it." The agent and coach walked away, Mike still in an animated conversation. Susie waved goodbye, laughing at the agent. The elevator door opened, taking Bigun and Eve to their floor where they packed, taking the next flight to Charlotte, then onto Charleston, and home on Malone Ridge.

Forty

Lillyanne Malone announced her arrival the following November with a loud cry from the master bedroom. Eve chose a home birth with a midwife in the big log home. Lilly had red hair and green eyes, like her namesake. Bigun doted on the handful that Eve presented him with. She couldn't take her eyes off the two of them, Bigun rocking her, humming an unknown melody.

Eve took the call from Marcy the next day, eager to convey her joy firsthand. Marcy and Cora had taken Lisa and Marie home the week before.

"Aside from not sleeping, we are doing well I'd say. Twins are so difficult. One is fed and finally goes to sleep, then the other one wakes, gets fed, then the first needs her diaper changed and on and on. I'm either feeding, rocking, or cleaning bottoms twenty-four seven. Cora's been great but she gets a break at work all day—I mean, not a break exactly, but you know what I mean. Don't listen to me whine, I—we love them, but enough about me. So how are you finding motherhood, Eve?" Marcy sucked in a big breath.

Eve laughed. "I'm sore as hell, I need a shower, and I need to brush my teeth. Lillyanne is sleeping right now, and she is such a doll. You will love her. I can't wait to introduce her to you, Cora and the twins. Susie sent the most beautiful running stroller but I can't even think about running right now much less walking. I'll call you later. I need to shower before she wakes. Love you."

"Love you, Eve. See you soon."

Eve finished drying off to the sound of Lillyanne's small noises from the bassinet near her bed. A car pull up to the lot in the back, the entrance to the tattoo studio. Bigun was back from running errands. She pulled on her robe and duck-walked gingerly to the bassinet. "Ouch. And I thought marathon recovery was torture." She scooped up the bundle and backed to the bedside, placing Lillyanne in first and then crawling in next to her. Lillyanne nuzzled her breast, content to nurse while her little eyes explored the world around her, finding her mother's gaze. Her small hand reached up. Eve took Lillyanne's fingers in hers. She gazed around the room, the master bedroom large and comfortable, the big pine timbers warming. The picture window overlooked the flower garden and Daddy's spot next to the rock-framed garden where Momma lay. Eve's new studio sat across the clearing. Her eyes settled on the framed charcoal of her from a different time, now set above the large stone fireplace mantle. The picture was a world away. Annie gripped tighter.

Opening her eyes, Eve saw Bigun sitting in the window seat with Annie in his arms. Annie moved, a little arm wave. "Can you get a diaper and the wipes? She'll probably need a change soon." Bigun laid her down on the bed with the supplies, and sat next to mother and daughter. The day was coming to a close, twilight filling the room as the sun began to set on the next generation of Malones on the ridge.

Acknowledgments

This work was completed during the recent pandemic, a time of much worry, struggle, and turmoil due to health concerns and protocols that prevented us from seeing loved ones. I also had a front row view of the social turmoil that took place in Richmond and across our nation. It helped me greatly to have a creative focus and be able to visit Eve, her family and friends in Nitro and Alexandria.

I want to thank my wonderful family, great friends, and trusted associates during these surprising times. First, to my companion, compass, and wife, Wendy. I am glad you are by my side along with Meaghan and John, Quentin and Bekah. You all delight us with your dreams, hard work, and thriving families. The little ones are the sparkling stars in our sky.

I'd also like to thank Joni Albrecht of Little Star, my publisher and friend. Your confidence is contagious and you have first rate associates. Cathy Plageman, you were a gentle and patient editor which made the process enjoyable. Wendy Daniel, your artistic touch brought Bigun's mural to life on our cover. Your combined support has been incredible. I'd also like to thank reviewer Gary Cohen, friend, interviewer, writer, and sage. It's been great catching up on college running and visiting your amazing library of celebrity runner interviews which (surprise) includes me and reviewers Anne, Lisa, Kim, Carrie, and Judi, champions all.

I'd also like to thank Erin Levens for helping edit my earlier drafts. You liked my characters which kept me going. Last but not least, my writing circle has been a big encouragement in this process. David L. Robbin, you are a master and your craft and enthusiasm for writing never ceases to inspire. Likewise, Jeff Barnes, it's been a joy to work with you and see you published. Here's to many more half price burgers, fine scotch, and cigars with you both.

CPSIA information can be obtained
at www.ICGtesting.com
Printed in the USA
JSHW022242091122
32870JS00002B/10

9 781735 887289